1953

THE SONG OF THE CAVE

THE
Song of the Cave

A TALE OF
RUTH AND NOEMI

Edward F. Murphy

THE BRUCE PUBLISHING COMPANY
MILWAUKEE

TO MRS. ALEXANDER MC CABE

AND

A GRACIOUS MEMORY

PROLOGUE

EARLY that night, a little heap of faggots was burning on the hillside and making just enough sound to emphasize the silence. And something kept whispering to an old shepherd's heart.

Seated on the hard dry earth, with a boy of seven beside him, he gazed along shadowy slopes at other shepherds watching their flocks, and saw each of them, under the deep blue sky and the winter moon, as a lonely waiting figure of Israel itself — silhouetted by sorrow against a never relinquished background of hope.

The flicker of the flames played on the two faces: the one so withered, the other so fresh. The boy clasped his hands over a knee and touched with his cheek the bony arm; and the old man smiled, glad that, when he should be sleeping with his fathers, his dreams would live on in this offspring of an only grandson who had died at Jerusalem defending the temple of the Lord from Roman outrage.

Both turned their eyes to the limestone houses of Bethlehem, vapor-gray in the valley below. "There," said the old man, "Rachel breathed out her soul in giving Jacob a son." He stroked his beard solemnly, reflectively. "In these very hills, David learned to play the harp that soothed Saul. The fountains beneath our walls have slaked the thirst of bravest warriors." His lips tightened.

But the boy, proud that the scenes of Rachel, Jacob, David, and Israel's bravest were also his, could feel no sadness. A love for place and people warmed him. He looked at the old man intently, because there was something of the depth of the sky in the countenance that had been molded by a lifetime of reveries. And, as he looked, the features suddenly were touched with a light that did not come from the glowing embers; a light softer and stranger than any he had ever seen. He glanced up, and a cry escaped him. He jumped to his feet and rubbed his eyes with his knuckles.

The old man also tried to rise but, even with the boy's help, could not; so, shielding his brow with his hand, he leaned back on the flat of the other and stared; for a star, infinitely brighter than raindrops in the sun but gentle as peace itself, had sprung from the womb of night, and its silver rays were reaching down toward the hills.

They trusted that the spectacle was real; and a feeling went through them that it had always been there, only that never before had they been ready or able to perceive it. And once more they sat close together, wondering.

"So beautiful and calm," murmured the shepherd, groping in his memory for a comparison. "It comes as *she* came."

The boy waited.

"I am thinking of one who blessed this land long ago. From the East she came, guided by Noemi the Good; and her glow is still on our people. She and this star make me feel that Israel may be larger than the land we know; for surely all souls — wherever they are — that see and follow the gleam of God are his beloved sheep. . . ."

"Are you going to tell me about her?" asked the boy, restive at the pause.

"She was Ruth, and here in Bethlehem she gave birth to Obed — him that became grandfather to King David." The old man's tone throbbed with reverence. "Behold!" He pointed to a ledge of rock on which the star was now shedding a luster like the very *shekinah*, the glory that once suffused the images of two adoring angels on the long-lost Ark of the Covenant. "There's where, just before sunset, we led the man Joseph and his wife Mary. The inn was overcrowded, and she with child! Could it be that Heaven, through us, chose that cave up there for them and is rendering it worthy? It

seems fairer, at this moment, than any palace." He paused.
"I talked with Joseph while we walked along and you led
through the steep pathway the little donkey Mary rode. I
knew from their having journeyed here to be enrolled that
they were of the seed of David himself, and I could picture
Ruth in that patient, beautiful young mother-to-be; Ruth returning from the far years to these hills. How often my father,
a Galilean fisherman whose words echoed the sea, told me the
story of the Moabite maid!"

The boy snuggled under the sheltering arm to listen, and
his eyes were on the cave outsilvering the moon.

"In the days," the old man began softly, "of one of the
Judges . . ."

And as he was speaking, the other shepherds approached,
drawn together by the light above and by that, too, of the
humble faggot fire which linked them reassuringly with night
as they had long known it in Bethlehem.

Some of them soon joined in the narrative, adding many
an interpretation and detail. Gradually the tale became
everybody's; and it flowed on beneath the star, reflecting the
boundless themes of love and truth even as a streamlet mirrors
in its very limitation the immeasurable heavens above it.

CONTENTS

THE SONG OF THE CAVE

Chapter One

THE MAN AND THE MUSIC

A PATH in the valley led from the house of Elimelech to that of Boaz. Brick-paved and grape-arbored all its length, it formed a cool tunnel of shade through sunlight; and the solace of intimacy might well have pulsed through it, for Elimelech and Boaz were kinsmen, and Hobab, Elimelech's only brother, lived a full day's journey away. But the path lay neglected, though nature itself, as if for some secret purpose, kept the vines leafy and, in season, filled them with heavy clusters.

Almost as long as Mahalon, younger son of Elimelech, could remember, Boaz had lived alone; but neither his parents nor his elder brother, Chelion, would say why. He could have tried to find out for himself from Boaz, save that a certain sensitivity restrained him; besides, he had been put under obedience to make no such advance.

One noon, while sitting with Noemi, his mother, on a stone bench in their garden and thrumming his crude triangle-shaped lyre of four strings, he remarked with all the archness of a persistent curiosity, "Such a sunny day as this should warm even the heart of Boaz." And, to his great surprise, Noemi did not change the subject.

"The only warmth he permits himself," she said, "is love for his acres."

"But how can he love land — mere land — like that?" The boy put the lyre down beside the bench and pressed his knees with his hands impatiently.

"A treasure is buried there, my son. . . . You have seen him near the almond tree that grows by the brook?"

1

"Many times."

"You must have noticed how unhappy he seems."

She raised a hand to her throat, her wide sleeve slipping down along the bare wrist. The little gesture somehow affected him deeply, and it prepared him for her next words.

She drew closer. Her sandaled foot retreated under the fringed hem of her woolen robe; her lids drooped, and the soft brown shadows beneath them seemed to increase the pallor of her high-boned, sloping cheeks. "This is your fifteenth birthday, my son," she said, "and you are now old enough to know." She sighed. "Some years ago — it seems only yesterday — Boaz came daily to us. We loved him more as a son than as a young cousin. He used to watch you and Chelion at play, and I could see that he was longing for the time when he would have a family of his own."

She glanced at two blue thrushes flying together from the tall, twisted oak in a corner of the yard. The tips of their wings almost touched and the unison of their motion was perfect.

Mahalon took her hand, his gaze shifting to the arbor the birds were seeking. "What was the treasure?" he asked eagerly.

"In Jerusalem, while on a pilgrimage, Boaz first met his Zora. Her brow was the color of wheat, her step was as light as the spring breeze, her eyes had the bright blue of the flax flower."

"Your own eyes are blue like that," he observed, forgetting his curiosity for the moment, or rather saving it for a fuller satisfaction, as boys do. He was thinking how fair she herself must have been in her girlhood, since so many traces of beauty still remained. He studied the mellow profile and the noble head. How white the veil that completely covered the hair and was gathered up under the slightly cleft chin! He tried to find just the right words to express himself and ease her mood; and his memory of a psalm that he had once heard sung in the hills, came to his aid. "Your face, O my mother, is as an evening window with a candle shining through."

She smiled, but her heart was too heavy with memories to be relieved by his praise. "When Boaz returned from Jerusalem to us," she said, "he appointed a deputy, according to the custom of our people, to secure the marriage consent from Zora's guardians. Your father readily accepted the mission and he had me go with him. We were successful and Boaz welcomed us back with boundless thanks; and soon the time of espousal passed with his building his house and planting his vines. He worked to the very last minute, and we helped him. . . ."

A sob escaped her, and Mahalon suggested, all too reluctantly, that she tell him some other time. But she went on.

"The wedding day came. Your father had gone again to Jerusalem, this time to fetch Zora; and that morning Boaz, in his best dress and turban, stood here with his groomsmen and a band of musicians, ready to set forth to receive her. At my request your father chose a special route of return, a little off the regular course, so that friends of ours might have an opportunity to see the bride. Oh, if I had let well enough alone! The countryside is not always safe; and, that day, three men armed with knives were crouching behind some boulders in the way. They must have seen the flower-wreathed donkey cart from a little distance and readied themselves. One sprang up and seized the reins. The others forced him and Zora from the cart. They eyed her wedding robes, her ornaments, her person. They tore the veil from her face. They — they took her — but your father fought them without weapons. Always remember that, my son. He made nothing of his wounds. He freed Zora and thrust her behind him, so that his body could be a shield. She clung to him, and he did not know that, yielding ground, he was edging her backward toward a crag. Some workers heard her cries from a distance and came armed with scythes and clubs.

The robbers fled; but not before Zora had reeled over the ledge to the rocks beneath. And your father found her. . . . Somehow he brought her back to us, holding her like a slain lamb in his arms. . . . You can guess the rest. It mattered not that he would have given his life for her. From then on, Boaz has not been himself. And it's not only your father he resents; he blames me, too, for that ill-fated path, and even believes that — that . . ." She could not bring herself further to disclose the suspicions of the darkened mind, and finished sadly, "Pain brought blindness. His bond with us is no more. So the vines thrive and the grapes ripen, but winter is the lasting season of his soul. Ceaselessly your father has grieved. Nor has his body ever quite recovered from the wounds he received that day."

"I am going to Boaz," said Mahalon, already on his feet. One of his fists was tight as he stooped and retrieved his lyre. "I should hate him — "

"No, no, my son!"

"But I can only pity him, the way you've told me all this. You want me to go?"

"Chelion went a year ago, but it did no good," she murmured. "Boaz wants none of us. Oh, my son, the sorrow of misunderstanding! If men only knew what is in one another's heart! They know their sheep and oxen better than their fellow men."

"Boaz should be made to know that we did him no wrong and that he needs us."

"Your father and I tried so hard. But we were resentful at first because we too were keenly hurt. Later — too late, when nothing could be done — we realized that we should have ignored our feelings. In his boyhood, Boaz had been badly treated by his elder brothers — now dead and gone. His kindly nature was terribly tried, you see; and the loss of Zora went so deep. Always we pray that, some day, one of life's many little miracles . . ."

Mahalon held his lyre firmly. "There are miracles in the hills," he said; "silences that seem to speak. They even sing!" He tapped his chest with his thumb. "You can hear them with something inside. And the shadows there have such hues at times! If I could get him to come with me —"

She rose. "You might invite him. As a boy, he was a shepherd like you. Shepherds learn much under the sun and the stars."

Her emotion under control, she turned slowly and walked toward the house, with the queenly bearing that always tinged Mahalon's love for her with awe.

It was the seventieth day before the Passover, the time prescribed by law for the sowing to begin. Through the winter, the boy had been marking each day with the sharp edge of a stone on the wall of the cave in the hills where he sheltered his sheep; and now, what with spring on the way back and the weather at its best, he felt a spirit rising in him to do something about Boaz. How could anyone remain depressed, with the sun absorbing the dews that clung to the lowlands and filling the air with diamonds?

He knew that Boaz, like Elimelech and Chelion, were to be found in the fields, perhaps resting from the heat, perhaps defying it in an eagerness to get a crop started, even though the cool of the morning and the early evening was better by far for the planting. As for himself, he had not been able to resist the temptation to steal away from his flock to spend a little time with his mother. Sharing an hour with her always doubled the pleasure of it. And what did it matter that their conversation, this bright day, had been sad? He was about to help Boaz, if possible; and, just as the removal of a thorn reduces pain, notwithstanding that the extraction itself is painful, so his mother must have found some relief in speaking forth the past. With such thoughts, he stepped more briskly.

He took to the arbored pathway deliberately, and the sunlight through the leaves dappled his head and shoulders with golden patches as he sped along. Soon he was standing in front of the house of Boaz.

The building was almost twin to that of his own home; a combination of mud and sunburned bricks, with blank walls to the left of a large central entrance, and with four small windows, wood-grated, set in those to the right. The chief difference consisted of an additional structure, with long vertical apertures, on the flat roof. He wondered if this was to have been the bridal chamber. A single palm tree, grown tall, brushed its fronds against the side of it.

It was not for even Mahalon's lively imagination to picture a welcome coming from any of those narrow windows. He could think only of an empty tomb. Needlessly a large black dog, chained at the gate, howled off any nearer approach; and shuddering a bit, the boy tucked his lyre even more securely under his arm and passed on to the open field.

Seeing Boaz, he hurried toward him, but stopped halfway. The man was as dour as his house. With an air of detachment from human interest, he seemed a ghost haunting the sod, rather than an actual person sowing it. His back appeared more hunched than bent, as he faced the breeze and dropped handfuls of seed from a basket held in the crook of his arm. The outline of his face — slightly hook-nosed, shaggy-browed, drawn-lipped — acutely etched itself against the glare of the sun. His short, armless tunic, girdled in the middle, revealed slim but wiry limbs. The scarf on his head was fastened down by a linen band and the folds dropped over his back and shoulders. His years could not have been more than a score and five, but he looked older.

Glancing from beneath his heavy lids, he straightened up and regarded Mahalon coldly for an instant. Then he made a gesture, as if bidding him begone; but Mahalon came nearer, holding his lyre in position.

Standing erect, his legs apart, his curly head flung back, he asked with a smile in which his even, white teeth glistened, "How fare the fields this day, O Boaz?"

"I have no time for speech."

"My father has often said that without speech we are locked in a cell."

"Your father!" The man's countenance hardened even more and the eyes narrowed.

Mahalon flushed. His fist clenched, but almost instantly the fingers uncurled, for he had surprised a yearning in the very surliness. "You have forgotten the real Elimelech," he found himself saying, and suddenly he smiled again. "Let me relieve you — somewhat — while you work."

"I want no relief."

"It is not good for man to be alone. Didn't the Lord himself say that?"

"Then why did he deprive me?" The sower's chest rose with strain, and his jaws bulged. The basket tipped and spilled some of the seeds.

"He did not deprive you — wholly. Soon the fields will be covered with wheat of the color of Zora's brow and as graceful in its swaying as her motion —"

Boaz stared. "You know about her — like that?"

"My mother told me."

Boaz averted his face. His bearded chin rested on an upraised shoulder, and a tremor ran through him. He was silent.

Mahalon stroked his lyre. A soft note like the sigh of a breeze came from it and lingered. "Does this remind you of her voice?"

Boaz stood still.

"I can play best in the hills, because of my sheep. But my best is nothing to what I want you to hear. Will you come with me?"

"Work must be done."

"And rest taken."

The man searched the boy's clear eyes, and his strong hand gripped the shoulder. "You seem wiser than your years," he said, trying to look cynical.

Mahalon took his hand and felt more tension than resistance in it. "The place where I'll bring you is not far."

"The seed has to be scattered. Plowed in afterward, and brushed over with the harrow. I have no time, I tell you."

"It will take so little."

"Every moment belongs to my fields. The earlier the sowing, the nearer the wheat." Then the lips of Boaz scarcely moved, though he still spoke. "Every blade will help bring her back to me. — Ah, no, I deceive myself. I always deceive myself. Spring means only shadows of what might have been."

Yet, almost without awareness, he had fallen into step with the boy. Over the muddied farm they trudged along, and soon they were ascending a ridge toward a rocky mound. At a cave in the heights, Mahalon paused. "The heart is lighter up here," he said, his hand on his chest, the strings of his lyre twinkling in the sun.

Boaz did not expressly agree, but the lines on his forehead had lost their heaviness. "Strange. When a shepherd boy, I, too, chose this very place as a little kingdom of my own. Here it was so easy, then, to dream —"

"This is as high as we can go. The nearest to Heaven."

And leading Boaz into the blue-green serenity of the enclosure, Mahalon pointed. On a bed of straw, gilded by the light from an open space in the rocks above, lay a lamb. "Emmanuel," he called low; and the little animal, rising uncertainly on its slender legs, came as quickly as it could to the bent form and warm touch. "See — he knows his name. *God-with-us*. You think it odd that I've named him so?"

"It is strange."

"Not at all. I can see the Lord even better in little things than in great. A sunrise dazzles my eyes, but Emmanuel fits right into my arms."

"Sentiment! Ours is the God of power."

"And peace. Often has my father told me that Gideon, the fifth judge of Israel, named the altar he erected in Ophrah, 'Jehovah-shalorn' — *God-is-peace*. This place is to me what Gideon's was to him. A shrine."

"It is but a stony hollow, and a vile one at that."

"Yet here, like me, you found dreams in your own boyhood. You said so."

A gleam came from the eyes of Boaz. He had been endeavoring to conceal the effect that the place was having on him, but now, involuntarily, he bent to pat the nuzzling lamb. "Emmanuel," he whispered.

Then to cover his embarrassment, he drew himself up and asked, "Have you forgotten that you led me here with promise of music?"

Mahalon's lips puckered. Seating himself on a flat stone near the entrance, he laid down his lyre, took the lamb on his lap, and ran his fingers through the wool. "It will be any moment now," he said, "when the wind stirs. You have to be in just the right mood to hear it well."

He pointed upward, and Boaz noticed that the opening above, through which the light poured in a great shaft, was crossed with thin fibers strung on a wooden frame.

"My big harp," the boy explained. "The wind has many fingers but no instrument; so I've given it one."

While Boaz stared, his tunic began to swell in a current of breeze. Then softly, slowly, strains as of a still distant but approaching choir came to the ear, mingling all the harmonic notes, now increasing, now diminishing, according to the energy that swept the cords. Time ceased to exist for him. Standing there, he thought of the sun drawing up the polluted moisture of earth and letting it descend in purity. All the consolation he had ever known seemed to return. And when the sounds died away, he could only contribute his silence to the stillness.

Mahalon, looking at him, asked, "Is it like Zora's voice?"

It was many moments before Boaz replied. "I cannot speak what I feel. I will return — and listen again."

Throughout the next months, the west wind kept moving over the hills from the Mediterranean. It refreshed the planters, made the earth moist, promised success for the planting, and, in the time of harvest, would help sift the chaff and let the grain fall thick on the threshing floors. And Mahalon, who had captured the music of it with his aeolian harp in the cave, now tried often to reproduce the same soft rustling sounds on his minor instrument and to compose little songs as he gazed from the hillside at the seething wheat fields below.

He was not so robust as his brother Chelion, and that was why his father, who loved him with an especial love because of his likeness to Noemi, had assigned him to shepherding. But, in some ways, he was stronger than they thought. Many a time he had lain at the mouth of the cave, where his sheep were folded for the night, and offered himself as a protection against a prowler. He had heard death in dismal, echoing howls. He had even felt its foot-padded approach. But it never occurred to him to mention this to his parents or his brother.

He had a means of defense for himself as well as his sheep — a slingshot with which he had once killed a wolf, gigantic, it seemed, as it sprawled in a still, gray mass before him. And after digging a grave for the carcass, he puzzled that life should be safeguarded by its opposite. Was there not some other way? After all, the wolf's only guilt had been hunger and an attempt to sate it.

Hunger. Mahalon himself experienced two kinds; the one

in his body, fitful and appeasable by the pressed fig cakes, raisin clusters, olives and cheese, with which his mother daily filled his wallet; the other in his being, born of his adolescence and underlying his every other need. But this second hunger, thus far, was undefined and mysterious. He could put the wind into words more effectively than his longing. Sometimes, however, when his parents looked at him, he had the conviction that they were reading his unrest and, in due course, would provide for his relief. He had sensed the harmony between them, too deep and assured for speech. Often his blood went warm to his face at the feelings within him; wistful feelings in which he fancied a veiled presence, white and slender, emerging from mist and coming nearer, like the music of the cave. His mother always wore a veil of immaculate white, woven from the fleece of lambs which he himself had preserved from every speck of dust and refuse. It matched her fineness and dignity. . . . Was there somewhere another Noemi, young, shining — waiting for him?

He recalled that, a year before, in the time of sowing, his brother Chelion, who used to like nothing better than fields springing from green to gold, and the opportunity of contributing the sweat of his brow to the wonderful effect, became strangely languid and uninterested in his work; and that the parents had made certain arrangements with Joachim, an old friend of the family, who dwelt at the far end of the valley. And the result was that Chelion's listlessness left him, for he became espoused to Joachim's daughter, Miriam. Presents of fine-spun garments were sent from the house of Elimelech to the future bride, the usual confirmation by oath and contract was made, and the betrothal was celebrated with a feast which all the neighboring folk, except Boaz, attended. But because of Chelion's and Miriam's youth, it was agreed by both families that the period of espousal be extended. If he himself, the younger, could but have such prospect! Still, he had his flock, his cave, his music, his excellent parents, his brother, and now Boaz — a friend. He was far from unhappy, for all his growing need.

Only once had his mood reached a point of envy. And that was on an evening toward the end of the previous spring, when a full moon hung low over the bearded wheat rising as rich and high in the fields as the seven-eared kind that appeared in Pharaoh's dream by the far-off Nile. For then the boy chanced to see the lovers, whose relationship at this stage was supposed to admit of no intimacy beyond that which could be effected through the medium of a third person chosen for the purpose. But it did not seem wrong to him that their yearning had brought them to each other. They had been often together in childhood days; and now that they were espoused, how could they be expected to keep quite apart? And so, on his way to night-watch on the hill, he paused beneath a tree and gazed at the couple. Chelion so straight and strong, with the same breadth of shoulder, the same rugged form, as his father's; Miriam so slender, supple, and frail. Hand in hand, they were slowly wading through billows of breeze-swept grain. And the boy admired even as he envied; but it was a smiling emotion, because the brothers were devoted to each other. Breathlessly he saw Miriam's long veil swirling from her shoulder to Chelion's and covering it seemingly with a caress; and Chelion's hand slipping from the clasp, only that his arm might encircle the waist. Their faces were a soft blur in the moonlight. Their figures blended, their lips met. And Mahalon, unseen, stole away.

A year ago . . . how time had sped and, now that Mahalon had found a friend in Boaz, was speeding! For hours each day, the two would listen to the intermittent music of the cave, and be drawn to each other, sometimes with flowing speech, sometimes with a yet more expressive silence. But Boaz kept his innermost stirrings to himself, and Mahalon could only guess at them. He hoped that the man's soul was healing; and the more he hoped, the more he cherished this lonely one who had proved a great capacity for love by fervently, almost fiercely, holding to memories. He felt that, if all happiness were his, he would have readily sacrificed it for him. He told this to Chelion, who warned, "Careful, my brother. The Lord may hear." But still thinking of Boaz, he did not mind; for those eyes of his friend were the seeking eyes of a lost sheep, and those hands were too often clutched as if to squeeze something out of the life that bereavement had left.

And here the harvest, the time appointed for the nuptials of Chelion and Miriam, was almost ready. This year the grain would set a record. A thin haze, dimming all the harsher notes of nature, covered the land with a visible peace. A family feeling spread everywhere and, one sundown, it was perfected for the house of Elimelech by a rare occasion. The arbored pathway once more became a living link between two homes. Boaz had once more walked along it.

"I bring something of what I've found out there," he said to Elimelech, motioning toward the hills. "My mind has become clear; my feelings are calm. Can you forgive me for the — past?"

"Lord of our Fathers be praised!" cried Noemi, as the men embraced. Her glance went for an instant to her younger son standing near with Chelion, and she nodded gratefully. "Our table is ready, good Boaz, and the lamps are bright. Let us believe that you have never been away from us and forget everything but the Providence that brings the longest night to day."

"Now is my cup of joy filled," declared Elimelech, his fingers running through his sparse gray beard, his slightly bald head flung back so that his gaze was upward, his features gently limned in the light. "What is there to add but the mating of our Chelion and then, in a swift year or two, that of our Mahalon? Come, let us gather around the board. This hour the heavens sing. Would that the whole world could know and share what is ours! Truly is our Bethlehem the 'house of bread.' "

"And more," said Noemi. "The cradle of blessedness."

But even as she was speaking, Mahalon seized Chelion's wrist. "Do you hear it?" he asked tensely, subduing his voice.

"What, my brother?"

"It sounds like a cry of evil approaching from over the hills. Does Satan begrudge us and — and —?"

Chelion released himself and slipped an arm around Mahalon's shoulder. "Don't speak that name or so much as think it. The hills are thick with grass, the sheep heavy with wool."

"And yet," said Mahalon, "I hear the cry."

Chapter Two

THE GREAT HUNGER

BEFORE morning, the west wind has ceased, and a sirocco from beyond the River Jordan and the Salt Sea was pouring its hot breath on the land. Sand clouds scudded the skies. A drought began and, through ensuing weeks, gave indication of never ending. Or so Elimelech thought, as he stood with his wife and sons on the roof of his house at a late hour one night and scanned the dark for a single star. The only light was the one that Mahalon held in his hand; a cylindrical clay lamp with a flat bottom, a ringed top, and holes through which the flame inside sent pale gleams.

And the father moaned, addressing his God. "With the east wind we are visited by ruin."

"Yet, in the flight from Egypt, was it not the east wind that drove back the waters of the Red Sea and made the dry land appear?" said Noemi, placing her hand on his arm.

"Dry land," he echoed, his pent-up feelings at last demanding release. He had been too rigid, too worried, for days. And he uttered the words again, nearly weeping. "I had thought that the only threat to our crop was the rodents or the too heavy dews. But this! What good are our sickles now? Our watersheds, poorly constructed, weakly supplied by our springs, have failed us. Our grain . . . in another week, it would have been ready for the cutting and sheafing." He raised a fist. "Bring me ashes to sprinkle my head, for the soil that kept life in our bodies is dying, and there is nothing for us but hunger." Shaking off Noemi's touch, he bared his chest and rent his tunic; and, reaching for a knife in his girdle, he might have slashed his flesh, only that Chelion seized one wrist and Noemi the other.

15

The sight was the more terrifying to Mahalon, because hitherto his father, in any situation, had shown control and restraint. Never before had the boy experienced blighted fields, though the fear of them had endured in the land; and he now recalled some of the elders mumbling about terrible times when not a blade of grass was to be found, and leafless black trees thrust themselves up from the burnt earth like contorted fingers of half-buried giants, and skeleton men poked in caked dung for undigested seeds. Had such times returned? He looked at his brother but could see only the writhing back and shoulders of him. He looked to his mother, but her face was turned. He did not dare gaze again on his father. He felt completely alone, not knowing how much of their concern was for him, the youngest. He thought of going to Boaz; but Boaz had been keeping too silent and aloof. He thought of his sheep. Then without a word, he left the roof, went down the stairway to the ground level, and dashed off into the night.

He still held the lantern. His eyes smarted with unshed tears at the grain stalks, lately so tall and promising, lying wilted on the powdery earth. A sigh sifted through the heavy black air as he groped his way. Sharp edges of rock cut his bare feet; briars scratched at his legs. His heart pounded in his chest. He quickened his gait, the lantern swinging wildly from the curve of his finger and revealing only devastation along the way.

There was no hope of melody to draw him on, as when he first led Boaz to the hillcrest; even though a languid breeze, hot enough to make his sweaty garment seem an extra layer of skin, was now sweeping the night. The cave had been silent for days; and now the howl of a wolf came to his ear. He had left his slingshot behind; it would have been of little use in the gloom. He knew, however, that unless accompanied by others of its kind, and unless emptiness gnawed its belly, a wolf was not apt to attack a human being; and this present howling seemed to argue a solitary animal. But this wolf and others must be hungry. Decayed remains of hedgehogs, mice, birds, and reptiles sparsely littered the ground. Wolves were devourers of carrion; but carrion as a steady diet was not enough, especially when living flesh was near.

He knew that they had all the cunning of the fox; that, when foraging in a pack, they would divide into parties, the one following the trail of the quarry, the other intercepting the retreat; that their caution made them regard every unfamiliar object with suspicion; that they would never pass through a door if they could leap over a wall; that they ordinarily would not attack a tethered animal, inasmuch as it might be bait for a trap. Applying this knowledge, he had made a door to cover the entrance to the cave, and, after leading his flock within that evening, arranged the rams in a protective circle around the sheep and tied their horns with loops of leafless vine and briar. He had felt that they should be secure, but the conviction had kept wavering.

Now he noticed that the howling no longer came from a single throat. It rolled in different tones and from opposite directions, as if an uncouth conversation were being sent across the night by several animals. Were they speaking in their own fashion about the nearness of prey? Far or near — he could not tell — evil sparks appeared. His hands, for all the insufferable heat, felt cold and wet. He thought he could hear his name being called from a distance behind by his father and Chelion; but he could not be sure.

At last, he was at the cave. He put down the lantern. His fingers found and were lifting the oaken beam, its ends high in two hollows, by which the door was fastened. A piteous bleating within whipped his effort to a frenzy.

Glancing over his shoulder, he imagined that he could see the scattered, lurid glares closing in and multiplying. Why was he opening the cave? Was it not folly? But he must convince himself that the sheep were safe, for tonight all space seemed alive with menace. And he must do something about the opening in the roof! Those cross strings, fine enough for music, were not strong enough for defense.

When he at last stood inside, the lantern, which he had again taken up, accented the dark for the moment; and then, as he held it before him, the ram-cordoned sheep were shown huddled to the right. In the middle of the floor, a young wolf sat on its haunches: fangs dripping with blood. The remains of what had once been the lamb he had named "Emmanuel" lay in front of the forepaws. With a swift upward look, Mahalon beheld the aeolian harp hanging in shreds.

He set the lamp aside, seized his shepherd crook from a corner, and swung it. The whelp leaped away and then, with a bewildered turnabout, sprang at him and knocked the weapon out of his grasp.

Repressing a cry, he plunged his fists down in time to grasp the neck. It strained and swelled. The tongue hung over the long jaw. The body rose on its hind legs, its claws flailing. One of the paws got below the boy's ribs and raked across the navel to the thighs as he tried to hold on.

A sudden flare covered the walls. Elimelech and Chelion, carrying torches, were hurrying in. As the wolf wrenched itself free, swirled, and streaked past them into the night, they dashed to Mahalon, whose abdomen was torn and bleeding.

Some other wolves had scaled the exterior, and shaggy-pointed faces were now poking down through the open roof. Mahalon, in the act of trying to rise, saw them first. "Look!" he shrieked at Elimelech and Chelion, pointing. Too confused to retreat, the beasts — three in all — dropped to the floor. Growling, they rolled on their backs and flanks as Elimelech and Chelion endeavored to prod them toward the doorway with the brands. One made a twisted, agile leap toward Elimelech's throat; but Mahalon, the haft of the crook again in his hold, had enough strength to get to his knees and strike. Then the cave spun, with bodies everywhere at once and the sheep panic-swept. The torches and the crook were knocked to the ground. Elimelech fought with the knife drawn from his girdle; Chelion, with his bare fists. Mahalon could give no further assistance. He shrank against the wall, holding his fingers to his groin and trying to keep from fainting.

There was much straw in the cave, and the rocks were overspread with dry lichen. Almost instantly flames were lapping them and, with burning spots on their pelts, the wolves took to the open. It was then too late to save the sheep. Scorched, halfblinded, choking from fumes, Elimelech and Chelion made every effort; but the flock kept static and immovable, awaiting fate. There was nothing to do but to get Mahalon and themselves out.

"We did our best," Elimelech groaned when he and his sons were in the open.

"And only for the worst," said Chelion, his arm dangling, ripped from the shoulder to the elbow.

Slowly, tortuously, they dragged their way down the hill.

Mahalon was unsteadily bearing one of the torches, grabbed from the flames. In the dying rays he saw his father's wounded chest, the matted beard, the ghastly face; and in horror he almost forgot his own injuries. He glanced back over his shoulder at the smoky maw of the cave and the glow thrown skyward from the roof. Those innocent lambs! Had they served a foreordained purpose? Was the Lord accepting the sacrifice, and would he be appeased? He thought of his lyre which he had left in the cave. Would harmony ever return to the hills, and the memory of this night be erased?

In the descent, Elimelech stood and stared. Out of the dark, a small blob of white seemed to be floating up from the valley.

"Your mother, my sons," he said. "She could not wait. Thank God she came no sooner!" He paused for breath. "She is the star! To think, I despaired of finding it, forgetting that the

Lord always sends such light as we must have in order to go on living." He raised his voice. "Noemi — Noemi —" And the call was as that of a spent and weary but grateful child.

Never had Noemi been more the wife and mother than in the days that followed. She scoured the fields and hills for stray, surviving bits of herbs to brew into a balsam potion. She treated the patients' burns and wounds with ointments of barley beer, sesame, and cedar oil. She even secured from a healer, with the last coins in the house, a salve which was made from the crushed body of a water snake and the pulverized udder of a cow: said to have the power to create an artificial skin for gashes. In the very excess of her service, she would not let her husband and her sons do for themselves even the little of which they were capable, trying to speed their recovery by conserving their meager strength, but contributing unwittingly to their helplessness.

They accepted with all gratitude the proof of her goodness; and they might have rallied, only for nature's continued mood. The skies lowered by day and blackened by night, and the cauldron heat kept rolling over the land. Not a single bird song was to be heard. Neither the sores of bodies nor those of spirits would heal. And Noemi compounded for the weakness that confined her family to their pallets, by drawing on some mysterious spring of energy deep within herself and performing not only her own duties fully but also those of the servants who had fled the household and the valley for the faint possibility of better conditions in the town. And, in addition, she gave every moment she could spare to the relief of her sick and worried neighbors.

"Rest, Noemi, and shame us not," begged Elimelech.

"To be needed is my rest," she answered. "Were twice as much effort required of me, gladly would I give it."

But she almost gave in to the strain the morning when Chelion, silent for days, attempted to rise — only to sink back heavily. She knew whom he wanted. The plea in his eyes was more than she could bear. "You never mention her name, my mother," he accused. "Why hasn't she come to me?"

Noemi turned her face away. She was still unable to tell him what had happened. Already, like Zora, Miriam lay buried, one of the first victims of a plague accompanying the famine. "The times are such that not even Boaz, so near, comes to us," she murmured, evasive for the first time in her life.

But one night, when the hour was darkest, Boaz did re-appear in the house of Elimelech. His head was shaven; his chin raw from the plucking forth of his beard; his face, haggard, his ash-sprinkled tunic hanging on him like a shroud.

"Flee this land of woe!" he cried. "I have heard today that, while we starve, the fields of Moab flourish. Go there, if it be not too late. Take my oxen and whatever else. I want nothing any more but to wait."

All listened in silence.

"The cave in the hills," he maundered on, his fingers clutched to his shoulders, his elbows digging his ribs, his eyes sunken and burning. "It is empty — worse than empty. No longer can I hear the — the voice. . . . And the almond tree by the brook is as sere as our soil. Go, while there's yet a place to draw breath."

"We cannot leave you," said Elimelech, "now that the past no longer divides us."

"But there is no future to bind us. And have no qualms about leaving me. I've too well learned to be alone."

"We could give you our house and land for the oxen," said Noemi, not too overcome for a touch of pride and independence. She would have her family accept nothing without some sort of return. She looked to her husband, and his eyes assented.

Then Elimelech held up his hands beseechingly. "If we go, Boaz, you must join us."

"No. What I cannot find here I'll not find elsewhere. Here I will stay. Someday I may hear the voice again. . . ."

Noemi came to him and touched his arm. "Believe, good Boaz, that somehow the Lord will reward the barren years, and reward them lastingly."

Elimelech's *amen* came deep.

"But no more than Boaz can I go," protested Chelion from his pallet. "Miriam needs me."

"She did, my poor son," said Noemi, "but now she needs none of us."

She knelt to hold him to her breast. And Mahalon, remembering the scene of his brother and Miriam in the moonlit field and thinking of the marriage that could never be, hid his face in his hands.

The next morning, Noemi and Boaz helped the invalids into the straw-bedded cart drawn up at the gate of the house, and then she took her place by one of the scrawny bullocks that would do the hauling throughout the long, slow journey ahead. So as not to add to grief, she told nobody about leaving, and there was no neighbor to see her off but Deborah — a sickly little woman with a girl child at her side — whose intuition had brought her.

"God guide you and bring you back to us," the woman prayed, weeping. "Now will the valley be bleak indeed! It is losing its best friend."

Noemi could not reply. She merely looked on her and the child with much love, grateful that they had accepted her help when she was able to give it, sad that there was no more to give. And the child's wide eyes seemed to absorb every detail of the parting.

Noemi's chin was firm, but her hand shook as it grasped the end of the short rope tied to the horns of the oxen. She turned to Boaz. "Won't you change your mind?" she pleaded. "Won't you come?"

He shook his head, and his pale lips opened like the edges of an old wound never really healed. "I want to see nothing of any of you again," he said. "My worst misfortune came from this household. Even the relief young Mahalon gave me was false. All your kindness — the covering of a curse! Would I had never known you!"

Then he turned and fled through the grape arbor — now a leafless stretch of twisted vines.

Noemi swallowed hard as she gave the rope a tug. She could see in memory the road along which she had persuaded Elimelech to take Zora on the fatal wedding day. A road that was still winding on, paved with sorrow.

In a rise of dust, the cartwheels turned.

Chapter Three

THE SIGN OF THE CROSS

AFTER days of pressing onward in an ever swelling stream of fugitives from the stricken areas, the family reached the upper rim of the Salt Sea where the River Jordan emptied into the weird waters below. They could not have gotten so far, had it not been for Noemi's resolute, steady spirit. Her pride had not let her beg for assistance along the way. It was she herself who assisted; here comforting a whimpering child, there bringing to parched lips what little water she could find or spare, now taking chill fingers in hers and transmitting courage, now composing the features of the dying or helping to bury the dead. Poverty itself shared spontaneously with her the crusts that kept life in her husband and sons. And at last fresh fields and tall grain, not too far off, were dimly appearing.

Many times during the journey, Mahalon and Chelion had tried to forget their pain and weakness, to aid their father, and to lessen their mother's exertion. But she so insisted on doing everything for them that they could only be resigned to inertness and wait. She might have been carrying them a second time in her womb, draining her substance into their being.

Elimelech lay pale and almost motionless on the straw of the ox cart. "Lift me," he murmured to his sons, as he felt the cool, clean morning air from the fertile highlands that crowned the northeastern shore of the sea. "Noemi, come closer and hold my hand."

He thought he could see the summit of Mount Nebo showing in the distance. "There on that height," he reflected aloud,

"Moses once stood, looking westward and longing to enter the Land of Promise. And here I languish, looking to the east, hoping that my family may find what I can no longer give."

"All of us shall find the end of the trial together," said Noemi quickly, increasing the pressure of her hand.

But, scarcely hearing her, he went on. "There in the land of Moab, over against Beth-Phogor, Moses sleeps, his heart rent like my own. There the prophet Balaam was led by the Moabite king, Balak, that he might look on the whole host of our people and utter a curse." His face convulsed. "To be cursed even by our own prophet!"

"But the curse was not uttered, my husband. Balaam predicted a great future for us."

"Is this that future? Our fields turned against us, our sons deprived of their inheritance, our lot cast among strangers."

"Does not 'Israel,' my husband, mean 'prince that prevails with God'? Could there ever be a prevailing, a victory, without a struggle? In the past, our people have many times been beaten to the earth, but have always risen. So shall it be again and again. The Lord's flail is on those he loves —"

"How he must love us! Worse than flailed, we are trodden like wheat on the threshing floor."

"But, as with wheat, only that the sweet grain be separated from the kernels."

"Oh, Noemi, my faith is as withered as this body. Speak on and restore me. What do you see in the strange misfortune of our race?"

Fatigue yielded to a sparkle in her eye. "Often the thought comes to me, my husband, that we of Israel live too much apart from other peoples. We have a treasure — the law of Moses, the Ark of the Covenant, the hope and promise of a Messiah. We've guarded the treasure well. But while holding ourselves from the worship of false gods, have we been eager enough to spread the worship of the true God? Ours is an in-growing race. It should be more — more outgiving.

And the Lord, in his wisdom, uproots and transplants us from time to time, that the truth we bear may come into other lives from our own. Is not mankind hungry for truth?"

"Hungry, indeed!"

"The Lord brought us into and out of the land of Egypt. During our wanderings, we have at least left traces of our treasure — crumbs from our table of truth. It is when we are too long in one place that our love of the land vies with our love of the Lord. How barren the life of poor Boaz, who sees only the soil and broods over it! To be up and bearing the living sheaves — the wheat of wheat — to those whose spirits are feeding on the husks of swine; this is our opportunity, not our pain!"

Never having heard such eloquence from her before, the others were all intent. They caught something of her vision and their faces brightened. "Wheat of wheat — behold the beauty of it in your mother, my sons," said Elimelech. "Look not on me who am but chaff, soon to be separated."

"Not so, not so, O my husband. In yonder Moab, we'll find nourishment for our failing bodies and share the unleavened loaves of our faith."

In exchange for one of the oxen, fit only for slaughter, a boatman conveyed them across the Jordan on a raft; and when they reached the other side, Noemi helped the remaining animal draw the wagon.

For endless hours she plodded ahead hoping, praying. At dusk she halted before a small boxlike dwelling near a great fig tree. At last her spirit had wilted, for the people of this land seemed to resent the influx of Israelites, and all her attempts to barter her services for a little bread and wine along the way had been useless. She recalled the boyishly ardent simile that Mahalon had once applied to her, and she begged the Lord, as she knocked at this last door, that the face of this house would be to her loved ones as "an evening window with a candle shining through." There was such a window, such a light, right before her; but her eyes were so blurred with the sweat dripping into them from her forehead that she could hardly see.

The door opened and revealed a girl holding a saucer-shaped lamp in the hollow of her hand. The wick, of cotton twisted around a piece of straw, gave forth a tiny flame and, in the radiance, Noemi noted the strong cast of face, the richness of lips, the dark shining eyes, the broad smooth forehead, the unveiled flowing hair as glistening black as the sorek grape. She indicated the cart with a slight movement of the head and extended her empty, bruised hands.

Silently the girl stepped from the doorway and played the rays of the lamp over the three men on the straw. Her gaze went to each wan face in turn. Then to Noemi she spoke, to the surprise of her hearers, in the language of Israel. "My name is Orpha. Here I live with Bahila, my mother: she a widow, I not yet a wife." For an instant her lips pressed together and her breasts rose, rounded and firm. "I have had to learn to protect her and myself from such as would do us harm."

"We bring no harm," said Noemi. "Behold our helplessness."

"I was but thinking," explained the girl quickly, "of the strangers who passed this way a year ago. My mother was alone in the house at the time. Not food, but money, they wanted. She had nothing to give. They beat her and left her lying on the floor. — It took months for me to nurse her back to bodily health. Her mind is still not recovered. I tell you this so that you will understand."

"Too well we understand," replied Noemi, all sympathy. "Our own kinsman Boaz has long been suffering from the deed of outlaws. . . . From Israel, the land of famine, we come. These are my husband and sons, ill in body but capable, with care, of regaining strength to repay whatever hospitality you bestow. And I — Noemi — will work for you in every way I can, if you let us stay a while."

Orpha set the lamp on a stone. "Good mother," she said, putting an arm around Noemi's waist and drawing the drooping head to her shoulder, "you yourself are almost as spent as they. Think only of rest. Enter our house. I am able enough to supply what help these poor men need."

And together they half carried, half led, Elimelech and Mahalon from the cart to the door of the dwelling. There the father and the son waited, their palms pressed to the walls for support, while Orpha went to Chelion. Waving Noemi aside, she assisted him all by herself.

It was possible for her to hold him to her almost like a child. The beating of her heart, the warmth of her breast, seemed to revive him from the torpor into which he had sunken. His eyes opened a little and emitted a flickering ray. At first he struggled weakly to free himself from the embrace, but then, with a sigh, he yielded to it.

Noemi, in strict accord with Hebrew custom, removed her own sandals and those of her husband and sons at the threshold. And since there was no *mezzuzah** attached to this house in an alien land, she herself, kneeling, uttered the night prayer from Deuteronomy: "Hear, O Israel . . ."

Elimelech, Chelion, and Mahalon also sank to their knees; and Orpha, with an arm still around Chelion's shoulder, listened to the solemn words: ". . . Jehovah our God is one Jehovah; and thou shalt love Jehovah with all thy heart, with all thy soul, and with all thy might. . . ."

"Your God," she asked when Noemi had finished, "this 'Jehovah' is truly one to be loved?"

"He is love itself," said Noemi simply, taking up the lamp from the stone and helping Elimelech to rise.

---

* A small metal or wooden box containing a prayer written on parchment.

Mahalon succeeded in getting to his feet by his own effort. Orpha kept to Chelion.

In the open doorway, a woman now appeared out of the interior shadows. She was small, angular, frail, and her face seemed part of the grayness of the mantle that covered her head and form; but, at the sight of the strangers, her eyes glittered sharply, and she drew back.

"My mother, these are refugees from Israel," said Orpha. "We must shelter them as long as will be needed."

Bahila's straight lips parted as if about to protest; but seeing how set was her daughter's intent, she said nothing.

Elimelech again sank feebly to his knees, and put his hands and forehead to the short stone step at the entrance. Noemi and Mahalon bowed from the waist. Chelion leaned on Orpha. "Peace be to you," they spoke together. And Bahila, commanded by Orpha's glance, approached to receive them.

They entered a large room, almost bare and dimly lit by two candles in niches. The floor was of clay, packed hard by years of use. From a carved chest in a corner, Orpha and her mother removed and unrolled two wool-stuffed sleeping mats and two goat's hair quilts. These they arranged on the floor for Elimelech and his sons. And drawing Noemi aside, Orpha whispered to her, "This is our only bedding. You and I and my mother can sleep together on the roof. The air is not too chill tonight, and our nearness to one another will make warmth."

After attending to the patients and sharing food with them, they bade them good night and ascended an outside stairway to the roof. Noemi had noticed that, as they were leaving, Orpha looked over her shoulder, her gaze solicitous for all three but mostly given to Chelion.

The roof was a small expanse of sycamore beams layered over with brush, reeds, and dried mud, and softly lit by a three-quarter moon high in the heavens. Noemi could see the outspread mat on which grain was customarily flailed; the space reserved for drying figs, dates, flax, and clothes; the oven for the baking of flat loaves of bread; and here and there, along the border where feet did not tread, tufts of grass and anemone which had sprouted from wind-blown seeds. It was all much the same as her own home in Bethlehem had been, and an ease crept around her.

"Tomorrow we'll build a booth of branches here," said Orpha. "Tonight the threshing mat will have to serve."

They lay down. And Bahila was soon sleeping or pretending. She had edged away and shrunken into herself. Orpha and Noemi remained awake, looking up at the sky and the stars.

"You say your God is *love?*" murmured Orpha.

"Love," repeated Noemi.

"The god of Moab is Chemosh," said Orpha. "His temple is not far from here and we live in the shadow. He sheds a great unrest and confusion. His face is that of a calf, and his hands reach out not to give but to strike and take. His belly is a molten furnace. . . . I've already heard of your God from a companion of mine, a girl younger than myself. But I could not believe —"

Noemi's eyes were closing. "I will tell you about him, if so you wish with the morrow's light."

"I do wish it. My companion will wish it too. How good it is that both of us have learned the language you speak! Israelites who've long dwelt in Moab taught us. Many of the Moabites know Hebrew, but few of us the Hebrew faith."

Moments passed.

"But how," she asked, "can you love a God who has deprived you of so much?"

"He has left me my family," said Noemi, her voice a thread of sound which vibrated with faith and gratitude. "He has led us to you, good daughter of Moab."

Orpha said no more. When she was sure that Noemi was at last sleeping, she rose, slowly crossed the roof, and descended the stairway. For the rest of the night, she sat on a low square stool in the room where the three men lay.

Elimelech's face was deep in shade, Mahalon slept with his head buried in the crook of his arm, and on Chelion fell the light of a candle in one of the wall niches. The girl studied his features and noted the pain in them. Twice, when his lids parted somewhat, she smiled gently on him. When dawn was slipping through the windows, she knelt and impulsively touched her lips to his brow.

"Miriam," he said.

She started.

His eyes were opening wide and she saw the loneliness in them.

"Speak to me — of her," she forced herself to whisper. "It will soothe you."

"There is nothing to say. She is gone — forever. But I dreamed that, for a moment, she came back and put her lips to my forehead."

"She will return," said Orpha, after a pause, in a voice that seemed strange to her own hearing. "Rest. I will help you as best I can."

Obediently his eyes closed.

In the days that followed, Bahila, used to receiving her daughter's every attention, sulked at the interest that was now being lavished on these people from afar; and her resentment fell chiefly on Elimelech whom Orpha, as well as the others, watched with a special concern because of his inability to respond to treatment. To her, he was the hub of the unpleasantness that had entered her life. If he were gone, would not his wife be gone too? Hour after hour she daily sat hunched over her grinding mill of black basalt, working the sun-dried grain to a fine powder with a stone that fitted her palm. And whenever Noemi tried to relieve her, she settled the more to her task, saying nothing. But Noemi could read in the very silence the questions: *Why do you let my Orpha, a stranger to you, slave for your family? Will the famine in Israel last much longer? Can you not leave us as you found us?*

There was a red-stone image of Chemosh in one of the niches of the house, and Bahila kept a lamp burning before it. The restless glow seemed to sharpen the white shell teeth in the cruel little mouth of it, to render alive the glass eyes in the calf-shaped head, and to smear with blood the naked figure, pudgy and potbellied, seated cross-legged on a low throne upheld by the back of a queer squatting beast. Elimelech, lying on his pallet, tensed every time he glanced at it, and he always covered his face with his hands and quivered as Bahila worshiped it many times a day.

"To eat of the bread of this house, is it not to share in its idolatry?" he complained one day to Noemi. "I want to be grateful for the hospitality, but my fear will not let me. Our fathers in Egypt yielded to a false religion and even clamored, after their release from Pharaoh, for some graven thing to adore; and Aaron made them an image not unlike the one in this very room. Let us go hence. Better to die than be defiled!"

Noemi, kneeling, touched his crinkled cheek. "We should have pity for a household and a land that know not the Lord of Israel," she admonished quietly. "Moab is in darkness and, like a child in the night, Bahila is afraid. Even as we fear contamination, so does she. We all require much understanding. And it is for us, in return for the good we're receiving, to give our light. Haven't you seen, O my husband, that Orpha no longer feeds oil to the lamp of Chemosh? A ray of our faith is already in her. Bahila, too, may change —"

But Elimelech, drawing her head down, whispered in her ear, so that his sons, lying near, might not hear: "The Lord's blessing is not for us, Noemi. I won't be able to bite my tongue forever. This Orpha is casting a spell on Chelion. I see him turning more and more to her. Seemingly she's neglecting her god, but only to win our son away. Woe is written on these walls."

"My husband," said Noemi, a catch in her throat, "the Lord sent us into this land and led us to this house. What comes of our staying is in his keeping."

But she herself, troubled within, found it hard to hide her feelings and muster enough courage to face the future. There was no turning back yet. What was there to turn back to? She could only wait and pray that Chelion's faith might not waver but rather grow stronger and help to repay Orpha's kindness with truth.

Like any girl in love, the daughter of Bahila shed warmth wherever she went, and her energy was boundless. She poured her spirit into Chelion and was bringing back to his countenance something of the look that had not been there since the loss of Miriam. As for Mahalon, he inclined to her as a brother to an unusual sister, and his gaze followed her with admiration in the midst of her many tasks. Even his mother, he had to admit, was not more efficient, and he was pleased at the bond so evidently developing between this Moabitess and his brother. And again he knew envy. Again a veiled presence, white and slender, seemed to be approaching him through mist.

"Where and how, my father, did you and my mother first meet?" he asked one evening when the tedium of lying and waiting for the return of health was too much for him.

A light came to Elimelech's face and his limbs relaxed on the pallet. His eyes turned in the nests of wrinkles that suffering had woven. "It almost seems," he said, "she was with me from the time my boyhood ended."

Mahalon looked at him eagerly.

"Our race has been rich in its women," Elimelech continued. "Sarah, Rachel, Rebecca, and so many others! The day is to come when a daughter of our people will bear the Messias and rejoice the land. We have lived on in a longing for him, and the worth of our daughters is a pledge that a fitting mother for him will be found." His lips closed, and the silence was like the aftertone of a bell. In a little while he spoke again. "Your grandmother, my son, did no evil all the days of her life. How she labored! — rising even in the deep of night to spin and weave and plan the comfort of her family, her every act a prayer, her mind never on herself. No hand was readier and abler in the vineyard than hers, no arms more given to lifting the weak, no tongue more steeped in charity." And Mahalon, in imagination, could see his father standing in dignity and hear him discoursing eloquently with the elders at the gates of Bethlehem.

"Her works praised her," summed up Elimelech. "And when it came time for me to wed, your grandfather well knew the wife I wanted. He found for me in a village in Galilee, called Nazareth, our own Noemi."

On the morning of his first day in the open, Mahalon made a discovery.

Still weak, he had gone a bit beyond the field behind the house, when it was necessary for him to lie down. His body, in contact with the cool earth, immediately felt better. A languor, induced by the fragrance in the air, possessed him. His eyes closed and he began to doze. But a small noise — a rustling of leaves — roused him; and, as he gazed in the direction of the sound, he saw a hand reaching forth from a leafy wall of silver olive trees a little distance away. It was a delicate yet capable-looking hand. Against the green of the foliage, it showed vivid and seemed to plead for assistance.

Quickly he was on his feet and crossing the intervening space. By that time, the long bell-shaped sleeve of a robe was also visible; then a form, a face.

Instantly he recalled his mother's description of Zora, whose brow was the color of wheat and whose grace was as that of stalks swaying in the meadow. He held his breath and stood still, lest the apparition fade.

The girl looked at him. Her large eyes had long, curling lashes, and their blue suggested clear water reflecting the sky. He noticed the rich but not too full red lips; the soft jaw lines; the small ears almost hidden by waves of unbound chestnut hair; the warm pure curve of bosom; the simple sun-bleached dress. Her bare, sandaled feet touched the ground lightly; her veil, which had slipped down around her shoulders, was as immaculate as Noemi's in Bethlehem.

"The branches caught me," she said, accepting his help, and bending as she put forth a fold of her garment to show him a small rent in it. With her other hand, she brushed back a tress or two of hair.

"Like Orpha," he said, "you speak the language of Israel."

She smiled and it was like sunshine released from within. "I enjoy speaking it."

"But your people — do they care to hear it?"

A shadow passed over her countenance. "There has been some thievery in these parts, and it is blamed on those that keep coming from beyond the sea," she said, looking away. "My people — some of them — are so bad that they get a comfort out of thinking others worse. They don't take the trouble to understand. But . . ."

"Yes?"

"I am sure that only good comes from Israel. Do you know a town called Bethlehem-Judah?"

"Why, it is the very place of my birth! It rests in the hills like a lamb in the arms of the Lord." His voice lowered. "Or rather it used to be like that. It's not the same now. The hills are bare. But how did you hear of it?"

She took a quick breath. "In my childhood, it was described to me by one who loved it more than all the other cities of

Israel. Sometime I'll tell you what he told me. And you
can tell me — everything."

"You would weep if I told you all. Have you ever been
hungry?"

"I've never wanted for bread," she answered gravely. "But
I'm an orphan. It is years since my mother died, and my
father soon followed her to the grave. They were everything
to each other and — me — and I've since had to live with my
uncle Jared, whose dwelling is not far from here. I wish
it were farther and that I didn't have to go back. He's
stewart to the high priest of Chemosh, and he thinks
Chemosh is angry at Moab for letting folk with another
worship enter here. He says a curse is going to fall on
us. That is why I'm forbidden to visit Orpha any more.
But I can't obey him in this, though I've tried. Orpha
is my closest friend. This morning I seemed to feel that she'd
need me, and I stole away."

"Let me take you to her."

As frankly as a child, she gave him her hand.

Slowly they walked toward the house, and he felt his
weakness lessening with every step. "What is your name?" he
asked.

"Ruth."

"Mine is Mahalon."

He hardly noticed when she withdrew her fingers, the act
was so gentle. And the morning light, warmer, brighter, fell
on them like a shower of blossoms.

They did not perceive that the gaze of a man, off in the field,
was following them.

Orpha and Noemi, seated on a bench beside the house, were
busy with flax, little bundles of which, already retted and
bleaching, lay on the ground. Chelion, asprawl at their feet,
was applying a wooden carder comb to some of the fiber;

and Mahalon and Ruth, as they drew near, could hear him saying to Orpha, "This will be spun and woven by my mother into something worthy even of a bride." They noted the glow in Orpha's look.

It was moments before the three were aware of them standing in the shadow of a tree. Orpha saw them first and, with a cry, she thrust her work aside, running to Ruth, throwing forth her arms.

Noemi let her flax slip to her lap, and pressed her fingers to her throat, as she always did when a keen sense of the past was upon her; for the young Moabitess reminded her no little of the Zora whom Boaz had lost. The same height, the same coloring, almost the same features — accentuated by contrast with Orpha's greater stature, darker complexion, and tenser type of countenance. And, thinking back, she could almost see Boaz as he waited, that distant day in Bethlehem. "Oh, if he could now behold this living likeness," she sighed to herself. But she had already surprised the luster in Mahalon's eyes and read the significance of it; and her relief that he seemed glad again mingled with a fear. Were the lives of both her sons to take root in this alien land? — And what would Elimelech think! She had left him lying on his pallet in the house, where he would be better protected from the rising heat of the day; hoping that quiet and repose might decrease his worry over the future. And here another worry was shaping itself to seize him. She wanted to go to him. She had a sharp feeling that he was calling, though there was certainly no sound.

Orpha was now leading the girl to her, telling the name, mentioning the value of the friendship.

Soon they all were comfortably settled, and a breeze from the open field blew around them. Mahalon, his eyes fixed on Ruth, who was sitting beside Noemi, had flung himself at their feet with Chelion. Ruth's gaze went from his mother to him and back again. Conversation flowed; and when at last it lulled, a little song of abundant harvests sprang to Ruth's lips.

But the song soon ceased, for a strange shadow began to float above them. It was that of a large gray-black bird, with gaunt wings and curled beak. They watched it circle above them, and then fly to the roof of the house, where it perched like a figment of evil, staring down, waiting.

From the curtained doorway, Bahila slowly emerged. She stood and swayed: her mantle gone, her robe rumpled and stained, her sunken cheeks wet with sweat, her hair hanging.

Instantly Orpha was at her side. She had seen that same facial aspect the day when Bahila was attacked by the marauders.

"What have you done?" she cried in her native tongue, seizing the skeletal shoulders and shaking them the way one shakes a child from the spell of a nightmare.

Bahila's teeth chattered. "I — I do not know. It came over me so swiftly." She pushed Orpha off and held her hands before her face. "Are these mine? And this blood. . . ."

A sudden thought, too terrible, struck Orpha. "Not his!" she almost screamed.

Bahila's jaw sank. "I remember — now. But the old man himself was to blame. He and — Chemosh." Her breath came in little gasps. "When I was lighting two lamps to our God to make up for your neglect, the old man chided me from the floor. 'Cease worshiping lies! There is no God but Yahweh!' I turned and saw his bearded face. I had no will of my own. Then it was done. I — I'd fallen on him and — and torn the throat. Chemosh must have used me. . . . Oh, why did you ever let these strangers into our house?"

Orpha thrust her aside, her gaze on Chelion with a plea that nothing — not even this! — be permitted to come between them. But Chelion and Mahalon were advancing with leaden feet, their thoughts only for what lay behind the curtain, and for their mother who must be kept as long as possible from witnessing it. They passed Orpha and Bahila blindly and plunged into the room.

Left with Noemi, Ruth clung to her on the bench. Noemi herself seemed turned to stone; but the young heart, so close, beating wildly, infused some of its energy and she was able to get to her feet. "Daughter," she said, measuring the space that separated her from the threshold, and pierced with a sense of what awaited her, "stand by me."

All was quiet now. Orpha had followed Mahalon and Chelion inside, and Bahila was gone. But Ruth, wondering whether her control could last and determinedly keeping her gaze from the doorway, suddenly uttered a cry.

"Look!" she bade Noemi, lifting her hand wildly. "No, no, don't!"

She tried to hold her sleeve over Noemi's face.

Bahila, who had swiftly ascended the stone steps to the right of the dwelling, was now teetering on the edge of the roof. The eeriness had returned to her face, and the stare of the vulture, as the creature again unfurled its wings, was following her every movement. And even as Ruth and Noemi called and waved frantically to her to step back, the body dropped like a sack of bones to the flagged terrace below.

Under the floating shadow of the bird, Ruth and Noemi hurried to the spot.

On her knees, Noemi bent over the limp form.

"Shall I tell the — the others — now?" stammered Ruth. "Or will you go to them yourself and leave me to help her until Orpha comes?"

"My place, for the moment, is here," said Noemi without glancing up. "Elimelech would have it so. He is now safe in the Lord, but Bahila still breathes." Her face was the color of bleached flax. "Go and fetch me a basin of water — linens, salves, my daughter."

Later, Noemi asked for an hour alone with her dead. And while the others held themselves apart from her, she arranged Elimelech's cold hands over the now quiet chest. She pressed her lips to the icy brow and kept them there, her arms wreathed around the neck and shoulders.

Mahalon and Chelion had gone into the field to prepare a grave. Orpha, having secured a neighboring healer, was administering with him in the booth on the roof to which Bahila had been carried. Ruth, standing beyond the draped doorway, waited.

She could hear the words that Noemi was moaning, but she was unable to move away. It was not only that woe had come to this Israelite family, but the fact that it had come to them from a Moabite like herself! And her pain was not lessened by Bahila's unaccountability. It increased as she caught Noemi's cry, "O my husband, you worshiped the Lord faithfully all your days; but, here in another land, you did not let yourself tolerate one who needed so much what we have so abundantly. Bahila was but cleaving to her faith as we to ours. She knew not Yahweh the Good — only Chemosh the Cruel."

And Ruth longed to be close to one who, bowed with grief, had no hatred but only understanding and forgiveness for the cause; one who had looked to her for strength and called her "daughter."

At last, incapable of bearing the separation any further, she pushed the curtain aside, hurried to the mourner, and knelt with her. She made another's anguish her own and, since tears fall more freely from the eyes of youth, she outwept her; so that, presently, Noemi herself was the consoler.

When they were getting off their knees, Orpha re-entered the room. Without looking to right or left, she went to the niche in the wall, seized the statue of Chemosh, and flung it violently to the floor. It broke into several pieces. "This I do in the presence of the dead," she told Noemi, pointing to the corpse, her nostrils quivering, her eyes ablaze, "because in life he would have had it so. Often I've seen how the image annoyed him, but I did not know how much."

Noemi took and stroked Orpha's hand, quieting her nerves. "Chemosh is now no more to you," she said, "but he is still alive to so many! We'll bury the pieces as Elimelech will be buried; praying for him and Moab that — that both may have peace."

Ruth shrank back against a wall of the room; for, thinking that she heard Mahalon's footstep, she had glanced toward the door and could not help seeing the glass eyes in the idol's calf-shaped head which had rolled to the threshold.

Those eyes seemed to be shedding a living malice.

Swathed and fastened with bandages, the head covered separately, the body of Elimelech was borne on the shoulders of his sons and lowered by their trembling hands into the grave. Ruth and Orpha kept their arms around Noemi, and they all knelt until dusk. A dun haze drifted around. Rain was beginning to fall.

When at length they rose and turned away from the grave, Chelion voiced a bitterness to his mother. "Why were we directed here by the Lord? Is this a just man's desert? — to be slain and to lie among strangers —"

Orpha hung her head at the word "strangers." And Noemi leaned to her.

"That is true," said Mahalon dully, turning his eyes from Ruth. His cheeks were drawn in, his shoulders down. "Cruel to our father, this land has been cruel to us. By tomorrow's sunrise, we must be gone."

Noemi extended a hand to Ruth, and the comfort of it was instantly taken. "Time will bring other thoughts," she said to her sons. "It will ease our sorrow and restore our gratitude to Moab for the good we have here received."

They did not reply. What was good when evil prevailed, or

what room could there be for gratitude where grief was so great? And to let their desire still go out to daughters of a land of death impressed them as utterly disloyal to their father. They were tempted to take their mother from the clinging girls and immediately to depart. But Orpha's eyes, full of pleading, were on Chelion, and Ruth's on Mahalon. The brothers stepped back. Then, with bowed heads, they walked side by side, wearily, toward the house; following the women and finding their only strength in her whose suffering was no less than their own but whose endurance seemed so much greater.

And Noemi was telling herself: "Had our departure been sooner, Elimelech might still be living. I have managed too much — and too poorly. I, who withheld myself from his wish, must now give in to that of our sons."

Yet the look of Ruth and Orpha wrenched her heart and she knew not what to do.

Later that evening, Mahalon, at a nod from his mother, took his place by Ruth's side as she was about to leave.

Ruth thanked Noemi not with words but with the extra warmth of her parting embrace. She then approached Chelion, sitting morose in a corner of the room, and laid a hand on his shoulder. He tried to respond, and would have gotten up, but she did not permit it. Orpha, hovering near, begged her to return often and assist in lifting the gloom that had settled on the house.

When Mahalon and Ruth were beyond the door, Noemi went to it and stood gazing after them. The two forms were not close but, while they moved across the field, the increasing distance, together with the tears in her eyes, seemed to bring them together. Her prayerful thoughts followed them.

"The moon and the stars are as bright," said Ruth, glancing up, "as if —"

"— they never had to look down on sadness," Mahalon finished for her. "But the brightness is as brief and uncertain as life itself. See. Over to the west, storm clouds are gathering again. Autumn and the rains are early — too early — this year."

She tried to comfort him. "Your father's spirit is living, and memory can always let you see his face. . . ."

"His face in death."

"You saw him lifeless for only a very little while," she said. "And he has been alive with you for years."

He could not answer this naïve reasoning, but it touched him, and he studied the profile in the moonlight: the smooth forehead, the delicate nose and generous lips, the long incurving line of throat. Silently they walked along.

Pausing, he gave way to an impulse and took her face in his hands; and shame that he had been trying to disprize her went through him. He searched her eyes. Serious and kind, they looked directly into his own, as clean as any of the dreams he had dreamed in the hills of Bethlehem. "How, in a land of evil, could you have kept without stain?" he asked in awe.

"Not all Moabites are evil," she said very low. "My parents were good, even as yours. And, in my seventh year, there came to us a priest from Bethlehem-Judah, who stayed for a time in my father's house. He gave me my first lessons in the language of Israel. He spoke of a God of holiness and truth, who would one day send a Redeemer. I asked him what that meant, and he smiled. 'It means love,' he said. Then he told of sin entering the world and, through sin, sorrow; and of him who would one day come to lead mankind like sheep back to the fold. He bade us prepare, as Israelites were preparing, for the coming. 'The barriers of race shall give way to the mighty stream of his love' — those were his very words."

Mahalon recalled what Noemi had said to her family during their first glimpse of the fields of Moab. "They could have been my mother's words," he murmured.

Ruth inclined her head. "After the holy man left us, my parents lived apart from the religion of this land and they reared me their way," she continued. "Ever since their death, my uncle has tried to force me back to the old beliefs." She trembled slightly, but her voice was steady. "It has availed him not. I still believe the man with the smile and the message."

"Are you free from faith in Chemosh?" Mahalon asked eagerly.

"I am."

"Somehow I knew it the first minute I saw you! Nothing but the trials of this day could have made me forget. . . . And Orpha?"

"Since we were children together, she and I have shared everything. . . . And didn't she, this day, destroy the idol?"

They resumed their walk. The light above now shone for Mahalon as if it would never quite fade away again. His countenance had smoothed. His arm went around her waist, but then, in reverence, withdrew. "You and Orpha belong to Israel — a larger Israel," he said. "If my father had only known!"

Soon they were at the entrance to the path that led directly to her home.

"Let me go the rest of the way alone," she said. "My uncle Jared would be angry to see us together."

"I must meet him sometime. Why not now?"

"Later is better. I should have time to — to try to dispose him."

"Will you be safe?" he asked quickly.

"As safe as ever."

He drew her to him protectively; then he took her fingers and raised them to his lips. They were cool, and yet a warmth was creeping through them to him. She stood silent. "To-morrow?" he asked.

"Yes."

In a moment, she was gone.

He watched her fluid movements through the lines of cypress trees and could not tear himself away. Something impelled him slowly to follow.

The clouds in the west were massing still heavier, but of this he was no longer conscious. A rumble of distant thunder hardly reached his ear.

When Ruth neared the house, she found Jared waiting in the doorway. He was holding one hand to his chest and the other behind his back. In the light of a lantern above the door, his face was marble-pale and cold. She made herself approach him, but she wanted rather to turn and flee back down the path, for the look of him reminded her of the vulture.

"You have disobeyed me," he charged. "That you have been to the house polluted with strangers, I know. You were watched. Bahila and Orpha are accursed."

"Stricken, but not accursed," she dared to answer him. "Death has been under their roof this day. Don't be vexed at me that I was able to bring a little comfort to their grief."

"Come nearer."

She took a faltering step, her veil slipping to her shoulders. The hand behind his back showed itself. A snaky length of hempen whip dangled from the wrist. "Nearer still!" he cried. "I should have no faith in your promises."

She fell on her knees. "I promised nothing, though I did try to obey you."

"But I will give you one more chance." The fist and the whip were poised. "Swear by the shade of Chemosh that you will never again set foot in that abode!"

"I cannot."

His muscles contracted. A dark hollow appeared at the base of his throat between the tight cords, and his legs, exposed by the shortness of his tunic, seemed as sturdy as tree trunks. He snapped the whip over her head.

"You would not care to have — this — on your flesh? It could be scarred forever — and what youth of Moab or *Israel* would then think you fair?"

She did not answer.

"Talk! Open your mouth!"

"By your love for my father — your own brother — do not torture me."

"Because of that love, I must save you from yourself. Your father and mother were false to our God and he destroyed them. You are favored in having been delivered by him to me."

His gaze moved over the faint curve of shoulder and hip, the soft mass of hair tumbling from the bent head, the whiteness of the nape of the neck where the tresses parted. He had been stirred before by her, and now her complete helplessness and the cover of night added to his urge. Because of her usual attitude of aloofness from him, he had come to think of her less as a blood relative to whom his best was due, than as a desirable property to be watched and, eventually, possessed. He had been waiting for her to offend him in some important way, so that he might discipline her severely and bend her will to his. Moab would approve his forcing her from contact with foreigners; and, if she should denounce him on any other ground, nobody would believe her. Was he not stewart to the high priest of Chemosh? Besides, how easily she could be silenced with fear! A certain satisfaction combined itself with his affected wrath. "I have let you live your own life long enough," he muttered. "Hereafter you must live mine. Get up."

Drawn by an authority as tight as a rope, she struggled to her feet and followed as he backed his way into the house. The room was large, but she felt it imprisoning and stifling her. Suddenly his left hand gripped her shoulder and tore away both her veil and the upper part of her dress. Frantic, she clutched her breast. Her skin shone with perspiration in the oblique rays of the door lamp. The whip rose, twirled, and fell, making long scarlet streaks on her back and arms. Through gritted teeth a moan escaped her and, at the repeated strokes, she had to scream.

His cheeks were mottled, his jaws rigid. He did not hear or see a third person in the room; and even if he had, the contrast of the intruder's physique with his own would only have made him feel all the more the master. But Mahalon had equipped himself with a heavy stool from under a table and was holding it by two of the legs as firmly as he could. He lifted it high and brought it down upon the man's skull.

Jared whirled; his knees buckled. The whip dropped from the hand as he fell.

The next moments brought a confused reaction to Mahalon. He wondered how he had found force enough to deal such a blow. A conviction both of guilt and virtue swept him as, in a daze, he saw Jared stretched out on the floor, like the enemy of his sheep that he had once slain with a slingshot. His fury was not spent, but chill beads of sweat broke out on his neck and forehead. No hero or champion, he was a mere youth aghast at what he had done, yet knowing that he had had no other course. His head ached as if many thorns were piercing it, and the feeling deep in him was worse; a griping awe at what he had done. Was it sufficient to justify him, that he had saved Ruth? He suspected that she would much rather have died than have owed her protection to this.

Then he saw her beside the prostrate form. She had drawn her tattered garment over her shoulders and arms and hurriedly brought an ewer of water and some cloths to cleanse and stanch the wound in Jared's head. Just what his mother would have done, he thought. Just what Ruth had seen her doing for Bahila. "There is life in him," she was saying in breathless relief. "He must not die."

He dropped the stool. "Why should such a monster live?"

"Would you have more trouble for yourself and all of us?" she asked rather sharply, without looking up. "Poultices, moist poultices of figs are a good remedy," she went on, "but your mother would know a better."

"I'll get her. We both need her. But I ought not leave you for an instant."

"You must go." She spoke with no unkindliness or ingratitude but only with the practicality that seemed so necessary. "Somehow I have the feeling of strange eyes on us."

"I can't leave you with — that." He pointed toward the body and instantly sensed what seemed a flicker of movement in the tallow face and fingers. He thought he heard a groan. Touched by a gust of breeze behind him, he turned his head and noticed the lantern swinging wildly from its chain between the parted, bellying flaps of the drape in the doorway; and the groan, as he heard it again, came rather like the sound of a rising storm. But he was not sure. "I will not go!"

"You must," she said, all her girlishness changed to womanly authority and assertiveness by the swift turn of events. "And it would be just as bad for you to come back as to remain. I'll manage somehow until your mother is with me. You have done enough for me — perhaps too much. His recovery and your safety — that's everything now."

Her face was white. He knew that the effects of the lashes were still stinging her flesh, and he wanted his mother's arms around her. His own could wait. He went to the door without another word and stepped out into the night.

The cypress trees appeared to be straining toward him as he hurried down the pathway; and the pale, sickly thoughts that emotional exhaustion brings were wrapping him in what felt like the folds of a winding sheet. He paused and looked over his shoulder, wanting to race back. If Jared should recover, Ruth would be more cruelly dominated than ever; and if not, the law of the land would seek out the killer and punish death with death. For some time he stood, now shivering, now motionless.

And then the rain was falling fast, an inky rain, drenching him, plastering his tunic to his skin. In the intervals between peals of thunder, he could hear the lathering of it on the rocks along the way and the foaming of the waters of a brook not far off. Except for flashes of lightning, he could see hardly more than an arm's length ahead, and the darkness seemed not only to surround but also to be soaking into him. Then he almost ceased to breathe, as a form, shapeless like a torn piece of the night itself, a segment of the very evil that permeated the air of this heathen land, came toward him. Incapable of retreat, he waited.

The figure was assuming the vague outline of a man. A hand reached forth and drew him to a sort of shelter under the branches of a tree.

"I am Manred, a slave to Banaias, the high priest," a voice said from invisible lips in the splash and hiss of the storm. "An intelligent slave who speaks more languages than one, and also reads motives. I have witnessed much this day."

"What have you — witnessed?"

"Things that make a slave a master." There was an acuteness of insinuation to the words. Each one, despite the noises, was incisively distinct. "I saw you bringing Jared's ward to Orpha's home this morning. I saw the old man's lifeless body before you did. Bahila's plunge from the roof . . . your father's burial . . . the hiding of a crime that could easily be fastened on the wrong person, unless . . ."

The voice stopped to let the implication sink in, and a pair of eyes, now distinguishable as the heavens lit up, smoldered in a pale face both shrewd and hard.

"What do you want of me?"

"Very little. — My master, Banaias, has a business sense. He barters lands and goods and receives cutthroats."

"But what can I do?"

"Just a simple thing. So simple that it should make you smile with instant willingness. You shall have Orpha grant a certain favor; not to me, a nobody, of course. Be not surprised at what I have to tell you. Nothing should surprise anybody in Moab. There is a man who plans to have a secret underground passage dug from an obscure spot — the obscurer, the better — to the treasury of the temple. This person is of high rank, none other than the councilor-in-chief to the king himself. He's conspiring with several others to overthrow him and needs gold to bribe the army. Oh, this land is a hotbed of intrigue! And one like me, cloaked in darkness, moves through many places, learning much. I am a thing to be used, and little do my users guess that, all the while, I am using them. I've won certain advantages for myself by passing on to the councilor a deal of information about the high priest and the temple, and I'll win more when I can tell him that the parcel of land he wants is his to do with as he wills. He has been having me seek a good site for the work to begin. Such matters, dangerous in the hands of free men, can be safely entrusted, it seems, to slaves. That's how I happened to be around this morning. Orpha's field is just right; surrounded by trees to hide the excavators, near enough to the temple to be convenient, far enough away to be unsuspected. Naturally he could seize it on some pretext or other; but that would be revealing. Orpha shall be paid well if she consents."

"But how could I get her to do any such thing?" cried Mahalon.

"Easily. She is taken with that brother of yours. I know this, from the way her eyes followed him. She would make any sacrifice to keep him from the consequences of what you have done this night. When you struck Jared, I was near, just as I've been near since dawn, giving you time and taking my own. An Israelite can do nothing worse in Moab than attack a citizen — especially one in Jared's position. And, whether Jared recovers or not, swift punishment would fall not only on you but also your family — your people."

All too well Mahalon felt the force of this. He pictured his mother and Chelion being dragged to the gallows or put to the sword because of him, and imprisonment or banishment for other refugees from Israel.

"But Jared was abusing Ruth," he protested.

"It makes no difference. You struck him." The voice took on a tinge of approval. "I don't believe you've killed him, but I wish that you had. As steward to Banaias and overseer of his household, he has been harder on us slaves even than the master himself. I hate him. But slaves can get what they want only by craft." He uttered an obscene oath and a small laugh. "So I won his nod this day, and a few coins too, by telling him about his ward and you. He believes I'm faithful, or rather that I'm afraid not to be, the fool! Tomorrow you'll begin paying me for helping to conceal your deed. Agreed?"

Mahalon's lips curled under his teeth and his nails dug his palms. The storm within and the storm without seemed to echo each other, and the sound of the stream, increasing, was like the beating of a drum. He well knew that Orpha, generous Orpha, would be all too ready to put his family's welfare before her own; but how could he let her run this extreme risk? When the temple should have been robbed, and the tunnel traced to her field, the secret would be out; and then — what then? The thought was replaced by another even worse.

"If I were saved by your silence," he said, "where would the profit be? If Jared recovers . . ."

"Need he recover?" The slave paused. "I might prevent it. That is, should you do as I say. Both Banaias and Jared have used me to spy, and I've learned the art to perfection, both for and against them. I come and go noiseless and unseen. My fingers on Jared's throat would mean no further speech or — breath —"

"You would kill — like that?"

"Why not? He's treated me, I tell you, worse than a slave; and my blood is far nobler than his! Know you that I was a prince before the Moabites came and drove out most of my people — the Emims — and yoked and branded thousands."

"I'll have nothing to do with your vengeance!" said Mahalon, the words twisting from his parched mouth. "Let me pass."

"Not without your pledge." The voice had turned flat and harsh. "I have told you much, because circumstance has made us associates and there should be an understanding. I have nothing to fear from you, but you have everything to fear from me. You're a slave to a slave until we're done."

"And after?"

"If I kill Jared for you . . ."

The voice ceased for a few seconds, but the very silence was a sentence in itself.

"I am waiting," said the slave. "Your response had better please me. I am armed."

For answer, Mahalon leaped desperately at him. The abruptness of the attack found the slave unready. The bodies went down together in the splashing mud and rolled over and over until they struck the trunk of a tree. Mahalon bore the brunt of the impact and lay stunned. The slave straddled him, his fingers gripping the throat. The uneven struggle would have ended quickly, but lightning discovered to Mahalon's swimming, bulging eyes a dagger which must have dropped from the slave's sash. Feebly his hand slid out and, without the slave's seeing, grasped the hilt. The contact with a means of defense gave him a measure of strength and energy. Writhing upward with extreme effort, he plunged the blade into the slave's side and, using the hilt for leverage, hoisted himself. The slave jerked back, let go of the throat, and somehow got to his feet, the heavy movement causing the knife to slash a deep lateral wound before it was plucked forth. He lunged off into the night. But Mahalon stalked him shakily and doggedly by the glares in the heavens through trees and bushes.

The progress was slow. Finally, however, he overtook him turning back at the edge of the wild brook. For an instant, the countenance was uncovered. It looked to Mahalon, as the eyes focused pleadingly on him, empty of evil at last and like that of a frightened boy. He lowered the knife. He pushed forward, but could not bring himself to strike again. The hilt slipped from his hold.

The slave, too weak from pain and loss of blood, was unable to keep his footing. He grasped at air and fell backward. Mahalon heard the sound of the fall as a separate note in the raging of the storm.

Another streak of lightning revealed the body being sucked under and carried by the current down the stream.

Noemi and Chelion, worried over the length of Mahalon's absence, left Orpha with Bahila and, taking lanterns, went out into the night to search. They found him, face down in the mire, overcome by strain and exposure. On her knees, Noemi held him to her and waited until he could speak.

"Ruth — go to her, my mother," he begged. "Touch me not. — I have blood on me, like — like Bahila." Then, gasping for breath, he told what had happened.

The storm had passed almost as speedily as it came, and the moon was flooding the sky with a white light. Noemi, despite all the pangs of what she had to hear and bear, showed a calm face. "You did not want to kill him any more than Bahila wanted to kill Elimelech." She tried to keep her voice steady. "Your purpose was to defend yourself and us, even as hers was to defend her faith." She rocked his shoulders in her arms. "Nor did you intend to injure Jared nearly so much as to safeguard Ruth. Your soul is but accidentally stained. You must go with me to the proper authority just as soon as you can."

"A little while ago, it seemed I was back in the Bethlehem cave, fighting wolves. . . ."

She soothed him with words that were as helpful to his spirit as Chelion's arms, to which she now yielded him, to his body.

"But Ruth — hasten to her, my mother," he begged again, pointing. "The house is over to the right of the road — just beyond the cypresses. She is alone with — with —"

"I will go while your brother takes you to Orpha's."

She rose and drew her cloak around her. The drenched veil caught the moonbeams and the plain material looked silken. Her form appeared through the damp, clinging folds of her robe and, as she moved away, the old queenliness was in her bearing.

Mahalon and Chelion followed her with their gaze, but could not see the lips now tremulous with pain, or the eyes filled with fear.

The next morning, leaning on his mother's arm, Mahalon walked slowly with her from Orpha's threshold through dewy meadowland to the temple of Chemosh rearing its four-tiered mass on the edge of Bethjeshimoth, the capital of Moab. It was the back of the edifice, forming a part of the town wall, that they saw first; and they looked with misgiving on the dark masonry laid in bitumen and set with pitch-dipped reed mats between every few courses. More awful even than they had thought, must the god of such a somber abode be! How might mercy be expected from his chief priest? Mahalon asked that they turn back; but gazing straight ahead and keeping her lips in a firm line, Noemi still led him on.

When they had passed through the gates near the right side of the temple, they found themselves abruptly in a busy tree-shaded square where, from tethered donkeys and camels, merchants were removing their goods and jabbering and gesticulating to one another. The façade of the temple, a structure of stone framed by two flights of steps, jutted deep into the mart. And when they entered the wide-open ground portals, a tumult of haggling all along the booths bordering the walls of a large hall greeted them. The interior was decorated in three tones: black for the underworld, red for the earth, and blue for the sky. Crates of fruit and cages of birds lay around in scattered heaps. Sheep roamed over the tiled floor, spreading the soil of their hoofs and tracking their dung. Men and women jostled one another in an effort to get near the vendors and examine everything before making a purchase or exchange. Many minor priests, in flowing garments and fantastic headgear, kept ready to pounce on defects and blemishes and make sure that Chemosh would get only the best of offerings. And Mahalon and Noemi contrasted the scene with the dignity and reverence of their own outdoor high place of worship and sacrifice in Bethlehem.

As they stood staring, a hush fell and all eyes turned to a marble stairway which a vestmented person was pompously descending. The broad face resembled a tight-fitting mask; the small almond eyes were caught between thick, lashless lids, like half-hidden, stolen beryls; the nose went down almost to the broken lip line, and a pale thick hand rested on the expansive chest. Every head bowed. And Noemi nudged her son, quickly deducing that this must be Banaias, the high priest, himself.

Mahalon recoiled, but only for an instant. He felt an overwhelming desire to have done with his burden of worry; to say his say and get gone, if possible, from this smothering place. He dashed forward.

Noemi's hands fluttered to her cheeks as she watched him elbowing his way to the great one. "Have I given him like his father to death?" she asked herself in torment. "Why must I sway the lives of those I love? Why can't I leave more to the Lord? O Elimelech, you taught our sons to think me perfect. What little you and they have known about me!" And she groped to a far corner of the hall to await the outcome.

Mahalon was at last face to face — he felt — with Chemosh himself. "Hear me, Your Highness," he implored in his native tongue, almost aghast at his own ability to speak.

A corner of Banaias' mouth stretched and his pupils seemed to leave their sea-green irises as he scrutinized him. "Ah, an Israelite," he said in Hebrew and the soft voice that usually goes with fatness. "Why come you here?"

"To tell about your missing slave and — myself."

The priest smiled wryly. "It is a morning of the missing," he drawled. "My stewart is absent as well as the slave. Curious, I would hear you briefly. Israel — and Israelites — have always interested me. Come." And, turning his back on the people, he ascended the stairs.

On a heavy pillow-strewn carpet in a circular, drape-hung, torchlit alcove chamber, he disposed of all formality by comfortably reclining; and he motioned Mahalon to do the same. A large copper bowl of grapes was near and he reached for a cluster. "Speak."

With downcast eyes, Mahalon gave his story. Certain that this personage could have no care whatsoever for him as a human being, he made no attempt to win sympathy, but stressed the slave's revelation of the royal councilor's intention to rob the temple.

The priest listened without interrupting, munching away and ejecting seeds and skins from his lips.

"I cast myself on your mercy and pray that no harm befall my family and people because of what I have done," said Mahalon in conclusion.

After a few moments, Banaias broke the silence. "I should not believe a word, only that there happens to be confirmation," he said. With a jerk of his thumb, he invited Mahalon to partake of the bowl. "I have spies to watch my spies." He smiled a little and his gaze flickered. "For some time I've known of this slave's sly doings; but, in many ways, he was valuable; so I waited." He rubbed his too smooth chin, revealing strong but yellow teeth. "Ah, yes; only this morning, it was reported to me that Ner, the councilor, closeted himself last night with six chiefs, in the latest of several such meetings. Without gold, neither conspiracies nor anything else can get far." He rose, all his inertness gone. His facial muscles had tightened again, his voice had changed, and he looked like a different man. "Your news brings matters to a head. I shall reward you. What would you have?"

"Your pardon," said Mahalon, also standing.

"Pardon for what?"

"I struck your stewart and wounded your slave."

"Both stewart and slave deserved what they got. I've been quietly searching Jared's accounts, and the best I can say for them is that they are as ingenious as false. You have saved me the trouble of striking him myself. Speak a better wish."

"Oh that my people, driven by famine from lsrael, be permitted to live here in safety and peace," said Mahalon, his eyes wet. "Especially my mother, who led me to confess."

"So shall it be, for no native has served Moab better than you, a youth and stranger, this day. What further? If I can grant it, I will."

"Permit me, then," said Mahalon, "a certainty that the maiden Ruth be no longer molested by Jared."

"But this is taken for granted. Jared has failed his stewardship and will be delivered to the torturers."

"I beg that he be afflicted no more."

"What! After his scourging this girl, whom you evidently like? And there is his disloyalty to me!"

"He can hardly be disloyal again. My mother cared for him until dawn, and thinks he will be disabled for a long time to come. He may never recover fully. Ruth told her he received a head wound in battle with the Emims some years ago, and it has never quite healed. Now with the blow I gave him —"

"What a difference between Jew and Moabite!" Banaias

mumbled. Then he put a hand on Mahalon's shoulder. "Were you a worshiper of Chemosh, you'd have made sure to deliver a fatal blow. At your age, I had done away with at least three enemies of mine and thought nothing of it."

"The law given by Yahweh to Moses teaches that man must not kill."

Banaias pursed his lips. "But how could one live without the help of death?" he asked with a shrug. "We kill animals for sustenance and men for safety. A law like yours is absurd. How easily a land subject to such a law, could be overrun by an invader! Because of your service, however, I shall let Jared live out what time is left him, and I will personally see to it that one of my household watches him so that, if he gets violent, no harm can come to this Ruth." He reflected a moment. "I would have you visit me frequently and tell me more about the strange ways — beliefs — of Israel."

Mahalon, bending, raised a fold of the priestly robe to his lips, for he was much impressed that such a man, bloated with indulgence, swift to revenge, still had good in him. And the good, by dint of unexpectedness and contrast, seemed large indeed. "Why, even Chemosh," he thought, "cannot be all evil."

He found his mother in the corner of the temple, her veil drawn over her face, her head bowed, her hands hidden in her sleeves. She appeared as distrait as Boaz on the unforgettable day of the family's departure from Bethlehem. What it must have cost her, he thought, to bring me here! A great gratitude, touched with pity, went out from him. If she would only let him be the protector instead of the protected! He felt that, as a protector, he could develop the confidence in himself that Ruth had a right to expect. He discounted his battle in the cave, his assault on Jared, and his dealing with Manred the slave, since those were but acts of desperation, signifying little or nothing with regard to the courage that he had once believed himself to be acquiring in the Bethlehem hills. And, much as he loved his mother, he began to feel a vague resentment that he had been rather deprived, by her care and concern, of the spirit that might have fitted him to be truly her shield and Ruth's. But, he questioned, where would he now be if she had not taken charge? Doubtless hiding in some corner of Moab, cowering, trying to elude the law, and, worse, causing his family and people to be prosecuted too. As it was, he had won favor for them and himself and protection for Ruth. Fate, like Banaias, had been kinder to him than he deserved. His cheeks flushed.

Pretending not to have noticed her mood, he took her by the hand and led her from the temple, telling her animatedly about his session with the high priest and the result. She listened eagerly, greatly relieved; but she could not help admitting a new fear into her heart when he went on to praise Banaias.

On their way back to Orpha's house, they noticed a large rock in a field, out of the top of which a slender tree was growing. And long lines of cleavage ran the length and width of the rock, for the tender roots, having worked down through, had proved stronger than stone. They paused to consider the sight for a moment.

"It makes me think of what Israel might do to Moab," he said.

"Rooted in stone," she murmured, "a tree can have only a limited growth."

"But isn't it enough, my mother, that our littleness is now working itself into the power of this land and our fortune rising above it? Even a limited growth is good, after what we endured in Bethlehem."

"Perhaps."

"Happiness lies ahead. The hand of Banaias is with us."

She tried to share his enthusiasm, but she was still gazing at the tree-topped boulder. "The fissures run in the form of a cross," she said as if to herself.

He smiled. "Even so."

"A cross is a dark symbol. — O my son, still is there evil in the air. Despite all my joy and gratitude for the Lord's blessings, I feel it, as your father used to feel it. Should we trust the high priest or anybody else in Moab?"

"Ruth and Orpha are to be trusted."

"I know."

"The high priest is our friend."

"So he seems."

"And a cross is not necessarily a dark symbol. Often, my mother, I've seen the sun weaving shadows into such a shape on the floor of the cave in Bethlehem."

Chapter Four

TIME — THE WOMB

A YEAR passed. Now it was another autumn in the land of Moab and the rains were due.

In the dawn of the first day of the season, Mahalon and Chelion stood, arms akimbo, appraising the results of their efforts during the dry season. Two additions to Orpha's house had been constructed: a chamber on each side, simple but sturdy, and good as the brothers could make them.

"Banaias is vexed at me for not letting him have his own experts work for us," said Mahalon, looking askance at Chelion. "His idea was an entirely new house; one worthy of a friend and favorite."

Chelion did not reply.

"A man like him hates hovels," continued Mahalon, unable to keep a testy note out of his voice.

"There are hovels aplenty in Moab. Banaias does not care for the poor."

"He would place us high among his people."

"To be sons of Elimelech and servants of the Lord places us high enough anywhere, my brother. We have saved our pride and independence by using our own hands."

Mahalon agreed reservedly. "But why shouldn't we be ready to receive from rich Banaias instead of taking from poor Orpha?"

"Orpha — our mother willing — will soon be my wife," said Chelion sharply, "just as Ruth is to be yours."

"We bring them so little."

Chelion frowned. "We are bringing them the fullness of the faith of Israel."

"True. But ourselves — what of ourselves?"

Chelion did not answer. He threw off his tunic, since the sun was already warm; and, in his loin cloth, he turned his attention to a near-by brick kiln. Mahalon, too, put aside all excess clothing. This would probably be the last day, certainly one of the busiest, of their labor on the house. All the finishing touches had to be made; for, once the rains started, little or no further progress could be assured.

Their physiques were poor. A scar ran livid along Chelion's thin arm from the shoulder to the elbow, a permanent effect of the battle in the cave. There was no freshness to the skin, and the face had the leanest of contours. As for Mahalon, his limbs, as pale as old ivory in the early light, were still those of a boy, though he had grown years older from his experiences.

"Would you say that our mother is with us in our plans?" he asked, picking up a spade to work some clay. "She has been glad to accept Ruth and Orpha as daughters; but as our wives? . . . I know that the days have been bringing them closer and closer together. Without her, what could Orpha ever do for Bahila lying so helpless, her bones refusing to knit? And what could Ruth do for Jared?" he reflected. "She wears herself out, caring for all of us. Should we add to her worries by having her decide our future?"

Chelion looked up gravely from the kiln at him, searching for a deeper meaning in the question; but Mahalon avoided the glance and seemed uneasy.

"We've nobody else to go to," said Chelion. "She fills our father's place as well as her own."

"Our father resented Moab, and she — she troubles herself too much over my friendship with Banaias."

"It is because she fears that, in your talks with him, you may imbibe some of his heathenism. Your eyes beam, my brother, when you speak the high priest's name. Bethlehem comes to your lips less and less."

"Bethlehem is closed to us."

"It will always be open to our spirits. Here in Moab we have taken only a makeshift abode for the sake of our bodies. Our hopes should turn homeward." Chelion's nostrils expanded. "When we return, God willing, we'll have sons of our own."

"Sons?" sighed Mahalon.

"The Lord will strengthen our loins to build up the house of our father. You'll sing again among your sheep, my brother, and I'll plow a soil that's not borrowed but rightly ours."

"But our parents gave everything to Boaz. We have nothing to attract us back to Bethlehem; not even the good will of our kinsman. He flung his hatred at us the day we left."

"Perhaps it was less hatred than greed."

Mahalon put down his spade. "It was not greed," he replied emphatically. "For a time, before the famine, I understood and pitied Boaz so much that I was ready to sacrifice everything for him, just as our father would have given his life for Zora."

"And now?" Chelion bent lower to his task, but turned his head a bit. "Your love for Ruth has lessened your sympathy?"

"No, my brother. I think of Boaz repeatedly, as if his life were still bound up somehow in mine. I'd be just as sympathetic with him, and perhaps more so, only that I can't forget how he treated our parents the last time we saw him. No matter how unhappy he was, he should have realized that he wasn't the only sufferer."

"The darkness may have gone from him since then, as it did before. I could forgive him, only that I keep thinking that he took advantage of our wretchedness, urging us away and getting possession of our property."

For a moment, Mahalon was silent. Then he took up his implement and sighed heavily, trying to discard all worries and misgivings. "Why should we think of yesterday instead of tomorrow? Moab gets brighter for us. Here we've found what Bethlehem couldn't give. Here we can flourish. We're acquiring the language — sharing the life — of another people."

"We are still Jews."

"But Bethlehem is no longer Bethlehem. The cave is ruined. Everything's ruined. Moab has given us Ruth and Orpha, a home, music once more —"

"Yet you've not made another lyre, my brother," said Chelion, wagging his head. "You haven't again begun to sing."

"Singing can wait until, our mother consenting, the fairest maidens of Moab are our wives and we are all dwelling under one roof."

A few days later, they approached Noemi to tell her of their desire. She had just returned from attending Jared with Ruth and was standing in the room where Elimelech met death. It was evening, and perhaps the red rays of sunset brought memories of his bloodshed. She looked so tired and weary that Chelion, stepping back, almost decided to wait until another time; but immediately he was expressing himself, for Orpha, having come from the field, was glancing in at the door before going to Bahila, and gesturing him not to delay.

"My mother, all authority over my brother and me now rests in you," he said. "Orpha and Ruth look to you, too. You well know where our minds tend, and we've waited long. Now, therefore, we ask, 'Have we your blessing?' "

It was a question that she had been expecting for months, but it still found her without an answer. She folded her hands on her shrunken breasts and closed her eyes, thinking of a pallid, bearded face and a warning, "Woe is written on these walls." Could Elimelech rest in his grave, if she agreed to what would bind the family to Moab? . . . But he had not known Orpha well, nor Ruth at all. With more time, would not his reading of the future have changed? She was un-

certain, for she could still hear his voice denouncing the
intermarriage of "the sons of light with the daughters of
darkness" and his stern insistence that only by the putting
away of foreign wives and the disowning of offsprings could
race-guilty Israelites return to the Lord. She was silent. But
then, as her eyes opened, other thoughts came to her, induced
by the mildness of the autumn evening, so apart from prob-
lems, so like the understanding smile of the Maker. Through
the parted curtains of the door, she glimpsed the heliotrope
sky, rain-washed and glimmering, and some doves seeking
their cotes, flashing their wings. She went to the threshold for
a better view, Chelion and Mahalon following.

A garden, which she had started in the spring, had resisted
the intense heat of summer and kept alive with promise. It
was near the great fig tree at the entrance to the house, and
already she could picture it, in a new April, brilliant with red
and pink anemone. So many other flowers, too! — sword lilies,
salvia, capers, mallows, loosestrife, and blue squill. Together
with her, Orpha and Ruth had loosened the soil and planted
seed and bulb; and now might they not be permitted, she
asked herself, to bring care and fulfillment to her sons? The
flowers of Bethlehem could thrive here in Moab: why not the
lives of Bethlehemites? Nature was the same in all men:
would the Lord have Israel different? The law against intermarriage was reasonably designed to prevent the adultera-
tion of light with darkness; but surely there was no law
against the mingling of light with light. Ruth and Orpha were
believers —

Chelion waited.

Still gazing into the young garden, she murmured, "So
be it."

Autumn and winter, dreamlike, melted away and the day
for the nuptials dawned.

Banaias had sent presents of finest linen and fruits. Many

of the Hebrew exiles, and also some Moabites, whom Mahalon and Chelion now numbered among their friends, came to celebrate. The two couples knelt near the silver olives where Mahalon and Ruth had first met, and then went to the space beneath the fig tree where Orpha had first found her heart going out to Chelion; and they gave themselves to the Lord before receiving each other. His response seemed to come to them in breezes scented with apricot and henna blossoms, herbs, and beds of spices. Noemi's hands moved above the bowed heads, as her eyes uplifted and her thoughts slipped back to the day of her own union with Elimelech, many Aprils ago.

Good rains during the weeks previous had softened the earth and let the crocus, the *halaz-zeleth*, thrust up its sturdy stems and bear its bright yellow bloom. And Noemi silently praised Heaven for decorating the wedding scene so profusely with this beauty which was more than beauty, for she knew that it contained a medicinal essence; and, too, she had made use of some of the honeyed juices for flavoring the cakes that were part of the waiting feast. "All God's creatures have many uses," she was thinking, "and he disposes everything well." Then she noticed a particular flower near the place where Ruth and Mahalon were kneeling; the flower that had been her favorite in Israel, and little bunches of which Mahalon had often brought her in his boyhood. Its delicate petals formed a six-pointed corona. Crude husbandmen back home referred to it as "dove's dung," she recalled; but her younger son, whose appreciation of nature had begun to show itself when he was only seven, had named it "star of Bethlehem." She smiled at seeing him now reaching down to pick the blossom for Ruth.

That night, she sat alone at the threshold of the house, lost in thought. There were misgivings which, all through this busy day and those that preceded it, she had tried to dismiss. But now, as if taking advantage of her extreme fatigue, they returned tauntingly and would not be further ignored. She had studied thoughtfully, during the wedding, the contrast that the earnestness in the young faces projected; a lasting pallor on the cheeks of her sons, a glow of health on those of Orpha and Ruth. And both the pallor and the glow were not mere aspects: they went deeper. The seed of Elimelech had lost its strength. But would not a great love foster the little vigor that remained, and bear fruit? Grandchildren of him who had gone! A longing for them ached within her. Could they ever be?

Chelion — was he not bringing more gratitude than desire to Orpha and mistaking the one for the other? As Boaz to the memory of Zora, was he still devoted to the memory of Miriam? Mahalon, the day he met Ruth, had seemed to be standing at the portal of peace; but, so impressionable, so ready to homage, could he ever be a satisfactory mate? Because of his part in the death of the slave Manred, and his assault on Jared, he regarded himself unworthy. Perhaps, thought Noemi, an attempt to offset his sense of guilt with a sense of importance was part of the explanation of his stubborn attachment to the heathen high priest. Her worry drove her to a general self-accusation. How much to blame she had been for years! But for her, Zora might have been spared and Boaz might have had his happiness. Elimelech would not have had his tragic ending. And Ruth and Orpha, if unattached to a declining family, could be sought by decent sons of Moab — there must be some such — and well wedded in time. Their arms were made to hold children. But now . . .

She tried to shake off the mood, reminding herself that, even if the union of Orpha and Ruth with her sons should be childless, it would represent a sharing of the truths of Israel with Moab. Under this roof, a sanctuary of Jewish faith and practice could be cultivated. Surely that would bring rest to Elimelech's spirit. And she would make all possible amends to her daughters by kindness and service. But even as she was thinking and resolving, she could see above the trees in the distance the walls of the temple of Chemosh, high, dark, ominous; and, fearing, she called on the Lord.

No answer seemed to come. The stars were cold, and a feeling of rejection and futility filled her.

It was then that she sensed a presence behind her and turned her head. Ruth was standing in the doorway, her hair streaming over her shoulders, her arms outstretched. "I had to be with you, my mother," she said. "When we bade each other good night, I read your look. I think I know your thoughts — your fears —"

And Noemi clung to the youngest member of the new family as to a pillar of strength.

When Mahalon and Chelion approached her the following morning to consult about the day's work, they saw a setness in her face, which, though they knew it not, was the result of her conversation with Ruth. "My sons are now men with responsibilities that their manhood must serve," she said. "Take counsel with yourselves in the light of the Lord, and may he grant" — her voice shook — "that it be not too late."

Somewhat disturbed, they looked at each other and blinked. But, that day, they worked better in the fields and accomplished more than ever before. And, while they worked, they talked much about agriculture; their minds reverting to the drought and famine in Israel, and a determination rising in them to keep their wives and their mother from any such affliction in the land of Moab. Hitherto, they had taken the productivity of the soil here for granted; but now, with new duties, they thought long and hard about this and remembered what their father had learned too late. He had told them in detail what could and should have been done; so that, in the next months, they dug and clay-lined a series of small storage pits which separately tapped the water table and were connected by tunnels with a deep-bedded spring.

Season followed season, and eventually to Moab, as to Israel, a time of hunger did come. The spent fields lay parched and the rocklike clods looked as if they would never open up to produce again. But the storage cisterns contrived by the brothers had gathered the waters from the porous limestone under the topsoil; and Moabites came to gaze enviously on the little area not far from the temple, which was not only golden hued with wheat but also gaily bordered with flowers.

Some complained to Banaias, the high priest, about this "field cultivated by unbelievers" and mumbled of alien magic. And Banaias summoned Mahalon to explain.

"It is no magic but a little extra care and provision," said Mahalon, standing before a delegation of citizens in the temple and using the language of Moab which, by now, he and Chelion and Noemi could speak well. "Want in Israel drove my family forth and taught me and my brother prudence. If you come with me, I shall show you just what we did to ward off the same plight here." And when, led by him, they closely examined the work that had been done, they were both satisfied and inspired.

Then, at priestly and royal command, there began a great overhauling and reconstruction of watersheds in Moab; and when the next rains fell, they were abundantly captured. The land became productive again and the people would have been more prosperous than before, only that Banaias and the king seized all surplus grain for taxes and sold it to neighboring states for gold.

Noemi was pleased at the foresight of her sons, which Moab had seen fit to imitate; but, as she saw the soil yielding so richly, she dwelt more and more on the fact that neither Orpha nor Ruth had yet conceived. She had hoped against hope, and now felt forced to accept the fact that her daughters would never be mothers. And she grieved for them as for her own flesh and blood.

Over her sorrow, however, there crept a consolation like
fresh vines upon a tomb. Orpha's house had indeed become
a religious center to the exiles of Israel and was shedding a
light in darkness. And the chief beneficiaries of that light were
Bahila and Jared, who, at length relinquishing Chemosh, gratefully accepted the peace of the Lord, and in it died. Jared's
estate had been confiscated by Banaias, but he gave to
Mahalon the full proceeds of a sale of it; and, at Ruth's suggestion, the money was spent on deeds of charity for the
benefit of the departed soul. And, inasmuch as the charity
went out not only to Israelites but also to needy natives, a
better interracial spirit developed, so that not a few Moabites
attended the devotional meetings in Orpha's home and gradually loosed themselves from the hold of their past. Even
Hebel, the new steward of the high priest, was among the
converts. "Though my daughters are childless," said Noemi
to herself, "yet are they, together with my sons, parents of
the true faith in Moab."

One evening, Mahalon, returning from a visit to Banaias,
brought news. Merchants from Israel, on one of their rare
excursions into Moab, had told him that Bethlehem was
definitely recovering from its years of want, and grain that
promised to be as high as the best hereabouts could already
be seen there. Also, according to the account, Boaz, about
whom Mahalon particularly inquired, had survived the long,
lean period and, devoting himself to his fields, was becoming
known as the most prosperous of Bethlehemites.

"He has land that should be ours," said Chelion at table
after Mahalon had spoken.

Noemi looked down at her bowl of bread and curds. "We
gave it to him in fair exchange for his cart and oxen," she
reminded.

"He took advantage of us."

"No, my son. Boaz cared not what we did at the time nor

what would happen to himself. But the Lord cared. He has sustained his poor afflicted servant and blessed him."

"We, also, are blessed," said Mahalon. "Moab has plenteous harvest and Banaias is still a friend to us and Israel. Only a short time ago, he had the king cast into his dungeon a Moabite guilty of a crime against a Jew!" His gaze went to Ruth, who was serving the meal. "We are protected. It is good for us to be here."

Chelion made a muttering sound and Orpha, seated beside him, patted his hand as a mother soothes a fretful child. He drew a little away, and a hurt look came to her eyes. She knew that his mood was harsh only because his feelings were tender; but tender for Bethlehem rather than for her. Her cheeks hollowed and her teeth sank into a corner of her lips as he said, "Too long have we tarried in this land of shadows. Without delay we should return to Bethlehem to reclaim what is ours — now that it is worth reclaiming." He glared at Mahalon. "The uneven bargain with Boaz is not binding. A house and acres for a yoke of oxen and a cart!"

"The oxen and the cart meant life to us, my son," said Noemi quietly. "Without them, we could never have reached our Orpha and Ruth."

The eyes of her daughters turned gratefully to her.

"But we can't leave Moab!" cried Mahalon. "Bethlehem was cruel to us and could be so again. The Lord would have us remain."

"Moab wasn't merciful to our father," put in Chelion, edging still farther from Orpha and striking the table with his fist. "And if the Lord wants us here, why has he not given us sons?"

The three women bowed their heads, and Noemi's sank the lowest.

Ruth laid a hand on the thin arm. Noemi, reading the meaning of the warm little act, covered the hand with her own, and her voice went to Chelion and Mahalon. "What the

Lord would have us do," she said, "can be discovered only in prayer and patience."

The following day, Mahalon went to the temple, hoping again to hold converse with the merchants from Israel and learn more about conditions in Bethlehem. But they had already departed Bethjeshimoth.

He remembered Ruth's interest in the city of his birth and, having lain awake a large part of the night, he had meditated to the point of admitting to himself that, like Chelion, he did want to go back. The hills, green again, would be gently alive with sheep. He thought of his pet lamb — the first victim in the cave. He pictured the cave itself, and a new harp strung across the blue space between rocks. He could see Ruth standing where Boaz had stood, her garments aflutter in a breeze, her face radiant with what she heard, spotless sheep pressing close, a newborn lamb — like a child — in her arms. . . .

The motherhood that had not been hers in Moab — might it be granted by the Lord in Bethlehem?

Preoccupied with such thoughts he was admitted by a guardsman to the alcove at the head of the marble stairs of the commercial hall of the temple.

In a half-light, Banaias was resting on a mound of colored pillows. He did not rise or even stir when Mahalon greeted him.

"Is Your Highness ill, or is it that Your Highness feels vexed at me?" asked Mahalon anxiously, searching the small, slanted eyes.

Banaias' underlip shot out. "I am disillusioned."

"But why?"

"You let me think you loyal. You received my confidence only to betray it."

"I do not understand."

"Those gatherings at your home have been held even more often of late. I did not mind until it at last seemed wise to have them secretly investigated. Chemosh put a warning in my ear."

"You did not trust me?"

"I wished to prove to my fellow priests, who brought complaints, that you were faithful. Vain intent!"

"Still I do not understand." Mahalon tried to come nearer, but was waved back. "There has been much gratitude — no disloyalty."

Banaias rose heavily and adjusted his robe. "Was it not enough," he said with a show of great injury, "for you and your brother to rob your wives of their Moabite faith —"

"Ruth and Orpha had inclined to Yahweh before we came."

"Without enticing others from our God? Several of my people, I am informed, have abandoned their beliefs and accepted yours. Among them, even Hebel, my own steward."

"But I enticed nobody." Mahalon was now pleading. "That I spoke to them often about the Lord, I admit. That I preached anything against Chemosh, I deny."

The high priest's breath made a whistling sound. "Cleverly you had your brother attend to that. His very words — 'Chemosh is vile and to be shunned like a plague' — have been repeated to me. You were with him, and you neither refuted him nor defended the creed of this land."

"How could I — belonging, as I do, to Israel?"

"You have been accepting the protection of Moab. You owe us honor."

"I thought my debt was mostly paid when I uncovered the scheme to rob the temple," he said, his hand pressing down on his wrist, his throat constricted and dry.

"Do not overestimate that service. I'd have found out about the traitors without your help. Few things remain concealed from me for long. I now know that you've been going among Moabites with sympathy, increasing their murmuring against me and the king, whether you intended just that effect or not. So — this land must be relieved of the poison of your beliefs."

Mahalon's cheeks reddened. Recklessly he let his feelings come forth. "There is no poison, but health and healing of the spirit in the truths of Israel!" he cried. Never having had occasion to defend his faith to the high priest before, he was now moved to make up for lost time; and the thrill of this particular kind of release emboldened him. "Our God is good and just, but yours is scandalous and malicious. Our ritual is clean — yours, obscene. Our doctrine has substance — yours, only shadow."

Banaias stiffened and his look was like a lash. "Go to your guilty house," he commanded. "And don't try to escape. You and your brother shall be watched."

Mahalon groped his way out. Life had suddenly become a dark cave teeming with peril. And those human lambs — Ruth, his mother, Chelion, Orpha, the exiles of Israel, the natives recruited to their faith — what would become of them? He might have known that Banaias' favor could not last. He wondered why it had been granted at all. But it occurred to him, that, in nearly all conversations, Banaias' trend of questions had been such as to indicate a much keener interest for the weaknesses than for the beliefs of Israel. Had he been used merely as an unwitting agent who, too grateful and callow, too spontaneous, would deal out more information than was obtainable from the shrewd, itinerant merchants of Israel or from the resident, usually tight-lipped Jews in Moab? Had he injured the interests of his people by telling things that his father and the elders used to discuss at the gates of Bethlehem? In any case, he was now certain that in the mind of the high priest some evil design had long been maturing, and that the man, at last ready for action, was seizing an excuse.

That night, he was awakened from a light, fretful sleep by a sound such as he had been hearing in fancy since Banaias' threat. He jumped up and hurried to the window of his and Ruth's section of the house. From down the road, a small company of soldiers, unarmed, but with their eyes glinting in the watery moonlight, like those of the idol that Orpha destroyed, were nearing the central doorway.

He stepped back toward the bed where Ruth was sleeping. He had told neither her nor the others anything about his encounter, wishing to spare them as long as possible and desperately hoping that somehow he could still smooth out matters. His first impulse on his return from the temple had been to go to his mother, who could have advised him; but she had been withholding herself so long from any affairs involving his and Chelion's manhood, that he had learned too well to keep silent and depend on himself. And now there was little self-reliance left as, kneeling, he gazed on Ruth's face in the faint glow of a candle on a small table beside the bed. He was thankful for whatever impulse had prompted him to have her put the taper there. How childlike she looked in repose! He bent over her, tracing the arched brows blending into the fine lines of the nose, and the lips seemingly molded by a prayer. That prayer, he was sure, had been for him. What meager good he had been able to do for her! A whole lifetime would have been insufficient for his wishes; and already his opportunity was ending.

He snuffed out the wick, suddenly unable to bear the sight to which, as a failure, he felt he no longer had a right.

Stirring, Ruth awoke and sat up. She put her arms around him.

"Mahalon, what is it?"

"I — I dare not think. But I must speak. Fast. The time is very brief. Listen carefully. Banaias has trapped me. For what purpose, I can only guess. I wish I could undo the harm I've probably done by speaking too freely to him of Israel — especially Bethlehem. He now knows the town as well as Chelion and I; possibly better, because he's questioned many other Israelites too. But while he's been learning all about us, I've been learning many things about Moab. He gave me entry to every section of the temple and didn't seem to mind what I saw, because, as I now think, he intended all along that I'd never live to tell. I was the worst kind of prisoner, not knowing my chains. But my eyes have always been sharper than my mind, and maybe they've caught more than he suspects. Though I never planned to be at all disloyal, I could not help pitying the people of Moab." He hurriedly drew out a small, folded piece of papyrus from his bosom and gave it to her. "Slip this into your robe and keep it always. It may prove useful, for it's a description of the secret place in the temple where the wealth that Banaias and the king have squeezed from the poor is hidden. It tells how to reach it."

Noises broke in on them. Disengaging himself from her embrace, he ran to the door. Those men must not pass over this threshold into the presence of his wife! He turned his head and saw her near. "Escape through the rear of the house," he begged.

But she was already clinging to his shoulder. "How can I leave?" she said. "I am yours and my place is with you."

A billow of voices drowned out her words. She shrank back, trying to draw him with her. He forced her off from him with the flats of his palms. "Go — go," he insisted, almost harsh in his fear for her safety.

A moment more and muscular forms, bathed in the light of a torch upheld by a hairy hand, were crowding the narrow entrance. Chelion was in the midst of them, his wrists held by two of the soldiers. Noemi and Orpha, death pale, were in the background. "Here he is!" cried one of the men, gripping Mahalon by the neckband of his tunic and thrusting his burly face so close that the rancid wine breath was an assault in itself.

Mahalon tore himself free, and his fingers leaped at the shaggy throat, burying themselves in it, feeling for the vein that held life. But the offensive was brief, for the man seized him by the hair with both fists and yanked his head backward so violently that the neck almost snapped. Then he flung him wide into the room, onto the floor. Choking and sputtering, he entered with his men in a rush behind him.

Ruth was trying to shield Mahalon; but he struggled to his feet, bent on resuming his attack. In a second, however, a blow on the forehead felled him again.

Chelion, wrenching himself from his captors, plunged at the men. And then the scene was bedlam. The women stood helpless, stricken by horror and anguish, just beyond the rim of the sudden circle, centered by the brothers, in which bodies were being welded into a single force.

Somehow Noemi and Orpha got to Ruth. Huddled together in a corner of the room, the three could not now see Mahalon and Chelion, but they could hear and feel them struggling on against hopeless odds, and were all too conscious of the merciless beating to which they were being subjected.

The voices of the victims dwindled to nothing, and yet the assault did not cease.

When the soldiers, breathless, panting, finally spread out a little, the aftermath was revealed in the smoky flame of the torch that was still being brandished by the hairy hand. Two corpses lay on the floor; the faces, ingrained with dirt from metal-soled sandals, were hardly recognizable.

Noemi clutched her daughters from the sight and held them tightly. For this had she remained in an alien land, fostering her purpose of serving the Lord by sharing the faith, trusting that her sons might live and prosper. Her teeth in her lips were cutting them, but she could feel only an agony of spirit, the futility of all hope. Sons and husband alike gone! Two blameless wives tortured! Elimelech had been right. That which was holy ought not to have been offered to heathen.

Finished with the brothers, the soldiers were turning to Ruth and Orpha.

Noemi's embrace became a frenzy. *Lord of Israel, not that, not that. By the blood of my sons, I entreat you.*

And while her lips were moving, there came a surge of other voices. She hardly heard, until Orpha gasped into her ear, "They are here! Our friends."

"Have courage, my mother," said Ruth, though she herself could hardly stand. "Mahalon and Chelion have proven themselves."

The leader was now looking through the window at a milling, furious group. Out of the side of his mouth, he said to his men, "We must go. Our orders were to come here weaponless and do away with the criminals but avoid tumult. Someone of our own must have betrayed us and aroused the Israelites from their beds. There are Moabites among them. This house has sympathizers everywhere."

Noemi found speech. "We have the Lord," she declared. "You — only Satan."

The ruddy glow of dawn was at the window. To her, it seemed the crimson shadow of the Gentile world itself; the shadowy realm where men were not brothers but beasts. Yet, even as she was thinking this, she felt rising within her an unruly pity for the blindness that breeds excess. And, from Ruth's plea, she was aware that, though her sons were no more, their ending had justified their existence. All the wavering, sighing, and fecklessness of their brief lives had passed in valor. The evil spirit still possessed this place, but outside a new day was breaking and the light of the Lord had led in loyalty the cherishers of his word; and good daughters were sustaining her now, just as they had sustained her when last she looked on Elimelech's face.

As the men left, the light increased. Alone with their dead, the women sank on their knees. Moments passed like hours. When the fullness of dawn was in the room, it was Ruth who covered the torn faces with her veil.

Chapter Five

THE PRESENCE OF THE PAST

THE high priest refrained from prosecuting Noemi and her daughters. He did not believe, at this time, in honoring the sex even with adverse attention. Neither did he bother, beyond publishing that Israel had shown herself an enemy to Moab by planting her spies here, to take measures against the Moabite converts or the still lingering Jewish refugees; for he and the king were now busy emptying prisons and pardoning suspected offenders to make additions to the army. It was being whispered from Bethjeshimoth to Iim that some sort of martial venture was being planned, and public opinion was divided as to whether it would be aimed at the haughty tribes to the east or at the again lush regions to the west. The latter seemed more likely, not only because of the proclamation of Israelite hostility but because of the seemingly inconsistent fact that Jews in Moab were now being almost coddled by the government. Was this for the purpose of turning them against their motherland and using them?

Left alone, save for the solicitous visits of the faithful, Noemi, Orpha, and Ruth spent a large portion of each day at the two new graves near Elimelech's.

Early one morning, Ruth and Orpha found Noemi at the end of a night-long vigil in the field of the dead. At their approach, she rose. Her face was ashen, and her garments flapped loose in the slight breeze around her wasted figure, as if they covered spirit rather than flesh. But her upper lip was rigid; and Orpha and Ruth could see that a decision had come.

"Only their bodies are here," she said, holding her sunken cheeks. "Soon they will be dust. But their shades are hovering over Jordan. I'll find them there." Her head sank. "Out of my life came little joy and much sadness to you, my good, good daughters. It is better that I go and that you forget. Hence, this day, I, who came into Moab still blessed with husband and sons, will leave it in the poverty that the Lord has seen fit to lay on me."

She turned slowly and began to walk toward the river and the sea. But she had gone only a short distance when she stood still. To her, as to most Israelites, no land seemed farther from home than that of a false worship; and now, though it was dawn, she felt so lost that terror seized her. Her face crumpled up with distress. How could she proceed without the assistance of these daughters whom shared sorrows had rendered even more dear?

She glanced over her shoulder and saw that they were following her. She tried to resume her steps and to speed them. But spent from her watching through the night, she had to stop once more.

Again she faced them. "Go," she begged, yet extending her arms. "Return where your mothers dwelt before you. The Lord deal mercifully with you, as you have dealt with the dead and me. May he grant that you find rest, each in a new husband's house!"

But they came to her, and she embraced them. She kissed each of them, and they raised their voices and wept.

"We shall go with you to your people," said Ruth simply.

Noemi sighed. "That you and Orpha should hold to one who brought such pain!"

"You gave me, in Chelion, my heart's desire," reminded Orpha.

Ruth slid her hand into Noemi's arm. Her eyes could not leave the thin, gray face; nor could she say as yet what she most wanted to say, but it was welling up in her.

"Return, my daughters," repeated Noemi. "Why would you accompany me? Have I yet sons in my womb, that they might become your husbands? Please go, since I am too old to have a husband. Even if I should say: I have hopes; if I should have a husband this night and should again bear sons, would you on that account wait until their growth? Would you remain single for them and not marry?" She tried to smile. "No, my daughters, for I am sorely grieved on your account, since the hand of the Lord has gone out against me."

Orpha stepped back a little, thinking. She looked into Noemi's eyes. "There are things to be done here, and I could do them for Chelion's peace," she murmured. "Never to remarry, might I not devote my life to preaching his faith to my people. I want to be with you always, but — but also I want to help Moab."

Noemi wrung Orpha's hand. "Great is your worth, my daughter," she said.

Orpha knelt for a blessing. Then, rising, she left without another word. Once she swerved a bit, as if expecting that Ruth would catch up with her; but Ruth was clinging to Noemi.

"Look," said Noemi, "she has gone back to her people and the peril of their false worship. Follow her. Sustaining each other, you could both resist evil and do good. She needs you."

"And does Mahalon's mother, more than a mother to me, need me not?"

"O, my daughter, I do. But what right had I to hope?"

Ruth held the bent head to her and declared, tears filling her eyes, "I know only that I cannot leave you. Whithersoever you go, I'll go, and where you stay, I'll stay. Your people shall be my people, even as your God is my God. Where you die, I will die, and there I will be buried. So may Yahweh do to me, and even more, if aught but death part us."

And all that she had to take with her out of the land of

Moab was the clothes she wore and the piece of parchment that Mahalon had given her before he died. It was sewn with finest stitches into the hem of her garment.

During the journey toward the sea, Ruth and Noemi saw many tents pitched on both sides of the highroad, and troops of soldiers maneuvering. But, unmolested, almost unnoticed, they paid scant attention. The world of men with its ceaseless recourse to arms seemed something to be forgotten.

Going slowly, they talked of many things with the freedom of complete trust, being adrift from all their old ties and having only each other. And Noemi learned that Ruth's union with Mahalon had left her without the fulfillment of marriage, because of his injuries which dated back to his struggle with the wolf in the cave. As brother and sister rather than as man and wife, they had lived together through the years. And finally knowing the deeper, silent meaning of Ruth's having come to her on the wedding night, Noemi marveled that a young bride, so deprived by fate, could have been strong enough to give another the very consolation that she herself should have received.

"But we loved each other, my mother," said Ruth. "Often he begged me to forgive him for joining what he called a barren life to mine, and grieved that he had only the hunger of his spirit to share with me."

They were at last standing where the waters of the Jordan emptied into the Salt Sea. Noemi looked on Ruth with a great love, and in the light of it she asked herself, "Why has the Lord so suited this body to bear sons, if motherhood is never to be?" But how might it be if the journey continued? Moab, where marriage was possible, lay behind. In the close-knit life of Bethlehem itself, where most minds were like Elimelech's and marriages with aliens were forbidden and unthinkable, how could a worthy mate for Ruth be found? She shook her head. "My daughter," she said, "we have come far enough. There is nothing for us both but to retrace our steps."

"No, my mother," replied Ruth quickly. "Bethlehem is your desire and mine. There Mahalon found music —"

"And lost it." Noemi's voice sounded a little strident. "He wanted to make another lyre but never did."

"Yet he never gave up hope." Ruth lifted her face in the sun. "He would have found his touch again, had he lived longer; and his music would have been finer, I know." She paused. "The night before he died, when we were standing at the window and watching the skies, he said that the stars were brighter for the very dark. And he said, 'I feel a shadow on me, but in it my memories of Bethlehem begin to shine.' He told me the dream that had often been his in the Bethlehem hills; a dream of life as a lyre, with the Lord himself stroking the strings."

There on the shore of the sea, she stood erect, taller with the exaltation of what she was saying; and her voice throbbed on. "Listening, I wanted more than ever to see the place that inspired such a dream, and almost felt that the time would come when the eyes of the world would turn to it. I longed to live there. And now that we are on the way, my mother, would you have us turn back?"

"Bethlehem might be unkind to you, my daughter," Noemi warned. "The love of God is there, but also a mistrust. . . ."

"Of strangers? But I'll not be a stranger. Already I am a Bethlehemite in spirit."

There was no gainsaying her.

A friendly boatman ferried them across the river on a raft of pegged planks, and when they reached the other side, they knelt upon the soil of Israel. Noemi gave thanks that the land was green again for others, if not for herself; and Ruth asked the Lord for the grace to serve this lonely mother well.

They were stirred from their prayers by singing voices. People were passing; migrant harvesters with their families, some going north, others south. Noemi and Ruth stood and watched them, especially the babies in woolen cradles on their mothers' backs. And Noemi thought of the days when she carried Chelion and Mahalon, just as small, into the fields of wheat and barley, and of the days when she, too, used to raise her voice in harvest song: a woman rich with husband, sons, and hope.

Ruth guessed her thoughts and realized that only a child, held to the sere breasts, could ever restore joy to them. And she, too, felt sadness, since this apparently was never to be. What union other than one with the Lord could she look forward to in the life ahead? What man of Bethlehem would incline to a Moabite widow! Moreover, a virgin she was and, in memory of Mahalon, a virgin she should remain. Orpha intended never to rewed: was not such an example of devotion to be cherished and followed?

They set their faces toward the southwest and moved on, Ruth subduing her pace to Noemi's languid steps. Almost always, when they stopped to rest under a tree or by a stream, somebody happening along would offer a few words of cheer and a little food. At night, they lay on the ground and wrapped themselves in each other's arms. The air was mild, the stars hung low, and not a sound of lurking wildlife disturbed them. And at length, in a rose-flushed dawn, an olive-bordered path led them to the ridge of an eastern slope. The morning star, paling, yet still sufficiently vivid in the melting blue, shone before them; and after looking up to it with gratitude for him who had brought them so far, they contemplated the town of their destination, the clusters of limestone cubes — the homes that Noemi knew so well. Bethlehem.

Soon she turned her eyes away from the simple serenity which she could no longer claim, and looked across the valley toward a place in the hills; a rocky mound, touched with the rays of the rising sun. The cave! And at the distant sight of it, a somber wave of memories rolled over her.

Ruth threw her mantle around Noemi's stooped shoulders and tried to cheer her. "Bethlehem is just as Mahalon pictured it to me," she said. "He likened it to a lamb in the Lord's embrace."

"I have seen the lamb slain," sighed Noemi.

"But it lives again, my mother!"

They next traversed meadows and were nearing the gates of the town. Noemi stopped near an almond tree growing beside a spring. She took hold of Ruth's sleeve and drew her to it. "It's not just an ordinary tree of its kind," she said with emotion. "It has been watered with a good man's tears. Here under these branches, Boaz regularly knelt, mourning his Zora just as Chelion mourned Miriam. True sons of Israel can no more forget their first love than the land that gave them birth. And their faithfulness" — she smiled a pensive smile — "is part of their stubbornness. Their blessed stubbornness! We have been called a stiff-necked people, but the stiffness is rather in our bosoms. We hold so strongly to what is ours, that we find it hard to understand — easy to misunderstand — the ways of others. And therefore others do not know us."

"But I know," said Ruth. "Mahalon often told me about Boaz. I wonder whether the downcast spirit of him has revived, now that the west wind is good to these fields, and this tree is green again."

Noemi had felt that she had no more tears, but still they were there. "Some wounds are healed only in death," she said.

"If death can heal, why not life?" Ruth broke a small twig and examined the glossy, luxuriant leaves. "Mahalon spoke of this tree and the anguish that its withering caused Boaz. Must not new foliage have brought new hope?"

Noemi's face brightened with a sudden thought. "It is a white almond tree," she said. "It blooms even in winter; a token, like Aaron's rod, that the Lord is with us always. The flower of your goodness, my daughter, was given me in the last of my days, a proof of his remembrance. And if he has not forgotten me, how could he forget Boaz?" She regarded her in a veiled manner. "Boaz may yet find happiness. . . ."

If Ruth caught the timid suggestion, she gave no sign.

And then Noemi's gaze turned upon two houses not far away. They were joined by a leafy grape arbor, but seemed as lonely as when she last saw them.

Out of the gates of the town, reapers were now trouping, ready for the day's work; men and women in garments that were homespun and durable enough to be handed down from one generation to another. Noemi and Ruth watched the procession; and, as it came nearer, Noemi fastened her gaze on a girl clad in a neat tunic which she gradually recognized as one that, years ago, she herself had made and, when it was yet new, included in a supply of clothing for a certain widow mother. "Rhea," she cried.

The girl's eyes widened. She stood, examining the old face, her attitude that of a person rapidly scanning a scroll for a certain haunting yet half-forgotten text. Then her face brightened. "Noemi!" she exclaimed.

Noemi embraced her. "You remember," she said, pathetically pleased and grateful. "And you were so little when I went away!"

Her voice carried, and some of the women stared. They interchanged quizzical glances and drew nearer. "Noemi — she who with husband and sons left Bethlehem in the early days of the famine?" asked one of the eldest.

"Call me not 'Noemi,' the pleasant one. Call me 'Mara,' the desolate, since the Lord has visited me with woe. I went away full, but he has rendered me empty, save for Ruth — this good and gracious daughter of Moab who has come back with me and would henceforth be one of us."

They peered at Ruth with ready suspicion. Two or three of them winced. A Moabitess, schooled in dark beliefs! How could such ever be one of them? They noted her comeliness and thought of their men.

Ruth's look was a plea for friendship, but they chose to interpret it as a pose, for they had heard that Moabite women were full of wiles. They returned their interest to Noemi with a swell of sympathy. To be accompanied only by a heathen was to be impoverished indeed. Worse than the loss of husband and sons!

Not yet knowing their minds, but bound up in her griefs, Noemi repeated herself: "Why do you call me by my former name, since the Lord has borne witness against me?"

"In truth he has!" said the first woman, eyeing Ruth again.

They formed a circle around the two, but pointedly ignored Ruth. They put many questions and learned what had happened to Elimelech and his sons in Moab.

"See what comes of association with aliens," said one. "Better to starve than eat their bread."

"Moab, with all its years of plenty, is still a land of lust!" said another.

"Thank the Lord that you've at last escaped!" a third told Noemi. "I'd rather be eaten by worms in Israel than live on the fat of Moab."

"You have returned to us defiled," said the first woman again. "How can we welcome you — with a Moabitess — into our homes, even though your need be as great as it seems and you look repentant? Hateful to the Lord is the mingling of Jew and Gentile."

"The mingling of good with good is no evil," replied Noemi.

"You call Moab good?"

"Sin is there, just as it is everywhere. But some Moabites are truly seeking God. Some have found him."

"You speak rashly. Have a care! Your days are far gone. Would you dwell with us as before, you must send this idolater away."

"She's no idolater!" cried Noemi, now thoroughly indignant, "but the wife of my dead son Mahalon, whose brother Chelion likewise married a daughter of Moab. She has turned to our faith." She thrust Ruth before the group. "Search her face. Her soul is in it. She's left everything to be with me."

"No one reared in vileness can ever be really good!"

"Does the mud soil the lily that springs from it?"

There was a small silence.

"Words, mere words. Now that the Lord's wrath has lifted from Bethlehem, we'll not tempt it again. Much as we want to help one whose bygone merit lives on in memory, we cannot receive you, unhappy woman, so long as she's at your side. We have our children to think of."

But the girl in the dress of Noemi's making put an arm around her. "Come with me," she said. "What Deborah, my mother, and I have, we'll share."

The women turned their backs and went on into the fields, but the girl led Noemi and Ruth toward the gates.

The keeper, bent and wizened, mumbled a bit as they passed. His interest was especially on Ruth. He did not recognize Noemi.

"Do you still wish to be a Bethlehemite, my daughter?" Noemi asked Ruth when they were well within the walls. "Those people have added shame to my grief."

"I will make them accept me, my mother," said Ruth quietly, smiling her bravest smile.

The little square house where Deborah and Rhea had found shelter during the famine was hardly more than a moldy old shed. It had belonged to a leper and nobody cared to claim it. But some vines twined about it, and their bright green was enriched by the very drabness. There were trees growing near; olive, fig, cypress and myrtle; and the air was fragrant.

As she removed her sandals at the threshold, Noemi thought: "How often I came in the past with aid for the widow! Now, a widow myself, I bring only my own want."

But Ruth had seemingly put out of her mind the attitude of the harvesters and she smiled again, gratefully, as Rhea took her and Noemi by the hand. She liked the tilt of the girl's head, the neat-coiled braids of copper-colored hair, the decent veil, the vivid thin face which could have been pretty only for deep shadows under the cheekbones. She knew that she had made a friend; and, with a mother and a friend, she felt that she should not fear.

When they passed beyond the door of wattle, they stood in a cool gloom, the only source of light being a tiny window.

"My mother," said Rhea to a haggard, gray-haired woman lying on a heap of straw, "the Lord has brought Noemi with Ruth, her adopted daughter, back to Bethlehem."

"Noemi?" The eyes deep in the almost fleshless sockets gave out sudden specks of light like fireflies in a tomb. "Not *our* Noemi. . . ." Deborah's arms, almost a skeleton's, reached out. She would have forced herself up, but Noemi and Ruth were already on their knees, their hands sliding gently under the stiff spine.

For moments, a thankful sobbing filled the room.

"Now I know why the Lord had me live on through the time of death," she was at length able to say, as she gazed on the two faces. "Now I can die, and in peace, knowing Noemi and an angel are here and that my child will be taken care of."

Noemi gave Ruth and Rhea a glance which begged them not to reveal by any word or sign that empty handed, poorer than the poor, she had returned. They could see in it an utter longing to be able again to give. Silently she stroked Deborah's brow until the eyes closed.

And when Deborah seemed asleep, Noemi told Ruth softly but fervently, "I must do something for her. She lived in the valley in the old days and was the only neighbor to bid me Godspeed when I left with my husband and sons. Somehow she knew. . . ."

Rhea overheard. "Do not think of help," she said. "I am good at gleaning, and there is food." She indicated a table with some bread on it. "Eat and rest. I'll go back now and work twice as hard but twice as willingly, and there'll be enough for us all."

"And I'll go with you," said Ruth.

"No — not today. You have come so far! Do refresh yourself with Noemi."

"To be with you out there will be my refreshment." Ruth's look was trustful. "Those in the fields have had time to reflect and — and change their minds. I believe that, within themselves, they wanted to be kind."

After she and Rhea had departed, Noemi continued to sit by Deborah. She, also, would have slept, for fatigue had reached the very marrow of her bones; but she could not relax as yet. She succeeded in putting the reapers from her mind, but other thoughts had their way. *The arbor, leafy again. The houses it joined. Boaz.* Was he still the brooder, or had new conditions brought hope — even a touch of happiness — to him? How was he treating the place that her family once called home? Her glimpse of it had revealed no neglect but only an air of solitariness. What a pity that it apparently was unused! She recalled how comfortable her family used to find it and what it had meant to them in the days that were gone forever. Dear scene of her union with Elimelech, birthplace of their sons, cradle of their every plan! Elimelech had built it in his youth with his own hands and imparted to it the very fullness of his spirit; trusted that it would enfold generation on generation and even endure to the day when the heavens would open and the Messias descend; invoked blessings on it over and over again. How often she had there spread honey on the family bread to symbolize the coming of a sweet and fruitful year! How often she had partaken there, with Elimelech and his sons, of the Paschal Lamb — symbol of unity of family, unity of nation, unity of

God with his people. And now, in this life of discord, estrangement, trial, and death, what unity remained? She thought of the unleavened loaves that she had kneaded and baked: no fermentation that would have signified decomposition; pure dry wheat as an emblem of the freedom from all foreign mixture which the true faith demanded. She moaned, realizing that, to save the failing bodies of husband and sons, she had exposed their souls to outrage in a strange land. Yes and, in the end, even their bodies too. By what right or authority had she dared to offer sacred beliefs to aliens? What good had come, or could have come, from it?

Her mind growing darker, she felt that somehow she had betrayed truth and tempted God. She had lent herself, however unwittingly, to the will of demons. All along, she whom others deemed strong had been yielding to sentimental impulses, positive and negative alike. She thought of the awful apartness imposed on Israel, the chosen, by him who made the sun, the moon, and the stars, struck the land of Egypt with plagues, parted the waters of the Red Sea, delivered the tables of stone on Sinai, and shattered the walls of Jericho! Had she not violated that apartness? No wonder she was punished, afflicted, rejected. But Ruth, blameless Ruth. . . .

And her daughter's brave smile came to mind like a star releasing itself from a cloud, and she began to think differently. "The works of his hand are indeed mighty, but what of his heart?" she asked herself. "He put tenderness in us, and surely his own nature is not harsh. Perhaps — perhaps it is given to some of us to feel beyond his might to his mercy. Surely his love, like the sun, shines on his other children even as on the chosen! Surely those who need him the most cannot be without his care, else why did he make them and imprint his image on them even as on the rest? Ruth's goodness is such that, all the way from Moab to this place, he seemed to be present in it, right by my side. Neither he nor she has abandoned me."

In utter exhaustion, but with the soothing that this last turn of meditation brought, she lay on the straw with Deborah. And then she slept.

And in her sleep as if inspired she saw Ruth — Ruth as the first flower of the Gentile world to be implanted in Israel. Ruth as the first ray of dawn opening the dark mystery of the East. Ruth as a proof that divine love sought sheep that were not of the fold, and that the Lord was not only in Israel but also where men knew him not. Ruth as a daughter not of Moab but of grace.

Meanwhile, Ruth was earnestly conversing with Rhea on the way to the fields. She wanted to know everything about this town of Mahalon's boyhood and dream. Those houses, for instance, lining the shadowy yet sunny narrow streets? Most of them had been built long ago, neighbor helping neighbor, with stones from the hills; and something of the set character of the builders, something of the timelessness of the hills themselves, had gone into the construction. Better times had returned so recently that only the young and plastic were thus far able to respond fully; most of the others — those who had somehow dragged themselves through the worst of the long siege of want — still bore the results of their endurance and, under their present hopefulness, were sick in spirit. Ruth would find out. She had had some inkling in the treatment already given her that morning. . . . What of Boaz? Rhea looked solemn. "No one understands him," she said. "He hasn't any intimates. He walks alone. We all feel for him. He has so much to make him contented, but seems the unhappiest man in Bethlehem. Some say he does not till his fields for profit at all but only for memories. I can't see meaning in that."

Ruth thought of the grave where a young bride slept, and of the wheat whose color and waving brought back to a lonely man the living hue of cheek, the fluid ease of motion. "Memories may be all that's left of life," she said.

More puzzled, Rhea went on. "He does not sell his grain. He is known to have become very angry when dealers from Tyre offered him a great price. He gives to the poor of the town and the countryside."

"Goodness is truly in him," said Ruth. Then she asked, "Does he ever visit the cave in the hills?"

Rhea stared, not comprehending.

"It was once his habit to go there with Mahalon," explained Ruth, "and there he used to find peace. The hills look so calm this day."

When they reached the fields, Rhea went to a group binding sheaves and hoisting them onto the carts that would bear them to a circular space of hard ground to be trampled by oxen. She beckoned Ruth to follow.

"Behold, the Moabitess is here again!" said the overseer of the female harvesters, jabbing the nearest worker with her elbow. This was the same who had taunted Noemi. Her face was sharp. "Why should unbelievers come to eat the bread of Bethlehem?"

"Moab fed Noemi and her family," challenged Rhea. "And Ruth, as the widow of Noemi's son Mahalon, belongs to us."

"A daughter of sin — one of us!" The woman threw up her hands as if calling down divine witness and cocked her ear to catch from the others a vocal proof that her horror was shared. It came, and she smiled grimly.

"A poison is under your tongue, Hagar," said Rhea angrily. "Have you no feeling for one who journeyed so far with Noemi and would now toil to feed her?"

The woman glared. "In my time, girls never spoke back at their elders and betters. If this stranger still thinks we'll let her tarry with us in these fields, she's not quick to learn." Her eyes commanded the others and received the approval they sought. "Our bread is unleavened; so is our way of life."

Ruth said meekly, though a spot was burning in her cheek, "I have foresworn the gods of Moab."

"The curse of having belonged to them — nothing can change or lessen it."

Ruth turned, her head bending, her tight-clasped hands hidden under the loopings of her sleeves. The hostility seemed too much, after all, for one who would have given years of her life for just a little of Bethlehem's kindness.

Rhea tried to take her arm protectively, and her snapping eyes told Hagar what she thought and felt. But Ruth, thanking her with a look, merely murmured, "I have not yet had time enough to prepare myself, nor have they had enough time to consider. I returned too soon."

And she left the fields of harvest, saddened for the second time since entering Israel, yet yearning the more to be accepted. She skirted the border of the town, wondering how she could return so soon to Noemi — what excuse she could offer. Then she began to feel as if a hand had slipped into hers and she were being led gently on, upward, to the solitude of the hills.

There were flocks of sheep like drifts of snow along the way. As she climbed higher, the cool air fanned her brow, and the sight of the sheep calmed her spirit. And soon she was nearing the point in the hillcrest on which Noemi's gaze, early that morning, had focused from the opposite heights.

Mahalon's voice was in her soul. "Here, beloved," it seemed to say. And she paused before a hollow in the rocks over which masses of briar were entangled in sorry proof of long neglect. The charred remains of what must have been a door lay on the ground, one beam transecting another in the form of a cross. Tears glazed her eyes as Mahalon's story — every detail of it — came back to her.

Tremulously she removed with her bare hands some of the tough vines at the entrance. The thorns pricked her fingers but she felt no pain of her own. It was his that filled her.

At last she stood in the interior on damp, moss-covered stones, and was surrounded by sweating, lichened walls; and down through the sky-blue opening above, a shaft of light descended, encompassing her. She raised her eyes and could see fiber shreds still sticking to the rocks and resembling blackened fissures in them. The remains of Mahalon's aeolian harp? She glanced at a heap of white bones in the corner — her lids closed and her fingers curled. Oh, to cleanse this cave of every sadness and restore to it the dream that Mahalon had dreamed, the music he had so often heard! She would come again and scrub each stone, three times with lye, three times with ashes, and over and over she would lave them with purest spring waters. She would weep while she did so, as Mahalon had said she would weep if he told her all. She would plait fresh strings of fiber for the aeolian lyre.

A new emotion began to fill her. The unearthly hand that seemed to have led her now might have been touching the very cords of her being. And in this moment it felt less like Mahalon's than that of the Lord himself. Though Bethlehem was rejecting her, she seemed to feel an assurance that Heaven was accepting her.

She knelt and gratefully offered her mind and heart. Hours passed as minutes. And when she looked up again, the patch of sky overhead held an early star.

In the dusk, a body brushed soft against her side. She gazed down into the quiet eyes of a lamb.

Their first night in Bethlehem, Ruth and Noemi sat on the doorstep of Deborah's house long after the lamp was extinguished. More than they needed rest, they needed each other. Ruth's mind was on her visit to the hills, and she was thinking of the cave of life itself where light and shadow, harmony and discord, hope and fear so strangely mingled; as well as the sky always above it, which seemed to shed promise that one day the mystery of the medley would be solved. She wanted to put this thought into words for Noemi, but decided to wait until the cave that Mahalon had loved was restored.

Inside the house Deborah and Rhea were sleeping. The only sound without was a faint stirring of wind and leaves. And Noemi, listening, told Ruth the parable that once was told by Joatham on the height of Mount Yarizim and had often been repeated in the households of Israel. "One day the trees went out to anoint a ruler over them, and they spoke to the olive, 'Reign you over us.' And it answered, 'Can I leave my fatness, which both gods and men make use of, to be promoted among the trees?' And next they addressed the fig, 'Come you and reign over us'; but it answered them, 'Can I leave my sweetness, and my delicious fruits, and go to be promoted among the other trees?' Downcast, they turned to the vine; but the vine also made demur, asking, 'Can I forsake my wine?' So the trees at last invited the humble bramble; and it gave them reply, 'If indeed you want me, come and rest under my entwining.' "

"What is the meaning?" asked Ruth, edging closer. "The bramble . . ."

Noemi's voice was low like the breeze in the leaves. "You and I have seen together the sorrow that crowns life with thorns. Somehow I believe that the Messias, when he comes, will lift this sorrow from the brow of mankind and make it his own. Then all our sadness will be seen as part of his glory; for there is no glory like that which relieves the suffering of others by assuming it. The bramble is, to me, a figure of a meek and perfect kingship such as the world has never, never known." She took Ruth's face in her hands and turned it to her. "Today I had a dream about you, my daughter. It made me appreciate afresh what you've done. You've left all things, and taken on another's burdens. You've been strong with a humble, silent strength." She pressed the cheeks. "Poor, misunderstanding Bethlehemites may see in you only a bramble of Moab, but I see in you a goodness that sets you apart. — Each passing day brings Israel nearer to the time of the great coming. Born of woman our King shall be! No one knows what woman will be chosen for this greatest of motherhoods, but I think I know the kind that will be chosen. . . ."

She looked directly into Ruth's eyes.

The following morning, Ruth decided to meet whatever humiliation the day might bring by going again to the fields. But Noemi, who had been informed by Rhea about the unshakable attitude of the reapers, tried to dissuade her. "My daughter, the Lord does not require this of you," she said. "You endured enough yesterday. Stay here with Deborah and me."

"And let Rhea alone support us? Would you think more of me, my mother, if I should hide away and cringe? You had Mahalon face Banaias."

"It was part of my weakness. Later, I resolved to interfere no more."

"And might my mother not be 'interfering' now, if she would have me remain here and withhold myself from becoming known?" Ruth smiled softly. "How can the women of Bethlehem ever know me, unless I keep going before them until they see that even a Moabitess can love and serve the Lord?"

Noemi, disarmed, went with her and Rhea to the door; but there she made another attempt at dissuasion. "Deborah seems weaker this morning," she said with a sigh. "Were it not well for both of us to watch over her while Rhea is away? By myself, I can do so little."

Ruth, turning, looked at Deborah, who was not lying on the straw but sitting up and partaking of some nourishment all by herself. "You often regretted, my mother, that you did not let Chelion and Mahalon do more for themselves when they were awaiting the return of health," she said. "Did you not?"

Though abashed, Noemi still did not surrender. "But you need more than yourself to deal with those women," she said.

"I'll go with you and speak to them. They'll know you very well when I am through! I was disheartened yesterday and could not express myself fully."

Again Ruth smiled a warm little smile which lighted up her whole face. "Is that the Lord's will?" she asked in a tone of affectionate teasing.

"No, it is not." Noemi's arms dropped and she stepped back from the door. "I crave his guidance, but this nature of mine has too much will of its own. Go, if you must and so God would have you."

Leaving the house, Ruth and Rhea were too interested in each other to notice a man standing not far from the doorway, or that he was following them at a distance as they walked along.

In the course of their conversation, Rhea offered to champion Ruth with even more vigor than before; and Ruth thanked her but did not accept. "Treat me before the women as if you do not know me," she said. "It is better. You would only make yourself angry on my account and turn them the more against me."

"But you have a right to be there!" Rhea's eyes flashed. "Is it not written in the law for the owner, 'When you reap the harvest of your land, you shall not wholly reap the harvest of your land, neither shall you gather the gleanings of your harvest. You shall leave them for the poor and stranger.'"

"I know," said Ruth. "Noemi and her sons told me many things that were taught them by the elders from the sacred scrolls. But I'll seek permission, for I would win favor." Yet favor seemed so far away that her face, now that Noemi could not see it, was troubled.

As they entered the fields, Hagar espied them and flatly turned her back. Rhea pulled Ruth's sleeve. "Glean, glean!" she whispered. "Defy her!"

But Ruth went to Hagar, touched her shoulder, and asked, "May I follow among the sheaves after the reapers?"

Her hands on her hips, Hagar whirled. Bending, she seized two fistfuls of the grain lying cut, and held them tight to her chest from contamination, while other women and some of the men came close, welcoming the distraction. "Get you gone, Moabitess!" she cried. "We are servants of Boaz who prizes his land too well to let anybody from Moab so much as step on it. There are other fields in Bethlehem."

"I wish to work nowhere else," said Ruth. "I have reason."

"Your reason is your shamelessness. Must we drive you off with blows?"

Ruth did not move.

Then a silence fell, and the harvesters, suddenly solemn, were looking not at Hagar or Ruth but just beyond, to a man who now spoke. It was the one who had been following. His voice had the depth and resonance that loneliness can give, but there was warmth to it.

"The Lord be with you," he said.

"May he bless you," the reapers replied in unison.

Ruth turned her head and had a sensation as of a picture within her coming to life. Surely this must be he of whom Mahalon had so often spoken. Surely this was Boaz.

"Whose maid is this?" he asked of a young man, the general overseer of the reapers. "Last night I saw her descending the hills. I followed her from a distance until she went into a little house in a humble street."

The young man told what little he knew about Ruth and threw in a few words of praise to please him. But Hagar, irritated, had to interrupt. "She's a Moabitess!" she said, putting an extra hiss onto the end of the word. "What good can come out of Moab?"

"Good went into Moab," answered Boaz. "I sent it."

To ease the awkwardness of the moment, the overseer hastened to add, "She came to Israel with Noemi, wife of Elimelech that was."

"Noemi?" Boaz started. "Here?"

Hagar spoke again. "Over in Moab, Elimelech and his sons met violent death. And now Noemi has indeed returned, not merely in the decent poverty that we'd all be glad to relieve, but with this —"

A flash of warning from Boaz silenced her.

He addressed Ruth. "Knew you the family? Chelion — Mahalon —"

"I was Mahalon's wife, my lord."

Hagar mumbled, but well under her breath, so that Boaz might not hear, "Moabitess!"

"Mahalon's — wife?" He came closer and for a minute could not say more. When he found his voice, he sounded different. "Listen, my daughter. Do not go into anybody else's fields to glean, but remain with my maidservants. Keep your eyes upon the best places not only today but until the end of the harvest. I command them" — his gaze sprang at the group — "not to prevent you. If you are thirsty, go to the vessels and drink of what is drawn."

His kindness, after the rejection by the others, overwhelmed her. She went down on one knee and bent her head. "Why have I found favor in your eyes," she murmured, "that you regard me who am a foreigner?"

He lifted her up, and the contact sent strange tremors through him. "The keeper of the gate had learned about you from some of the harvesters," he replied, "and last night he told me what you did for your mother-in-law after the death of her husband and sons, and that you left your household and your native land to come with her to a people hitherto unknown to you. But he is slow of wit and weak on names, and did not seem to know that your mother-in-law was our Noemi. Not until now did I myself know. Noemi, so good! Elimelech and his sons, so worthy!" His lips twisted and his brow furrowed. Only Ruth could now hear his hushed words. "I judged her and them wrongly. May Yahweh requite your deed and may your reward be complete before the Lord of Israel, under whose wings you've come to dwell."

She answered: "I have found grace in your eyes, my lord, for you have consoled me and spoken to the heart of your handmaid."

"Your name?" he asked softly. "I have not been given it yet, but I — think it could be 'Zora.'"

"It is Ruth, my lord."

"Just as fair. . . . Ruth. . . ."

His hands reached down, as if to take hers, but then they slipped to his sides and he turned away. Almost blindly, he moved on.

The servants stood gazing after the tall, spare figure and the odd set of the shoulders — the one elevated, the other slanting. The sun was touching threads of silver in the strands of dark hair.

"Well," said Hagar sourly to Ruth, "your Moabite witchery!"

Another woman drew her away.

Then, at a command from the overseer, they all resumed their work, except Rhea, who sidled up to Ruth. "You are very lucky," she said. "Casual gleaners are usually forbidden the best parts of the fields while the sheaves are still lying around. They have to wait for them to be carried off to the threshing floor, before they may gather the leavings. But you can go where and when you will, and help yourself. That's what he meant."

"He is good," said Ruth.

"The better harvest is a week or two away. Only barley — the bread of the poor — is here. I hope he will be as well disposed to you when the wheat is ready."

"He held to his memories for years." Ruth's gaze was in the direction he had gone. "Can his goodness change in a few days?"

And she stooped in gratitude, taking from the soil her first *shemal* — all the grain that a single hand could hold. The stalk heads were heavy. She raised them to her lips and murmured, "Bread of Bethlehem — house of bread."

She followed in the wake of the female servants for the rest of the morning. And when the sun was directly above, she heard his voice again.

"Ruth!"

She looked once more into his face, and this time she made a quick yet detailed survey of it. The blue-gray eyes; the sensitive nose; the black beard flecked with white, covering but not concealing the hollowness of the cheeks; and the hair of the head straggling unkempt from under a somewhat soiled turban. But she saw him less as he was than as he could be: handsome, upstanding, nourished, comforted, hopeful. Given a single hour, she might have cleansed the turban to the whiteness of foam, mended the tears in the striped mantle, fixed the too loose straps that held the cowhide sandals to the ankles. And how gladly she would have laved the tired, calloused feet —

"Draw near," he said, motioning toward some harvesters.

She knew that his ire would be aroused against them if she revealed in any way her realization that they still did not want her; so, without a word, she went to them. He followed, and they stood together beside a fire of dry grass and thorns into which some of the best grain, not too ripe, was being held by the still attached stalks until the chaff should burn away and the kernels be sufficiently parched. A cloth had been spread on the ground. Ruth and Boaz assisted the others, with sticks supplied by Hagar, in beating and winnowing the ears now thrown on it. When all was ready, they sat, and Hagar served them first. They rubbed the grain on their palms and ate in silence; and the women furtively studied their countenances. Glances were interchanged when Boaz held a cup of cool and refreshing vinegar mixed with spring water to Ruth's lips. There was knitting of brows, and Hagar frowned her darkest.

Ruth ate little. The portion that Hagar had given her was ample, because the eye of Boaz had been on the serving. But she was thinking of Noemi and Deborah; so, discreetly, she slipped the larger part of her helping into her dress.

When the meal was over, Boaz rose and repeated his command of the morning and added to it: "She may glean among the sheaves, and you shall not oppose her." His glance darted at Hagar and, going to her, he whispered, "You and the rest shall draw out some ears from the bundles and leave them for her."

Then he walked away. But Ruth had a feeling that he would not go far. When she returned to her work, she was tempted several times to look and see, but refrained. Perhaps it was mostly his affection for Mahalon or his respect for Noemi that had caused his kindness, she thought. Perhaps, having thrust from his devotion a Bethlehem that had given him so little solace for long, he had too readily been attracted to a stranger who happened to bear some resemblance to Zora. Perhaps, before the wheat harvest, he would indeed have forgotten that he ever met her.

She tried to put him from her mind. Once, unintentionally she did raise her eyes as she picked up some especially rich grain that one of the reapers must have accidentally left behind. And there he was, a short space away, watching.

He nodded that the grain was hers. And he smiled in the half-ashamed, self-conscious manner of one caught enjoying the success of a childlike ruse; but it was enough to make his whole countenance bright.

She gleaned until the sun began to sink behind the hills and the reapers were making ready to quit. Rhea joined her while she was beating out what she had gathered. "Never has anybody done better, nor nearly so well, with a single day's work," she commented. "Why, you have almost a bushel there!

I thought I was your only friend in this field, but there must be others. Someone must have helped you."

Ruth smiled. "Someone did."

Noemi, attending Deborah, had thoughts of Ruth all that day. They came in a stream which flowed now forward, now backward. From the little that Deborah could tell her in answer to queries about Boaz, she inferred that he was much the same as when she last saw him: dour, distrustful, bound to self by sorrow but given to impulses of generosity which probably relieved his unhappiness just enough to enable him to bear on. Knowing that it was to his fields that Rhea had taken Ruth, she could not but remain disturbed. What if he should be there in person today — they had to meet sometime — and vent his moodiness on her? What if he should order her away? But Noemi found herself dismissing this idea as improbable. She remembered how she herself had felt, the first time she met Ruth; how affected she had been with the resemblance to Zora. She pictured the two discovering each other: Boaz awakening to the fact that, though Zora lay buried, beauty still lived; Ruth drawn to the abjectness which her nature could never resist. And the picture began to take on perspective and detail. She fancied Ruth and Boaz wading through tall grain, just as, back in Moab, she had often seen her and Mahalon; their forms uniting in the distance, a bond weaving itself.

But realizing the possible absurdity of such a notion, she erased it. Boaz must be in his mid-thirties by now. Melancholy had undoubtedly continued to age him beyond his years, whereas Ruth's habit of forgetting herself in a concern for others had preserved in her the freshness of youth. They were far too different for mutual attraction. Moreover, here in Bethlehem, every obstacle would be thrown between them.

Noemi wondered a little why she herself had never recoiled from *nokri* or non-Jews. Maybe it was because her girlhood had been spent in Nazareth which, as a crossroads town, received many transients. Some of those aliens who used to stop at her father's carpenter shop on business had been very kind to her, and she grouped them naturally with the other good people she knew. They must have believed in goodness; else how could they have practiced it? Thus, she recalled, she had reasoned in those early days; and the reasoning still seemed right to her, notwithstanding her somber experiences in Moab. Was not the Lord good, and did not all goodness both come from him and lead back to him? Bethlehem, unlike Nazareth, lay too secluded from other peoples and had not learned any too well that God's love and the love of God could be wide. It needed some great lesson. But, whatever the explanation of its stern attitude toward *nokri*, Noemi had to admit to herself that the fact of prejudice must be faced, and it would stand like a stone wall, no matter how much Boaz and Ruth might conceivably be drawn to each other.

Besides, did not Ruth, like Orpha, seem disinclined to look again on any man? And had not Noemi herself resolved, years ago, to yield no more to her tendency to manage lives? But that resolution was now old and the effects of it had been as unhappy as those that followed her previous attitude. Just as Deborah wanted to see Rhea settled before her death, so did Noemi desire Ruth's good fortune. To be able to advance it was the last blessing that she would ask of life and the Lord.

What might she do? Go to Boaz and sing Ruth's praise? But Ruth needed no praise: her worth could speak for itself, except to women who would not listen. Well, then, ought not Boaz be firmly informed that, though he possessed Elimelech's estate quite legally, he still had a moral obligation to provide a frugal existence for the remnant of Elimelech's family, now that the fields were producing again? Soon both the barley and the wheat harvest would be over. The soil, at its best, could yield more crops than one a year; but, in the times between, the poor might again know the pinch of hunger. In this little house of Deborah's, there were four to be fed. Noemi felt, from yesterday's evidence, that no help could be expected from outsiders, even if she and Ruth should go into the streets and beg. Something had to be done, and she must swallow that strangely persistent pride of hers in order to do it. Deborah had told·her that Elimelech's only brother — Hobab, who used to dwell a day's journey from Bethlehem — was dead. There was only one person to whom she could turn; the one who had urged her and the family away and cried from the depths of his soul, "Had I never known you!"

With such thinking, she waited for Ruth's return from the fields, praying the Lord that the faithful daughter be spared further humiliation this day. At whatever cost or contrivance, Boaz should be approached. Rhea's generosity was not to be imposed upon. Ruth must be placed under the protection of the most prosperous, hence most influential, townsman, who alone could save her from want and insult. But how could she — Noemi — bring herself to sue for this favor? Would Elimelech, Chelion, and Mahalon have her crawl back to Boaz?

The room had filled with dusk when the door opened on a flood of early moonlight. Ruth and Rhea were back.

Noemi rose from her place beside Deborah on the straw bedding.

"See, my mother," cried Ruth, displaying the results of the day's work. "And there's more, too." She placed her gleanings on the table and drew forth the portion of the noonday meal that she had kept. "The Lord walked with me out there."

Noemi's eyes could not believe the abundance. "Where did you really glean today?" she asked quickly. "Blessed be whosoever had regard for you!"

"And what regard!" Rhea's voice rang. "O Noemi, you should have seen. He could hardly tear himself away from her. He had the look of a sheep finding its first green pasture.

He stayed in the fields until sundown just to be near her!"

She would have gone on, only that Deborah needed her attention.

"Yes, my mother," said Ruth, "it was he — Boaz."

Noemi's lips parted but she was speechless for the moment. Here she had been puzzling and planning all day, thinking that it was for her to bring two lives together; and all the time, the Lord had been taking matters out of her tired hands into his own —

Ruth embraced her. "He was kind," she murmured.

"Blessed be he by Yahweh who has not ceased to show mercy toward the living and the dead!" Noemi pressed her cheek to Ruth's. "If the Lord has been with you this day, must he not have been with us all through every other, whatever the darkness? One night long ago, Boaz, led by him, came to my family to restore his friendship. And now the joy is repeated through you, my daughter."

"God takes his time but never fails," said Deborah from her pallet.

After Ruth assisted Noemi to a bench, the only piece of furniture beside the table and a chest, she lit two lamps instead of one, feeling that an extra light could be afforded now.

"For the past and for the — future?" asked Rhea, coming close, her eyes twinkling, her face rosy in the glow.

"Both for Bethlehem," said Ruth, placing the brighter in the window and gazing out into the starry night.

Again Noemi spoke. "It would be well, my daughter, for you to live with the maidservants of Boaz for the rest of the harvest. You could save yourself from moving back and forth, and there would be more energy left for your work. This one-room house is rather cramped by the four of us. Rhea has to return each night to be with Deborah, but you don't have to worry about me. I feel almost young again."

Ruth knew her mother-in-law too well not to detect the significance in the solicitude.

"You are silent," said Noemi.

"I am thinking, my mother."

A little later, when they were about to partake of their evening meal, they heard a step at the door. A long shadow fell and stirred upon the floor; and looking up, they beheld Boaz entering. His first glance was for Ruth, but he went to Noemi.

She could not rise, and he knelt and bent his head to her knee.

Her fingers touched his hair, his brow, his tear-wet face.

As one who had lived life long and relived most of it, she remembered each note of his last coming for forgiveness; and now she gave practically the same greeting as she had given then. "The table is ready, good Boaz, and the lamps are bright. It's as if we never lost you."

The barley harvest soon ended. Then the wheat was ready, and the gathering of it was more important than the mining of gold would have been.

From a leafy booth on a small hill, Boaz watched his laden fields by night, but it was not the grain that claimed his thoughts during these vigils. Among his maidservants, down there in the velvet dark, lay Ruth. Obedient to Noemi, she had come to make the fields her home until the last sheaf should be taken in. And each night was wondrous to him because of her being there; each day sunny with the sight of her.

Slumbering or awake, he dreamed of her; his second and even fairer Zora, his fresh existence, his new-found spring.

The almond tree by the brook, so like the peach in form and blossom, seemed to exhale Zora's approval of this new love. And he would have been thoroughly happy, planning to restore Elimelech's estate to Noemi and surround her with comfort, only that there was an elusiveness to Ruth which he could not understand. There was nothing franker than her friendship, yet she seemed to him to be withholding something of herself. Was she still given to Mahalon's memory, as he had been given to Zora's? But might he not make her see what he was now finding himself believing — that the dead bequeath their hearts to the living?

He wanted to talk with her about Mahalon but he could not find speech. He had never forgotten the youth who captured the harmony of another world, and it was mostly the memory of him during the years of Bethlehem's woe that had finally tempered his outlook and made him long for an opportunity to repair all wrongs. He would not have neglected their little retreat in the hills, only that he had continued to fear the forlornness of it. When the soil started to yield again, he would have gone to Moab to bring him and the others back, but for the conviction that he had forfeited every right. Ruth must have discerned in him a love for one whom she herself had loved; and this thought served to increase his trust that he could win her. Would not Mahalon, who had shared his music, want it so?

His day's joy began when he descended the hill each dawn to rouse the harvesters; for there in the fields he could find Ruth, already risen, beating out the grain that had been left from the previous evening; and he wondered whether, like himself, she had been more awake than asleep in the night. His gaze would eagerly follow her salvaging the early hours, cool and fresh, with a variety of tasks such as attending to the children of the servants, washing their garments in the brook, and preparing the breakfast that would be eaten in midmorning. She had a way with the little ones which could be explained, he was sure, only by her wanting a child of her own. They turned to her even more than to their mothers and were responsive to her every glance or touch. He could see that she was steadily winning their parents. Even

Hagar no longer frowned but merely looked perplexed. And, while the workers took advantage of the four rest periods of the day, he noticed that Ruth still found too much to do to sit or lie under the shade trees. All her activity, though, appeared so effortless, so self-effacing, that it shed a certain serenity, and he was confident that it did not interfere in the least with her personal thinking. Was her mind on him, just as his was on her?

They were seldom together and their conversations were always brief. She seemed to prefer this. His glowing secret, he suspected, was diffusing itself to the field hands. And soon it would be no secret. After the end of this wheat harvest, he would put his plea, since she had no blood relative in Israel, directly to her. As for Noemi's approval, he was sure that he already had it; and any disapproval on the part of Bethlehemites could be strongly ignored.

A breeze from the Mediterranean kept blowing far inland. Like any of his menservants, Boaz would stand on the threshing floor, tossing bunches of wheat with a wooden fork and letting the chaff be separated and the heavy grain fall. Occasionally Ruth would pause to join the children gazing wide-eyed at the process; but what attracted her was the great change in him. His cheeks seemed fuller and had a touch of color, and his eyes had lost their sadness. Zest rippled in his movements. The scarf on his head, tied down with a linen band, shimmered from very whiteness in the sun. She had washed it herself when she found it discarded near the brook, and he took pride in keeping it from the least stain. His black hair, with its streaks of silver less noticeable now, was smooth. The peculiar slant to his shoulder had gone. Whenever his eye met hers, he smiled, and she smiled back.

Soon came the final day of the harvest. Reaping, binding, threshing, winnowing and sifting, all were over. From dawn to sunset, carts hauled off the grain from bursting cribs into the town and the villages beyond. This season, Boaz was sending some of it even to more distant places; and stately camels, five of them in a chain, had been led by a driver on a small brown donkey into and out of the fields. Their humped backs were piled with well-filled sacks, their bronze bells tinkled to their stepping, their long necks were laced with blue beads to keep "the evil eye" away. The children followed them, clapping and shouting. And Ruth found her own voice mingling with the glee, her own hands clapping. Never had a day passed more speedily and pleasantly.

With a sense of work well done, she made ready to return to Noemi in the evening. In less than an hour, the valley would be a great bowl of starlight. Regretfully she looked up in the direction of the cave in the hills. The harvest had deferred her plan to restore it; now she intended to spend much of her time where, she felt, the Lord's answer to the problem that had taken possession of her might be found.

Rhea was about to join her; but, seeing Boaz drawing near, she slipped away.

Then he was at Ruth's side, relieving her of the sheaves she had just knotted into one bundle. With his eyes he asked permission to accompany her. Whatever the conventions of his people, he could not forego this opportunity to have her all to himself.

Children and parents, already on their way and well ahead, glanced back and waved to them. She turned more than once to look at other children who, happy with all the stir, were making it difficult for their mothers to get them together and started; and she noticed how many of the grownups were deliberately loitering, as if the fields, to which they had given so much of themselves, still held them. A calm was on her face and that of Boaz. They needed no words as yet. And so they approached Bethlehem.

Just outside the gates, Boaz hesitated. He put the bundle down and took her two hands. He held them below his chest and considered the tapering fingers, oblivious of his surroundings. The harvest had been hard on those fingers, but the twilight poured itself over them like an ointment and softened them. Gradually his gaze lifted to her face. It did not meet her eyes. It must await her response for that. "The Lord of the harvest brought us to each other," he said. "Would he have us go different ways, now that the crop is in and the poor have food?"

She glanced back to the fields. They were an expanse of purple, and a mistiness, perhaps in her vision, perhaps the result of the mingling of the day's warmth with the cool of evening, was blurring them from view. She next looked to the hills, and her look lingered on them. If she could lead him there, as Mahalon had once led him. . . .

But the dusk was deepening and the cave was not ready.

"Do not answer now," he said quickly. "You've known me too short a time perhaps."

Turning to him, she saw his stark fear of a refusal. Her nature recoiled from hurting anyone, especially this lonely man. But how else could she make an honest effort to have him understand the stirrings within her? The call of a realm more real to her than the world around them both; the desire to relinquish all desire save that of her soul for union with the Lord. And yet her longing to accept the love that Boaz was so humanly and earnestly offering seemed beyond her ability to resist.

But the cave — it would help her in time to dispose him and herself. The lyre might be remade to sing to him again of a realm beyond the senses, in which all perplexities could be solvable by selflessness or dissolvable in an ecstasy not of flesh. He had heard that music once. She herself, in far-off Moab, had early caught what might have been a strain of it in her soul; for, one day in her childhood, when the priest from Bethlehem-Judah with the shining smile and message gave her a present of a shell which came from the great sea in the west, she had held the object to her ear. The call of something everlasting seemed to issue in silvery accents from it. She had never been able to put the impression into speech, but now it seemed to her that the sound had converged all the scattered notes of experience into a single suggestion: the sigh of creation for the Creator — the echoing answer from above. Was not this what mankind needed to sense most of all?

These thoughts, still seeking words, drifted formlessly through her mind as she stood facing Boaz, trusting that he and she might eventually be strong enough to conquer impulse and accept only the kind of happiness that exceeds physical ties.

And now night had fallen, but a strange unrest was in the air; and suddenly Ruth found herself quaking, for, high up in the tower that rose from the town walls, a sentry, dark against the sky, was blowing a curved *shofar*, or ram's horn. She had heard this same sound — the opposite to that of the sea shell — in her early days when Moab was on the eve of one of the many wars it waged or suffered. She remembered the horrors that the long, wailing blast then heralded: the screams of women and children, the oaths of men, the clash of arms in the streets, the hurled torches, the spread of flames, the desperate shelter in secret places, the dragging forth of the helpless, the shame, the blood. From her spirit had been driven, by the outrage of her senses, all desire for a world that could be so violent; and there had risen in her a passion for the gentle, the peaceful, the good, which her virginal union with Mahalon had largely satisfied and his cruel death increased. This was why, deep within, she felt unfitted for any earthly future and hoped for a life of deeper union with the Lord under whose shelter she had come to dwell, as Boaz himself had said.

"Has war reached even here?" she thought, listening to the clarion. "But no! Bethlehem is apart. These people have taken nothing. They've no enemies —" Then she remembered with a stab of pain the soldiers, the tents, the maneuvering that she and Noemi had seen during the journey out of Moab.

The gatekeeper was wildly swinging a lantern with one hand and beckoning to her and Boaz with the other. "In, in!" he cried. "This day we learned that men were marching from along the inner sea, but we supposed they were merely harvesters homeward bent. Tonight a messenger from a village to the east has just warned us that they have weapons and seem to be from Moab. By now, they must be at the hills. Are many of our own still in the fields?"

"Not many." Boaz was urging Ruth through the gates. "The horn will speed them. I'll go back to help."

"And I with you," said Ruth, turning around. "The children —"

"No, you must not! Join Noemi. Hurry."

"Some of them are so small! I can get them together and —"

"I must shut and bar the gates," groaned the keeper. "They've been open too long already. The elders have just sent a command."

Boaz again insisted that Ruth remain within; then, thinking he had persuaded her, he swung on his heel and disappeared into the night.

She stood peering into the darkness that engulfed him. The gates were closing, and something else was closing also. Was it life itself? She felt conscious of people behind her, and she thought she could hear Rhea's pleading voice; but she was mostly aware of the narrowing space between the great portals. There was hardly a minute for choice. Noemi or — Boaz and the children. Friendly hands were seizing her. She tried to shake them off. They withheld her the more. Struggling, she broke away and worked herself sidewise through the opening just before it completely disappeared with a creak and a clang. A fold of her breeze-swept dress was almost caught. She stood alone.

Fighting off fear, striving for control, she faced the direction of the fields. Memories of Mahalon's last flight to the cave, which he had often described, came to her. Would all Bethlehem be ravaged like the cave? Was the quiet, regained music of its living to cease? Were little children to be slain — slain by her own countrymen? She hastened to overtake Boaz. The mere nearness to him helping to get the others to some place of security would bring strength. But now, as she sped, there was a hush in the air, for the ram's horn had abruptly ceased. The promise of starlight which the earlier skies had given, was not yet fulfilled. The gloom had increased. Once or twice she thought she could discern a shadowy figure; but she dared not break with a call the strange command of silence that seemed to have fallen on the night.

Having gone over the winding road to the fields only three times in broad daylight and twice in the half-light of evening, and each time abstractedly, she was not at all sure of herself. It ought not have taken nearly so long as this to get there; and why had she not met some of the harvesters, some of the children, if they were hurrying toward Bethlehem? Had Boaz headed them off into a detour, the better to safeguard them? What else could he have done, with the town gates closed? Maybe he was leading them around the walls to some section of the western hills. Perhaps to the cave! Except in the town itself, no better shelter could be provided.

And then a fresh emotion gripped her. If he had gone to the cave, she would be utterly exposed and defenseless, unless by herself she could quickly get there too. She whirled. Trusting to instinct and prayer, she bore on and, before long, was climbing a slope. A faint glow, as if from some banked fires, was spreading above the summit. She sighed her relief. Boaz and the remainder of his servants, with the children, would be waiting on the farther side of this hill. They must have by-passed the cave in favor of open spaces.

Suddenly a hand fell on her shoulder. A man's voice with a high pitch to it smote her ear. "Who are you, woman?"

She trembled from head to foot.

"Are you of Bethlehem?"

Her tongue clove to the roof of her mouth.

"Speak!"

"I am of Moab," she caught breath enough to reply, as a bulky body pressed close. "But I belong to Bethlehem."

"Bethlehem belongs to Moab. By tomorrow's sunset, in the name of Chemosh, we'll have taken it. And then — Jerusalem!"

Chemosh.

For Ruth, that one word sprang out from the others. It trailed memories of the death scenes of Elimelech, Mahalon, and Chelion. It renewed every fear and revulsion she had ever known. Heard by her for the first time in Israel, it seemed to conjure up the monstrous god himself. Fearful for Bethlehem, she felt too for the people of her native land who were slaves to that awful name.

The man was seizing her arm. "You shall come with me. A Moabitess from Bethlehem! Our wise Deity has been working well for us. You must know much."

"I know little. I — I'll tell you nothing."

There was a harsh laugh. "We'll see . . . why came you into Israel?"

"It is the land of my dead husband Mahalon."

"*Mahalon.* Him that, with his brother, Chelion, was slain for treachery and blasphemy in Moab? Then you must be Ruth, whose father and mother were faithless to Chemosh and whose uncle Jared took on Jewry before he died."

His hand was now under her chin, tilting it upward. By this time, the moon had appeared and was sending down some light. Ruth's blood ran cold, for she recognized him. As a child, she had first seen that big heavy figure in a chariot drawn by a span of coal-black horses; and she had never forgotten the arrogant, sea-green stare, the long snipe nose, the evil lips. At the sight, she had run and buried her head in her mother's robe. And recurrently in her girlhood she had witnessed this same personage, ruling processions in the streets and presiding over ceremonies in the temple, which Jared forced her to attend. Three or four times he had "honored" Jared with visits, during which she hid in Orpha's house. Once, in her fourteenth year, she returned too soon from her refuge, and Jared made her submit to a presentation. Never could she forget the feel of that clammy hand or the gaze that trickled like foul water all over her. Later on, when Mahalon called the man "friend," she had shared Noemi's unrest and striven in vain to convince him that his confidence was mistaken. And now, here in the hills of Bethlehem, he had returned to her life, leading an army against a people whose love she sought. For this had he been temporarily kind to Mahalon and other Israelites in Moab, despising them as he used them.

She was face to face with the high priest Banaias.

Chapter Six

A PROPHET SPEAKS

ANAIAS and his soldiers had entered Israel in ordinary workday tunics, so that they might look like peaceable folk coming from beyond Jordan in quest of food and shelter in return for honest labor, just as many Jews themselves, a decade before, had gone over, with whatever household goods and implements they could carry, into Moab. All armor and weapons had been carefully placed in carts, covered up with sackcloth, and paddled on rafts across the narrow, northern part of the Salt Sea. He was confident that no Israelite would suspect the real nature and purpose of the expedition and that he would have the advantage of making a surprise attack. He felt that he well knew the weakest spots in Bethlehem's defense.

It had irked him that, when his wagons were passing through a tiny village on the way toward Bethlehem, some of the coverings had got loose; for it was possible that a few of the workers in the fields had glimpsed the military supplies. But he made himself think that Jewish eyes, hazy with dreams, were hardly capable of noticing much detail. Also, the clarion from Bethlehem at sunset had disturbed him; but he interpreted it as a call to some sort of harvest or religious assembly, rather than as a warning against a suspected enemy. And, anyhow, what could the town do? It had no standing army, no militia, no provision for a prolonged siege, no tactics beyond swift marches and sudden sorties of a citizen brigade.

He had arranged his plans slowly and thoroughly, having for several years cherished the idea of a western conquest to offset the territorial shrinkage of Moab which had once extended as far north as Mount Gilead but had been driven southward by the Ammonites. It took all that time for him to reduce Hotham, the Moabite king and son of a strong and valorous father, to such a weak and dissipated state as could offer no obstacle to the ambition. Before succeeding to the throne, Hotham had been approached by some visiting priest from Bethlehem-Judah, who prated about serving an invisible god with justice and truth, and fallen under the stupid spell. The young monarch consequently began his rulership with so many high ideals that Banaias was affronted and rendered fearful that the worship of Chemosh might weaken in the land. It was then that a hatred for the town in Israel which produced the troublesome priest, and a desire to aggrandize Moab by a capture of Israel, began to possess Banaias. And now he was well on the way. With the taking of Bethlehem, two aims would be accomplished: revenge on the town which, as a center of pure Jewry, seemed to embody a special menace to the religion of Moab; and, secondly, the securing of enough material of war, in addition to what had been brought across the water, to assure the success of an attack on Jerusalem. That was why he had not taken the high road from the sea to the so-called Holy City. Bethlehem first, and after that the biggest prize of all! With the very heart of Israel cut out, the winning of the rest of the land would be an easy matter. Then in triumph he would return to Moab, sweep off the throne the effete Hotham whom he had left behind, combine the offices of kingship and high priesthood just as he was now combining the latter with generalship, and rule the people, body and soul, with the very might of Chemosh. What an era lay ahead! There was such an accumulation of gold in a deep dungeon of the Moabite temple, and so much more to be wrested from Israel, that it might be feasible also to spread the kingdom of Moab as far into the east as the Tigris and the Euphrates. He would be a god himself!

And so, on that night before battle, he had betaken himself from his men to stand alone and gloat over the valley and the town soon to be his initial prize. It was then that Ruth strayed into his presence.

He immediately thought of spilling her blood in a pleasant little libation to Chemosh before the full flow that would follow tomorrow's sunrise. But, on the other hand, it might be better to let her live. And she was beautiful. Vaguely he remembered having seen that face, some years ago. He had tucked the memory away for future reference. Had he not somewhat fostered the notion, at the time, of presenting the king with a young concubine to assist in further softening the royal life and character? But, it came to him now, he had never made this gift because of a suspicion that such a girl might restore Hotham's virtue instead of losing her own. Moreover, he now remembered Mahalon's praising his young wife Ruth in the course of some of those private conversations in the alcove of the temple. Strange that he had never urged the Jew to bring her to him or even given the matter any thought. Well, the Jew's body was slain, and here was a chance to perfect the punishment by torturing the Jew's soul — if disembodied souls could still see.

Holding Ruth's arm, he roughly led her over the summit of the hill and, with a sweeping gesture, indicated an encampment on the slope. "My surprise for Bethlehem," he said.

She tried to break away from him but was caught with both his hands, which were like steel. "Has Bethlehem turned you into a fool?" he asked.

Dragging her toward one of the banked fires near the border of the bivouac, he flung her on the ground. Soldiers all around sat up and stared as he squatted and again addressed her.

"Why were you wandering in the night?"

She had inferred, from his having chosen the far side of the hill and thereby screening his approach, and from his mention of a "surprise," his belief that Bethlehem was still in ignorance. She must not disillusion him. Moreover, if she should tell him about Boaz and the harvesters locked out from the town, he might send a company to search for them and take them prisoners. She endeavored to rise but said nothing.

He bent, his face coming close to her, the embers shedding a red luster on him as on the image to which Bahila used to burn lights in Moab. He took her left wrist, spread the fingers apart, stroked each one.

"Your husband once told me of two cities — Sodom and Gomorrah — and of two individuals — Nadab and Abihu — who were punished with fire," he said slowly. "It would seem that the god of Jews favors this element. And you favor this god."

He brought the wrist forward until the finger tips almost touched one of the embers. "Still favor him?"

She squirmed, her eyes bulging, her wrist unable to move in the viselike hold.

He made her feel the incandescent surface through its thin layer of gray ash.

"Still?" His tone filled with mock worry, and, sliding his grasp to her elbow, he jabbed the entire hand down. The embers hissed. Her skin shrank, every muscle contorted, tears trickled from her squeezed lids. No sound escaped her knotted throat and lungs, though the need of an outcry tore at them like talons.

He himself was finding the heat too great. His own hand felt a touch of the agony he was inflicting. His sleeve scorched, and he thrust her from him. "This is only the start," he muttered, getting up. "You are the first Moabite woman I've ever seen without good use for a tongue. Useless things should be plucked out. But I can wait — a while. Waiting is a habit of mine." He stood now with his arms crossed and his legs apart, looking down at the hand. Suddenly he gave an order to two gaping soldiers. "Take her in charge but trouble her not. I'll deal with her myself when she's sensible. Meanwhile show her how well we are capable of treating a *true* daughter of Moab, now that she has a taste of what comes from being false. Get some unguents. Anoint and bandage her burns. She's shivering as if she hasn't had enough warmth yet. Kindle a special fire for her, and throw a cloak around her — there's the purple velvet one in my tent, that I'll use when I enter Bethlehem. It will be a reminder to her of my all-embracing power."

Her veil had slipped from her head, and her long hair, shining in the ember glow, was fully exposed. Stooping, again he ran his fingers through it; then, energetic with further inspiration, he reached toward a neighboring golden-apricot tree, some of the boughs of which swung low. He broke off blossoms and deftly plaited a coronet. Holding it before him, he placed it on her and in a falsetto voice declared, "So shall you be queen of my campaign against Israel, if you choose wisdom."

Boaz had indeed thought of the cave in the hills to the west of the town, and there he hurriedly led the stragglers. His spirit sank lower at the sight of the desolation within, and he regretted his years of neglect. But he noticed that the briars at the entrance were pushed aside as if somebody else had recently been here, and somehow this made him think more poignantly of Ruth.

He tried to console himself that she was in the walled shelter of Bethlehem where she would be safe, if anybody could be safe this night. As he stood with the harvesters and their children huddled around him like sheep, he felt almost that he could hear her calling him. The night wind seemed to whisper, then to sigh.

Restless, he could not remain here idle, however much these people needed the encouragement of his presence. He went to the mouth of the cave and gazed down at the town in the valley. It lay deathlike in a pool of dark, without a single ray from any window. — Ruth must be with Deborah and Noemi, but worrying about the children. How he wished he could reassure her! They would be better off here; but Bethlehem itself, was it to become a grave like the one beneath the almond tree? Life would be over for him, if the town should fall. Catastrophe must not be! Yet how could a man, unarmed, do anything to impede or prevent it? Bethlehem, just recovering from its long period of want, was very weak. The enemy had chosen the time for attack well. Unless the Lord intervened. . . .

He fell on his knees and there at the mouth of the cave prayed for Ruth and Bethlehem and Noemi. And, in the midst of his prayers, it occurred to him that the Lord's usual answer came not in miracles but in a strengthening and enlightening of the spirit to do what was necessary. He rose with a resolve. Even alone, he might and would attempt a blow. Yet he was tormented, because the keeper of the gates had suggested that the invaders were from Moab, and Moab was the native land of Ruth. The woman he loved belonged to the enemy of his people. . . . But, with Noemi, she had left them forever.

As his gaze crossed the valley to the eastern hill opposite, he saw the faint rim of light. On the farther side, the Moabites must have pitched camp for the night. If so, the light was from their fires. Soon it would be even fainter, and the army would be sleeping. Life had made a creeping, crawling thing of him for years. He was part of the earth on which his eyes had been so long fixed and with which he had so long struggled. He could find his way over it even in utter darkness. And if he could get to the leader, who surely would be in a conspicuous tent apart. . . .

Rising, he turned to the refugees and told them to remain here quiet and careful, while he set forth on an errand against "those Moabites." With a promise to be back in a few hours, he disappeared silently into the night.

He had proceeded only a little way when he felt that

someone was following. Pausing, he glanced over his shoulder and was able to make out the features of Hagar, the overseer of his maidservants.

"Forbid me not, my lord," she begged, coming close to him. "I am restless like yourself. I hate Moab, not only for what it would do to Bethlehem, but for a reason of my own."

"What reason, Hagar?"

"Only a few months ago, my family lived in peace, and everything was bright, with the fields giving again and the people learning to smile." She talked hurriedly, tensely. "But my hopes came to an end when my husband, a merchant and as good a man as ever served the Lord, was slain without cause by a Moabite during a journey into that horrible land. I learned about his death from an eyewitness who escaped and got to Israel. The attack in the deep of night, the mutilation, the theft of all his goods. . . ."

He touched her shoulder. "I did not know, Hagar," he said. "I wondered why you were so harsh toward — Ruth. How little we know one another!" His voice shook. "Noemi and Ruth. . . . Their loved ones also lie in Moabite graves."

"I could pity Noemi."

"And not Ruth?"

"I do not want to be against her. She's been showing herself mild and good. But — but she is a Moabitess."

"A cruel god rules the land she fled, and he is honored with the worst in men. But some souls despise him, and they must shine all the brighter for the shadows they pass through. Ruth proves that."

"Be it so." She tugged at his sleeve. "Do let me go with you. I seem to see your mind." Her eye glittered. "If you could cut off the head of the captain of that army —"

"I have no sword. But these hands —"

"I'd like nothing better than to receive the thing and bear it to our people. I'd have my son, Rei, spit on it."

Boaz stepped back, gloomy, depressed. "Hagar, we have

just come from a cave where I once heard music from above. I thought it sounded of peace and good will to men. Now — this!"

"There is no peace, no good will."

"True. But some day —"

"We are living now. Without cause, the Moabites would grind us in the dust. War, on our side, is holy. It would be cowardice to hold less."

"You are right," he said.

"May I come?"

"You may come."

They found their way down the hill, half-circled the hushed town, and, furtive as animals, ascended the other heights, over which the glow had already become slighter. As they neared the top, they wormed their way on their hands and knees, avoiding by a good margin a sleepy sentinel whose upheld, wobbling spear glistened in the pale of the moon.

"Remain here," cautioned Boaz when, from beneath some bushes, they gazed down the slope spaced at brief intervals with tents and with fires which were nearly dead. Only one, apart from the others, still flickered bright.

Hagar pretended not to hear his repeated command and continued to follow his every move. Soon they were deep along the left flank of the encampment and close to the one fire that had much life in it. The trunks and low-sweeping branches of trees concealed them.

They expected that here by the flames the leader would be sitting, mulling his plan of attack; but their approach showed their mistake. An arrow in the flesh of Boaz would have been kinder than what now confronted him. For a second his eyes locked tight with a pain keener than any of the many he had known.

There in the ruddy light, Ruth herself sat, a mantle draped over her shoulders, her head bedecked with blossoms. Two soldiers were offering her fruits and wine. And Boaz and

Hagar beheld only the profile, so dark against the light that the agony was invisible. They mistook the twisting of the lips for smiles.

"You see — you see," said Hagar in a half hiss, half whisper.

The small sound caused Ruth to glance from under her lids as far around as was possible without turning her face. Boaz, reckless, had thrust his head and shoulders from the foliage, and his look met hers.

She almost uttered a cry, but instantly she substituted a coughing so as to draw the attention of the soldiers fully to herself.

"The smoke of the fire is in your throat," said one of them. "Come, just a sip of this *Keruhim*. It will do you good. Clears the gullet in a second." He held a flagon toward her. "It's liquid gold. We got it fresh from a vintner on the way here. Better than any we make in Moab."

"Maybe she'd rather have this *Phrygia*," said the other, tilting his own flagon. "It's as red as blood. Banaias himself calls it the best in the world."

"There is still a better." Ruth forced a bantering tone into her voice. "Wine for the heart. . . . Sit closer to me and hum some of the songs of Moab."

She did not risk another sidewise glance. The merest sign might betray Boaz, and the same fate that had been inflicted on Mahalon and Chelion would be his. Anything but that! Her torment was now less from her hand than her imagination and memory. Every note of the brothers' ending came back to her, and she begged the Lord that Boaz would leave before he could be taken. But externally she kept calm and motioned the men into positions which would cut off any view of the lower branches of the trees behind her. For further effect, she joined in their humming.

Boaz was so overcome that he could offer no resistance to Hagar's urge to retreat. His body was bathed in sweat. Why had he ever mourned Zora? Why should he mourn any woman? None was to be trusted, if the best of all could be as this.

"I hated her justly," said Hagar, when they had crawled a sufficient distance away. "Something told me that behind that innocence of hers a serpent was coiling. No woman ever really fools a woman."

"There must be an explanation." He puzzled miserably. "But I — I cannot see. She knew I wanted her to remain within the walls. She must have known I'd gladly die to save her. She needed no help. She saw me looking at her and turned her eyes back to those soldiers. . . . Wine for her heart."

"She's from Moab." Hagar's voice had the sound of a snapped twig. "Her blood called to her own people and she went. This meeting of hers with them in Israel might well have been prearranged. And who can tell what secrets of ours she brought! She wasn't with us long, but long enough to learn whatever she wanted. Wine and fruit — ha, fire would be too good for her. Humming and smiling, the black-souled witch! . . . You're in no state for any deed here tonight, my lord. Let me get you back to the cave, if I can."

An overpowering desire to be far from the source of anguish made him listless to her words but all the more pliable to her will. There was enough energy in him to rise; and, letting her take his arm, he moved on dazedly by her side.

When they were again in the cave, he sank to the floor. The refugees gathered around him, equally sympathetic and curious.

"Thus has the child-faced Moabitess done to our generous lord," Hagar told them fiercely. "And he loved her, as we all could see. She's passed over to our enemies to work our ruin. She sits carousing with them. We saw her with our own eyes! The vileness goads me. I am going back."

"She could not have forgotten Bethlehem — me," moaned Boaz. "Our eyes lied to us. She was taken by her people against her will."

"For one taken against her will, she looked very much at home in that camp." Hagar tossed her head and shook with scorn. "Flowers in the hair, a rich mantle around her, soldiers plying her with refreshments; and she enjoying it all. My lord, tear her out of your mind."

Abruptly she turned and plunged off again into the night.

When she reached the camp once more, she found the Moabitess, still in the same spot and position in which she had last seen her. But the details were different. The long-haired head and the graceful shoulders were drooping; the mantle had been discarded and stains were visible on the simple dress; the blossoms no longer served as a coronet but were scattered around. A coil of linen, also stained, lay beside two overturned and empty flagons on the ground where the two soldiers had fallen into a drunken sleep.

Then she saw the burnt hand in the lap of the Moabitess.

Crouching under the low branches of a tree, she studied the situation. Slowly her bewilderment vanished, and she knew that here was no betrayer of Bethlehem and Boaz but a victim of Moabite cruelty which, not content to torture, had gone on to mock.

In tremulous shame, she called as distinctly as she dared. And Ruth, wondering, turned her head.

"Here, come to me."

Ruth crawled on her knees and her good hand to the space beneath the tree. And, finding herself in Hagar's embrace, she was able to shed the tears that fear and horror had withheld. She tried to tell what had happened to her, but Hagar pressed a hand to the lips. "Not yet, poor soul," she said. "We need distance from here."

The sentinel on the hill had thrown off his drowsiness. They could see his dark figure outlined in the moonlight; and he was beginning to move, as if suspicious. It would be perilous for them to tarry any longer, but they could not go over the hill without being detected. They had to creep down along the edge of the camp. Flat on the ground, one with the shadows, they progressed by inches. Finally, they were below in a leafy shelter, and could stand and talk freely.

"Now," said Hagar, sweating and breathing heavily, "tell me everything."

But Ruth could only say, "Where is my lord?"

"In a hill cave across the valley."

"Yahweh be praised! He is safe."

"He is suffering. He thinks you false, as did I when with him I first saw you up there. What else could be thought?"

"O Hagar, did he believe that? Didn't he know my only will was to save him?"

Hagar adjusted her robe and hid her face. "In stress, how can anybody think rightly? That mantle — those flowers —"

"And this," said Ruth, trying to lift her left hand. "I couldn't bear the touch of anything they gave me. When they fell asleep, I tore the bandage off."

"He did not see, because of the folds of the cloak. But here we wait while Bethlehem is threatened! So much needs to be done, I'm in a daze. Boaz was to have made an effort to slay the leader but became as helpless as a child. After getting him back to the cave, I returned, only to find you in this wretchedness and learn what a misjudging fool I've been." She cast a look of discouragement up the hill. "I'd thought I could steal into the leader's tent and — and perhaps use his own sword on him in sleep; but now, with this proof you give me that even a Moabitess can be loyal to us, I'm as weak as Boaz."

Ruth touched Hagar's arm. "You could go and assure him of my loyalty," she said. Then she asked, "Is Jerusalem far from here?"

"Too far. Ten miles or so to the north. Why would you know?"

"Help might come from there, if I could tell the dire need —"

"Who would listen to a woman?"

"Boaz must have listened to you. He let you come."

"I forced myself."

"I can force myself, too. It is not only Bethlehem that's threatened. Banaias, the high priest of Chemosh, told me that Jerusalem is next." Ruth stooped to free her dress from some briars in which it was caught, and found herself thinking of the day when a similar small accident brought Mahalon into her life. Then it almost seemed that he was actually with her again, for her fingers were touching the folded piece of parchment that he had given her on the night of his death and that she had sewn into the deep hem of her garment.

"But, if you got there, whom would you go to?" asked Hagar.

"To the Lord's high priest."

Hagar breathed audibly. "You are too poor — too unprepared. Those who seek him for favor should be anointed with oils and spices."

"My purpose will be my preparation."

Hagar, reflecting, stepped from the shadowy shelter. She again scanned the hill on which Banaias and his men were sleeping. Aggressively she took a few more steps. Now she was standing fully exposed in the moonlight. A moment later, an arrow from the bow of another sentry in the lower section of the camp whistled through the air and lodged deep in her breast. She fell forward.

Ruth saw. Then a cloud floated beneath the face of the moon. Under cover of the shadow, she went and drew Hagar back, terror lending strength and preventing an outcry. She propped up the limp shoulders with one arm and she might have tried to extract the arrow, only that the victim was bidding her, "Leave it there. My — my penance for my hate. Go — save yourself."

Ruth knelt and held her closely.

"To Jerusalem," Hagar was gasping. "You are no Moabitess. Handmaid of the Lord —"

Ruth stayed by the body, trying to breathe life back into it. When at last the fact of death had to be admitted, she knew there was nothing left but to get to the Holy City. If God should permit her to come back, with what reverence she would lay these remains to rest! But what if she should not live to see Bethlehem again or even to reach Jerusalem? What of Boaz whom Hagar might have enlightened? Oh, if there were some way of sending word to him in the cave!

Commending Hagar's soul to the Lord, she kissed the brow, rose, and passed on stealthily through the dark. Shaken to the core, she was sharply awake in every sense. Knowing only that Jerusalem lay to the north, she tried not to think of distance and forced herself to speed. But soon, the strain too great, she stumbled and fell.

As she lay helpless, the injured hand hurt almost as much as if Banaias were still holding it in the flame; and the pain within her was just as great. Would it not be wiser, she thought, to discard the idea of the city and, if enough strength returned, to seek the cave? Otherwise, when the news of her seeming treachery should be noised about, Bethlehem would recoil from the very thought of her, or would hold her in memory as an example of the tragic effect of trusting an alien. And Noemi — would she not have to believe like Bethlehem and Boaz?

But suddenly Ruth was sure that neither the city nor the cave could be reached, for she heard someone approaching, and she was unable even to rise, much less to run. She almost ceased to breathe and had a sensation of sinking into a grave.

A man began to speak, and the pity in the voice startled her more than harshness would have done. She had to look up. "Woman, fear not," he said. "I am Achaz, humble son of a humble father. I would help you."

He was raising her gently to her feet. In the moonlight she could see from the breadth of cheekbones, the shape of nose, the mildness in the eyes, that he was an Israelite.

"Why would you help me?" she asked faintly.

"Because the Lord loves the wayfarer and wishes that such be received as the sons of Jacob were received in Egypt. You are not a native?"

"Yahweh is my God. Think not of me. Bethlehem is imperiled. This night enemies are gathered against her."

"Then it *is* true, Yahweh help us! Rumors of men bearing arms and coming toward Bethlehem did reach my village, but they were vague. Gifts of grain from the good Boaz were delivered to us, as if all were well. And we rejoiced that our poor could eat. The last load arrived just before sunset and we sang, with gratitude and blessing for our benefactor, until our candles were low. And seeing the joy of my people that neither the Lord nor his servant had forgotten them, I could not lie down to rest. I wanted to be near Boaz and, even if I'd have to wait in his fields until sunrise, tell him our thanks."

"Boaz is dear to me, too, in the Lord," said Ruth, weeping. "I, also, would give testimony. Smitten and unhappy, he waits in the hills."

"I'll go to him. Tell me just where I'll find him."

A sudden hope came to Ruth. Here was a messenger, clearly sent by Providence, who could bring Boaz the solace of truth, though the sadness of Hagar's fate would have to be mingled with it. She needed but to tell him what had happened. Better still, she could have him assist her to the cave. But if she should do this, there would be neither time nor energy for the journey to Jerusalem. She could not do both. Perhaps she could do neither. But she must choose.

For moments, she was silent. Achaz saw the luster in her eyes dying. He gazed with shock and sympathy at her burned hand, but had no way of knowing that the heart of her was in a worse state. Carefully he held on to her and steadied her with his arm.

"You cannot remain here alone in the open," he said. "Where shall I bring you?"

Then she spoke directly and frankly. "Will you lead me to Jerusalem?"

He looked at her in astonishment.

With the relief that decision always brings, she explained, as briefly as possible, the events since dusk; and she mentioned the parchment concealed in her dress. "If we could get to the Lord's high priest," she said, "we might induce him to come here with soldiers and confront Banaias, the high priest of the Moabite god, who commands that hill." She pointed back. "Perhaps bloodshed would be prevented on both sides. With Banaias solemnly informed that Moab's treasure is in danger of falling into the hands of Israel, would he not have to withdraw to try to protect it?"

The eyes of Achaz livened, but his brows came together. "As the crow flies, the distance to Jerusalem is not great," he said. "But on foot it is, and you have no strength."

"I'll find it."

"The night will have gone and the attack on Bethlehem begun, maybe ended, before any good can come of our going."

"No good can come from our standing here."

His arm still sustaining her, he said no more but turned to the north.

When they had proceeded a half mile or so, Ruth, for all her determination, was exhausted. "Give me the parchment and, if you insist, I'll go alone," he said; "but without you, the chance of success will be slight." He regarded her sad earnest face and again her maimed hand. "No one could disbelieve you. As for me, how can I leave you here by yourself? How —"

"Listen!"

A low rumble could be heard, coming nearer. Soon, in a rise of dust, there appeared a chariot drawn by two magnificent horses.

It was most unusual, in that period of Israel's history, for horses to be used for any purpose other than battle; and

Achaz would have feared the sight greatly only for the Jewish features of the short, sturdy driver. Leaving Ruth, he ran forward, signaling. The man reined in his snorting animals and listened. "My brother in Yahweh, the good woman yonder is too enfeebled to reach Jerusalem on foot. If so it be that you are going in that direction, would you take her?"

He scrutinized him from under bushy brows, while the animals, restive, flung their long manes to the breeze and stomped the soil with their unshod hoofs. "What is her concern in Jerusalem?" he demanded sharply.

"To seek help for Bethlehem."

The man's look of suspicion faded, but one of worry showed itself. "If our forebodings for Bethlehem have real cause," he said, "only from Jerusalem could strength come to us. My mind has been turning there since sundown. A Babylonian traveler at my wayside inn loaned me — Abdon by name — this chariot and span of his when he was shaken from sleep by my groans. 'Go and assist your people if you will, and can, but let me rest,' he told me."

Achaz glanced over his shoulder at Ruth. "She is not of us but no one is more with us. She has that in her keeping which might save us. Take her to Samuel, our young prophet and priest."

"I will. But only on condition that you yourself come with us. Two men may be few enough to protect a woman this evil night."

Achaz went to Ruth and helped her to the conveyance. He and Abdon placed her between them. And then they were moving northward again, this time with a velocity which, to Ruth, seemed that of wings. The night opened up like a new world, and the hills slipped by like shadows.

They held to the low roads and encountered no obstacles; and well before the hour of dawn, they were heartened by the sight of the city. Under a now cloudless and spangled sky, it lay in a purity and calm which appealed to Ruth almost as an externalization of the ideals within her. The gates were but lightly guarded, and with very little questioning the three were permitted to pass through. Soon, after leaving the chariot and the horses to the care of an innkeeper, with whom Achaz was personally acquainted, they were ascending a winding street, past immaculate buildings of hewn stone, sheened with the moon, to the summit of Mount Zion on the western side of the town.

In those days, the Ark of the Covenant was enshrined in Cariathiarim, where it had been taken after the Philistines seized it from Shiloh and later, aghast at the power of the trophy, returned it to Israel. Abdon had told Ruth this when she spoke to him, at the prompting of Achaz, about the treasure of Moab, the secret of which was hers; for the subject of "treasure" had stimulated him to enthusiasm for Israel's own most precious possession which, he maintained, exceeded all the wealth of the Gentile world. And he had described the Ark in detail: the sturdy chest of acacia wood, two-and-a-half cubits long and one-and-a-half broad and deep; the overlay of gold; the golden rings through which passed the golden staves wherewith the chest could be borne in solemn procession by the Kohathites, so called from Kohath, the second of the three sons of Levi, from whom the three principal divisions of the Levites or personal guardians of Israel's treasure derived their origin and name; the sculptured figures of two adoring angels, the only images in Israel, atop the chest; the priceless contents — the very stone tablets of the law given by the Lord himself to Moses on Sinai, a pot of the manna that had fed the wanderers in the desert, the rod of Aaron with which were performed the miracles that demonstrated the presence of God to his people. And Ruth had listened intently to every word.

She found herself looking across the city to a height in the eastern section, on which the moon seemed to be concentrating its light. She was alone, because the two men were gone to try to effect an admittance to Samuel himself, who dwelt here on this hill of Zion. And while she waited, she felt as if discovering a link between her life and that uniquely beautiful eminence on which the outline of groves of trees against the bright sky resembled a great high crown. It was the same sort of stirring that she had known when first she saw Bethlehem and when first she entered the cave; and it was followed by a thought — a hope — that there on that peak of the chief city of Israel the Ark itself would be one day enthroned to express a vital symbolism to the nation and even the world.

Then her mood took another turn. If blessed with motherhood, she reflected, she would have fostered her son as a living tabernacle of the Lord and longed to have him glorified in Israel, but only that the Lord might have been glorified in him. She closed her eyes and pictured this son that had not been and perhaps could never be, as grown up and standing in Jerusalem, full of zeal for God and his servants, planning to house a people's dearest treasure in a temple surpassing the great one of Moab as much as a star surpasses a stone.

A voice behind her, deep and melodious, was speaking: "Daughter, Abraham once stood on that hill opposite, ready to sacrifice his son Isaac for the love of the Lord. Sacrifice is the proof of love."

She turned and her gaze met two eyes which might have been Mahalon's before the days of torment and blood. They were as clear and clean as a child's. Only gradually did she become conscious of notes other than the kindly, penetrating look itself: the slope and spirituality of the face; the calm, spread lips; the thin, long nose, slightly bent at the bridge; the smooth, high forehead; the flowing beard which, like that of Boaz, was flecked with a premature silver; the spare, dignified figure; the priestly robe. And she knew that this man was he whom she sought and whom Achaz and Abdon must have readily succeeded in finding. Samuel — prophet, priest, judge of all Israel.

She knelt to him. He extended his hand over her bowed head and he let it slowly descend to help her up. "I had already seen you in what these our brothers in Abraham said," he told her, motioning toward Achaz and Abdon beside him, "and now I know some of your thoughts." He smiled and she thought of the good priest of her childhood who had given her a sea shell. "There has come to your soul the same desire that has been in my own since earliest youth. You would that, one day, the Ark of the Covenant be entempled on Moriah — a name which means 'chosen of Jehovah.'"

She was startled at his insight. "But I — I was dreaming even more than that, Your Highness," she said, blushingly confused. "Why such feelings should have come to me, the least of the Lord's handmaids, I know not."

He looked at her injured hand. "The Lord is pleased with you, my daughter, for you have passed through a great ordeal. But now for the purpose that brought you to me! I would examine the papyrus of which your companions have spoken."

Having already removed it from the torn hem of her dress and placed it in her bosom, she gave it to him. He studied it closely in the light of the heavens; and when he lifted his face, she could see resolution there.

"Go to the tabernacle, my daughter," he said. "I have left word with one of the holy women who serve it, to receive and care for you. Remain with her and wait for me." And he answered the eager question in her eyes by adding, "Until I return from Bethlehem."

Bethlehem. Help for Bethlehem. He was going to bring it! Her spirit exulted. But a wistfulness was in it. She wanted to ask permission to accompany him, because of Boaz and Noemi. He read her desire and told her softly, "It may be wiser that you take some rest. And here, hidden for a while, you can better choose one of the two paths in life that lie open to you."

His knowledge of her personal dilemma amazed her further, but it was less this fact than his sympathy and solicitude that thrilled her.

His glance went again to her hand, and he touched it gently.

There seemed to be healing in the touch, and she gazed at him with equal gratitude and reverence.

To draw her attention from himself, he spoke quickly. "In Bethlehem, I shall no doubt see those that are especially dear to you. Have you a message for me to give them?"

Boaz and Noemi. She could have Samuel assure the one of her loyalty and the other of her safety. But he had directed that here she remain hidden until his return; and she was all too well aware that, if they should learn about her, nothing could withhold them from trying to come and persuade her immediately to go back with them. She suspected that Samuel's knowledge, great as it was, did not extend to this. Or was he testing her? What a consolation and solace it would be to have them! A blessing, however, that must somehow be surrendered; for, with them near, her choice would be all too humanly swayed; and it was the Lord's will, not her own, that should matter. But how mysterious his will! As he had once called on Abraham to sacrifice Isaac, was he now calling on her to sacrifice, at least temporarily, her loved ones?

"Mention me not," she replied to Samuel, "nor permit these others to speak. Until I know what to do, it is better that I be as if lost. — There is Boaz, a good man of Bethlehem, who wanted me for his wife; but he now thinks me untrue to him and Israel, and so, if he is not otherwise informed and the Lord should desire me solely for himself, it would soon be easier for him to forget me. There is Noemi, my second mother, to whom my life is so knitted that my love for her vies with my love for him who brought us together. But I have seen her striving to discover and follow his will, and I know she would have me do the same."

And Samuel said, "Amen."

She bowed to him and Achaz and Abdon, and looked toward the tabernacle a little distance away. But once more her eyes turned to Samuel. "The faith of Israel is not unknown or quite unaccepted in Moab," she said. "If the treasure of the temple of Chemosh should fall into Israelite hands, ought it not be given to the people from whose toil it was taken? This would prove the nobility of Israel to them and attract many more sheep into the fold."

"You speak justly and with inspiration, my daughter. I will remember. But I see a further wish in you."

"Orpha, my sister-in-law in Moab, is devoted to teaching our beliefs. May she be sought out and aided in her mission? It is her only comfort. She lives on a little farm not far from the gates of Bethjeshimoth. She could direct any agents of Israel well."

"She shall be consulted and assisted," he said. "But still I see desire in you."

"The body of Hagar, who was slain this night by a Moabite arrow, lies in the shadow of the enemy's hill near Bethlehem. Will Your Highness have it buried with honor?"

"I promise."

Thankfully Ruth passed on to the tabernacle, and at the entrance to it a mild-faced matronly woman was waiting to welcome her.

Spent by the sweeping emotions of the night, but relieved by Samuel's pledge, she slipped into the ready embrace, content for the moment with the prospect that help would be sped to Bethlehem and Hagar remembered and the worship of Yahweh better advanced than ever before in the land of Moab. But no sooner was she within than she thought again of Noemi and Boaz.

Chapter Seven

TIME — THE TEST

TEN days passed.

Ruth spent them mostly on her knees, combining prayer and meditation with physical exertion. Over and over she scrubbed the floor of the tabernacle with her one able hand, cleansing the very cleanliness, and at the same time trying to clear herself of every possible effect of the existence that had been hers in Moab. To remain here for the rest of her days, atoning for Mahalon's mistaken and calamitous devotion to Banaias, would be a precious privilege. Moreover, to have belonged to a race that produced both the savage slayers of two brothers and the present enemy-in-chief of Israel, implied — she believed — a personal taint which could be removed only by self-denial and immolation. The solemnity all around her, shutting out the world, harmonized with her intent, but her heart still cried for Noemi and Boaz. Must this torment of longing continue unabated? Must she leave Bethlehem behind like a brief day's lodging? If so, she would accept the need as part of the price to be paid. It was so small a price, comparatively with the end in view; but what made it so large and depressing was her constant awareness of the suffering of those who loved her and whom she loved.

Her thoughts kept turning back, and not the least of her yearnings was to be able to perform the task that had to be deferred: the restoration of the place in the hills where Mahalon heard his music and where Boaz might yet find peace.

140

On the morning of the eleventh day, while she was doing for the tabernacle what she would have done for the cave, an arm slowly raised her up and she looked again into the eyes of Samuel.

"Bethlehem is saved, my daughter," he said.

"And Noemi — Boaz?"

"They, too, are safe but sorrowing. They spoke only of you when I met them, and I learned much." He paused. "How I wished to be free to tell them about you! Have you decided to remain here in service to the Lord, or to seek his service otherwise and elsewhere?"

"There is a cave —"

"I know. Boaz told me it served as a shelter for those who were locked out from Bethlehem on the night of the invasion. I made it a point to visit it, and there I prayed for you and him and Noemi, that you three might not long be debarred from happiness. Heaven has marked that place, my daughter. It is a spot where two worlds could meet and touch; a tabernacle of nature waiting as if to be filled with the Holy Spirit. It should be watched over even more than all the tents of the Lord in Israel, for Satan is doubtless seeking to wrest it to himself. But it has been revealed to me that its value will remain hidden until the fullness of time. Would that there were someone in Bethlehem to serve as an angel guardian."

She marveled at his word.

Leading her to a side chamber, he spoke on. "I sent good men over the shortest route to Moab, with instructions that they seek out Orpha and work with her in using the parchment you gave me. I have already the good news that the treasure of Chemosh now lies cached, until it can be properly dispensed, in a dried-out cell of one of the underground cisterns that your husband and Orpha's husband built. The taking of it never could have been conceived or effected without your help. Orpha put my men in secret touch with two of the Moabite officials who had come over to our faith; and so, in the dead of night, they gained entrance to the temple of Chemosh, overpowered the guards, took the keys, and made their way straight to the dungeon: removing all the coffers of gold through a rear portal which opened into a field beyond the town, and taking the treasure to her house, where they hid it in Mahalon's room —"

"— and mine," murmured Ruth to herself, thinking of the night of the last communion.

"— until, at her suggestion, they decided on the cistern. We now have the king of Moab at our mercy; and, from what I know, I think he would rather be under our thumb than that of Banaias. No war of conquest can be waged against us in the foreseeable future, and Moab as well as Israel will have a long peace." His eyes uplifted in thanksgiving, and then returned to Ruth.

"As for Bethlehem, the threat to it had begun to wane even before I reached there with reinforcements. This was due to Boaz." He ceased for a second, noticing her avid attention and expression, studying it. "The night you were taken, his anguish at the loss of you restored and whetted his wrath against the enemy; and, when Hagar did not return to the cave, he went forth a second time. Repenetrating the camp just before dawn, he found Banaias in his tent and killed him with his bare fists. The deed was almost noiseless, and without hindrance he escaped back to the cave after searching in vain for you. When my men and I arrived that morning, the Moabites, leaderless, were in confusion. They would have rallied and somehow gone on with the siege, but we surrounded them. The Lord prevailed. It remained for me only to reassure the town and direct a lengthy series of ceremonies and holocausts in gratitude for the deliverance. Would that I could have given some special comfort to Boaz and Noemi! But you had charged me not to speak of you, and Achaz, Abdon, and I respected your wish. So Boaz and Noemi remain mystified by your disappearance. He thinks you have fled to Moab and forgotten him, and she lives only for your return."

Ruth could not speak.

"Have you made your choice of paths?" he asked again, a little embarrassed at having told her so much so quickly, and seeking to shift her mood.

For moments more she was silent. Then she said, "The Lord seems to have chosen for me. But if you approve, I shall visit Bethlehem — for the last time — to repair the cave and console my mother. Surely God would not deny me that. Once I told her that, wherever she was, there I'd be." Her voice broke. "Yet she is close to him, as I am trying to be; and shall we not be united in him? But Boaz . . ."

"The Lord is helping you by instilling the patience without which a soul could never be perfect. Go to Bethlehem, my daughter. Await there a yet clearer manifestation of his will, no matter how long it may take."

She stood in the sunlight streaming through drapes of fine-twined linen. "I shall go and await it. But meanwhile, shall I be strong enough in spirit — to face Boaz?"

"I have faith in your readiness," he replied.

"But what can I say to him? If I tell him how I was seized by Banaias while attempting to get to the cave, and how I did what I could for Bethlehem, he will love me the more. And that would only renew and increase his pain when I'd have to — to reveal the vocation that appears to be mine. Is it kinder to keep silent?"

"It is not only lips that speak."

His eye was on her hand. The healing had progressed rapidly, but the flesh, still terribly scarred, was all too eloquent of what she had undergone. Feeling his gaze and knowing his meaning, she drew down her sleeve.

"Be of good cheer," he said. "You have brought peace to this land of your adoption. Because of you, Boaz was moved to deal swift and hard with the enemy chief. Because of your coming to me with Achaz and Abdon, the Moabites were prevented from reorganizing themselves and attacking Bethlehem. May Heaven grant you a portion of what you have gained for us! I will send you back with a guard of honor."

"I wish no honor," she demurred. "Let me go alone and on foot. There are many things I must think through, and I can best do so in solitude. Besides, if I went with honor, I'd be received with honor, and that would not be good for this faulty soul of mine. You spoke, Your Highness, of patience. Do not deprive me of further opportunity to try to practice it."

Then she knelt to receive his blessing. But he knelt beside her. "The Lord bless us both," he prayed. "And may he reserve his particular favor for those you love!"

When she was bidding him farewell, he said, "Orpha sends you and Noemi warmest greetings from Moab. She longs for you both. Her good works increase there and the worship of Yahweh is enhanced." He waited a moment, again searching her face. "Have you ever thought of returning to your native land?"

"Orpha will always be very dear to me and Noemi," she answered slowly, "and morning and night we three have prayed for souls beyond the Salt Sea. But having been led into Israel by Heaven, how could I ever leave?"

He did not reply.

It was twilight when she neared Bethlehem.

She paused at the sight of a star already shining above the hill of the cave. The light seemed to her to be the shining of the Lord's directive finger; and, much as she wanted to be with Noemi, she turned from the town gates and forced her steps on toward the western height. But it was not all an effort. Something was drawing her, something akin, maybe casual, to the beauty of the dusk. The air was warm and fragrant as if, from unseen thuribles, incense were drifting through it. The higher she went, the lighter her spirit became, though her limbs were heavy with fatigue. And when at last she reached and entered the cave, she sank gratefully on the mossy flooring of stones.

A soft darkness smudged out the ravages of time and neglect, and the star that had led her was beaming down from its setting of silver-blue through the open space in the rocky ceiling just above where she lay. She crept from the rays into the shadows. Almost instantly she was sleeping a dreamless sleep which might well have lasted until dawn, only that, in the course of the night, a sound awakened her. Boaz was at the entrance to the cave, his bent head almost white in the moonlight. What had brought him here at such an hour, she could only surmise. Perhaps the very isolation. Perhaps memories of Mahalon. Perhaps the same strange weaving of destiny that had originally drawn him and her together. Or was she seeing him merely in a waking dream? No, that could not be. His grief emphasized his reality.

She must go to him. But it seemed to her that, if she did so, she would be turning her back on the Lord; for, close to Boaz in his present state, she would have to let him cling to her, and she knew that, once his arms were around her, freedom to await "the clearer manifestation of the divine will" according to Samuel's counsel would end.

Had Boaz come into the cave, or had she remained under the rays of the star, he would have seen her. As it was, he remained unconscious of being observed, and his soul lay open to her like a raw wound.

She thought of Abraham ready to slay his son for Yahweh, and of Jephthah sacrificing his daughter to the demands of an oath. But such examples could not render less poignant the crying need of Boaz for comfort.

Now sitting up, she was about to rise. Already, however, Boaz had risen and turned. Stiffly, he was groping his way back into the night.

In the early morning, she found a spring on the hillside not far below the cave. Kneeling, she gazed on the bright, clear flow and threw back her mantle. Samuel had given her the garment as a parting gift. It was of such a singularly fine weave that, at the touch, she asked herself: "Can I use it to bring some of this water to the cave?" She swept it from her shoulders and sank it in the stream; then she drew up the edges and saw that the seepage was slight.

The overhanging branches of a cedar were reflected on the smooth surface of the spring, and she looked at the tree itself, recalling what Boaz had said to her one day during a lull in the harvest when he found her gazing at the woody height in the distance: "We call our cedars 'the trees of God.' Sometimes the boughs of a live cedar, touching those of a dead one, grow into them and give a new life." Comparing her life and his to the trees, as Noemi might have done, she had pondered those words no little. Much had died in him; much to which she could give renewal. She wanted supremely to please the Lord; but could he be pleased if she denied herself to his servant? Last night, she had seen a soul bereft and desolate. She intended to restore, if she could, beauty and melody to the cave: ought she not endeavor to do the same for that soul? Surely she would soon see Boaz again, and under less emotional circumstances. Surely there would be a way of adjusting their lives to the higher will.

She kept thinking this as she fastened a corner of the mantle on the bank with a stone and let the folds float. She thought all the more while she gathered some of the needles, a half inch long, from above the thick tan cones on the twigs of the cedar. Next she plucked a supply of aromatic leaves from a bay tree and, returning to the spring, drew out the mantle and pinned the leaves as close and tight over the inside as she could do with one hand, making it almost completely moistureproof. Still meditating on what her attitude toward Boaz should be, but bent on rendering immediate service to the cave, she gathered the edges of the mantle together and scooped up an ample portion of the pure water as in a large wineskin.

When she again reached the cave, she poured out the offering on the floor, in the first of many ablutions. Each stone, she determined, should be made to shine in memory of what Mahalon, Chelion, and Elimelech had here suffered; in memory of the music that here used to soothe Boaz; in memory of what Samuel had said: "A tabernacle of nature waiting as if to be filled with the Holy Spirit. . . . Would that there were someone in Bethlehem to serve as an angel guardian."

After scrubbing and scrubbing, and resolving to return many times for the same purpose, she dug with five fingers a grave in the soft earth beyond the mouth of the cave and placed in it the bones of the sheep that had perished in the holocaust so long ago; and she thought of the human sheep that had lived on, only to die even more terribly, and of one, still living, whose life resembled an abandoned cave.

Before she left, she knelt and begged the Lord to accept her as an instrument of peace; that, where there was misunderstanding, she might shed light; where there was cruelty, kindness; where there was rancor, forgiveness; where there was despair, hope. She did not ask for solace, but only to be able to console. And her last thought on leaving was of Boaz.

When, with bowed head, she was entering Bethlehem, the keeper of the gates recognized her. For a second he was silent, while the things he had heard against her recurred to him. His old eyes, inflamed, widened. "Moabitess!" he cried accusingly, almost of a mind to lay hands on her and hurl her back. But the meek look of her withheld him, and he let her pass, his brow wrinkling. How could she, who had betrayed the town in its neediest hour, appear so unblemished, so blameless? Satan — that was the answer! The same dark spirit that sped her to her own people when they had the advantage was returning her here.

If she had her mantle with her, she would have hidden her face in it; but it was back in the cave, spread out on the floor and drying under the rays of the sun from the cleft in the roof. And now her hair was fully exposed in what, she suddenly feared, passers-by might consider an immodest display. She thought of going back to the cave immediately, but her need for Noemi would not let her, and she hurried on toward Deborah's house. To get to it, she had to pass through a busy street; and, though she tried to keep inconspicuously close to buildings, a woman — one of the harvesters who had been so harsh during the former arrival with Noemi — saw her and screamed, "Traitress!"

Others heard the charge and some of them shared the recognition. All bristled; for Bethlehemites, with their memory of the threat of siege so fresh, were still in a highly nervous state, and it had become common knowledge that the alien called Ruth, after finding favor with Boaz, abused his trust by stealing away, doubtless with vital information, to her countrymen in the hills. *Traitress.* The word spread. Many eyes were now on the shrinking figure, and forgotten were Samuel's exhortations that gratitude to the Lord for Bethlehem's deliverance be not marred with any deed of excess. This woman's shrinking was only feigned, else how could she be bold enough to reappear in the town she had wronged?

Ruth tried to hurry. Several followed her. She tried not to hear the phrases and half sentences thrown at her and suddenly she felt herself being surrounded. A blow fell on her arm, another on her shoulder. She sank to the ground, her hair undulating around her, her body turning to ice. She believed that, if these people could see her injured hand, they would have pity; but somehow, despite her stress, she could not bring herself to force their sympathy, and resolutely kept her long sleeve down.

Then a man's voice rang out: "You beasts! Freed from the cruelty of the enemy, would you be just as cruel yourselves?" A form bent over her, an arm slipped under her waist, and she was being eased to her feet. She knew her rescuer even before she saw his face.

The people quickly dispersed, and without a word he led her where he knew she wanted to go. At the door of Deborah's little house, she tried to thank him, but his expression silenced her. She could feel only the dull, dead fact of his life closed to her, and the feeling so stunned her that it was impossible to avail herself of this second opportunity, to set his mind clear. She had wanted to be free to offer herself to the Lord, but not with a freedom like this; not a freedom that could strike love mortally and leave only the regard that might have been had for any stranger in distress. Boaz did make a movement as if to take her hand. But that was all. He opened the wattle door, then turned and hurried away.

Noemi and Rhea were within, preparing the noonday meal. When they saw Ruth, they stood speechless, notwithstanding their persistent faith that she would return. She went to Noemi's arms. Rhea brought water to bathe her feet; but catching a glimpse of the burnt hand as the sleeve slipped back from it, she uttered a cry. Noemi also saw. Deborah stared red-eyed from her pallet.

For moments, there was not a sound. It was Noemi who at last broke the silence. "My daughter, I knew that the Lord had only borrowed, not taken, you from us."

Ruth clung to her as on the day they left Moab and as on the night when with Orpha they had to look upon death.

Rhea got them seated; but not until she had laved Ruth's feet and forced a little bread and wine into her, did she let her tell what had happened.

They listened as if to a voice from another world, Deborah half-rising and cupping her ear with her palm, Noemi necessarily interrupting with many an exclamation.

"Boaz has just saved me from the people," said Ruth in conclusion.

"He's been saving all of us," said Rhea, smiling through her tears. "We needed his help badly. The foolish ones were against us because we had harbored you. You'd think we had some kind of disease! Only for him, I might have been scourged in public for what I said to them." She looked into Ruth's eyes. "He wanted to take us to live in Noemi's old home, but she refused to go until you could be with us. Now that we really have you again —"

Ruth glanced away sadly. "He wishes me near no more."

Rhea threw back her tawny hair with both hands. "That's nonsense," she cried. "As soon as he hears what we've just heard —"

"I couldn't tell him. Oh, how I longed to! But I — I couldn't."

"Why not? He, above all, should know."

"Even if he did, it might relieve his pain only to increase it."

"But how? I do not understand."

Falteringly Ruth explained that her stay in Bethlehem might have to be brief, for the Lord seemed to be calling her to a life of tabernacle service in Jerusalem, and seemed also, from the circumstances he was permitting, to will that she make no disclosure to reinstate herself in the regard of Boaz. She admitted that, as yet, she was not quite sure of anything.

Rhea was not satisfied.

"I can appreciate your readiness to give yourself to the Lord," she said. "I saw you as his handmaid the moment I first met you. But aren't we all trying to be his servants? And why should your love for him mean more suffering for Boaz? You were serving Heaven when you helped Bethlehem: would you be failing Heaven, if you helped Boaz?"

"You know too little, Rhea," chided Deborah. "You talk too much."

"But nobody has a right to cause unnecessary grief," retorted the girl warmly. "The Lord is not pleased with that."

"Stupid one! Can't you see that she loves Boaz? I knew it from the look of her when she opened our door and I caught a glimpse of Boaz departing. You haven't lived long enough and you're too dazzled with ideas of earthly happiness for insight, my Rhea. Whether we cause suffering or not, it comes. All we can do in life is follow whatever light God sends us."

The girl, appreciating what her mother had endured for years, lying ill on the floor, worrying about the handicap to marriage that she was occasioning for one who must care for her, and awaiting the end, made no comment.

Ruth looked to Noemi. And Noemi drew a deep breath. "You have borne so much, my daughter," she said, "that surely the Lord will grant relief. He tempers the wind to the shorn lamb. Haven't we always found it so?"

"Always," murmured Ruth.

Noemi re-embraced her. "Your hand must be treated without delay," she insisted.

"It started to heal when Samuel touched it, my mother."

"Bless him! But the healing will be complete when I apply my own remedy."

"I am going right out and tell everybody what you've done for Bethlehem," said Rhea to Ruth decisively.

"No!" begged Ruth. "I did only what the Lord had me do, and it is for him to reveal it beyond these walls in his own way and time, if he sees fit."

Rhea frowned with vexation; but Noemi, still thinking of Ruth's hand, looked wise and even hopeful.

Weeks rolled by into months and winter gave way to spring.

At first, Ruth would glance eagerly toward the door whenever she heard a footstep. But always it was only Rhea returning from some errand; or a certain wordless manservant, who at regular intervals brought provisions for the family from Boaz. Never Boaz himself.

She prayed at Hagar's grave, but had to discontinue her visits to it when, one morning, a young man discovered her there and, with a curse, drove her away.

She went daily to the cave for the purpose that only she and Noemi knew. Noemi would have gone with her, at least occasionally, save that a growing feebleness confined her to the house. Sometimes, when she looked more pale and worn than usual, Ruth tried to remain at home to take special care of her; but Noemi would not hear of this and always urged her forth. "This body of mine is a ruin that cannot be renewed," she would say. "Go, my daughter, where you can do good. It is the greater kindness to me, for you are doing what I would do, in the light of what you've told me, were I able. My every thought is with you. I bless you for remembering Mahalon and pray that harmony will be your reward."

And Ruth busied herself with restoring the cave. She made each stone glisten, and she succeeded in stringing fibers across the frame in the hollow of the rocky roof, just as Mahalon had done and as he had often described. Would that Boaz, she thought, had been moved to do this! But no music, as yet, came from the touch of the wind on the cords; and Boaz seemed to have drifted yet farther away from her.

Resentment, a deep current of it, swirled around her in Bethlehem, and all the love that Noemi, Rhea, and Deborah bestowed could not keep her from feeling it. Several times she had caught sight of Boaz passing in the streets. His shoulder again had the old slant to it; his tunic and turban were shabby, his hair unkempt, his face clouded. He hardly noticed the salaams and greetings of the people and seemed quite unconscious that, from the highest to the lowest, they would have laid their all at his feet. And the more they saw his wretchedness, the more they blamed the Moabitess. Their inability to punish her, because of his definite but remote protectiveness, irritated them and whetted their desire to have her away. It was not only her past guilt that enraged them, but also her present parade of meekness and modesty. Never had any of them known such a persistent deceiver.

And Ruth, though understanding their attitude, was at a loss to deal with it. To tell them what she had done for Bethlehem, or to show them her hand, would have been inconsistent with her resolution of leaving the matter to the Lord, and it would have seemed like a boast or challenge. She tried not to mind being despised, but could not help being disturbed at the harm that her despisers might be inflicting on themselves; and, as for Boaz, the thought of him kept wringing her heart. Several times she was almost ready to cast every scruple aside and go to him frankly and abjectly. It was so hard to await "the clearer manifestation of the Lord's will" according to Samuel's counsel; so easy to interpret her own will as Heaven's.

One morning her feelings overflowed and control was swept away. She walked, then ran, toward the house of Boaz. When she neared it, he was standing at the gate, feeding his dog as if the little act meant everything; and a sense of the loneliness and emptiness of his life penetrated her heart. Seeing her, he turned, entered the house, and closed the door behind him. Her gaze lingered on the blank walls of mud and stone and then rose to the structure on the roof, which, as Mahalon once said, had been intended for a bridal chamber. She noticed the solitary palm tree bending its fronds above it and was filled with sadness. She looked again at the door. If he had not closed it on her! If he had left it open just a little. . . .

She spent the rest of the day in the cave. Striving to reason with herself, she seemed to see the estrangement as something that could and should be settled. At a mere word from her, she felt, Samuel would hasten from Jerusalem with consolation, guidance, and testimony that could dispel the clouds from Boaz and restore faith, just as she herself had restored this cave. But — was this the way the Lord really wanted it? And the realization smote her that not yet was the cave fully restored, for not yet had the music that used to give it meaning returned.

Kneeling on the stones in the light from above, she was able again to view rather dispassionately the strange trial that the Lord had sent her and Boaz. Rays of understanding in the dark mystery of pain came to her, as they had often come before; rays all the brighter for the gloom. She remembered her conversations with Mahalon on this very subject of light in darkness. She appreciated pain as opportunity for the patience without which, as Samuel had indicated, a soul could never attain perfection. What pain was doing for her, could it not at length do for Boaz? Was the Lord preparing him and her for an eventual union of souls, superior to time, place, and the flesh, such as she had had with Mahalon in Moab?

It was not at all that an ordinary union repelled her. On the contrary, she felt its attractiveness so keenly that she had to make the strongest effort in order to resist it. She knew the beauty of the bond that had existed between Noemi and Elimelech, having seen the afterglow of it in Noemi's eyes. But Noemi and Elimelech, both of Israel, had had to make no awkward adjustments to each other; whereas Orpha and Chelion, of different races, had never become fully united. And Ruth knew that, if it had not been for a common ground of spirit, she herself might have missed the harmony that had shed joy through her years with Mahalon. He had taught her that, though flesh failed, higher needs and impulses could be satisfied; and she had come to put her faith in the spiritual phase of love. Was not this what the Lord intended for her? Just as the present sadness of separation from Boaz was serving to quicken her own sense of ghostly values, would it not also, in time, quicken his? And again she felt sure that the breach could not last. Somehow, when it should have satisfied its God-appointed purpose, it must end. She had never forgotten Noemi's express repentance for yielding to a natural impulse to shape events and manage lives, and ardently she wished to avoid any such tendency in herself. She must continue to try to leave Boaz and the future to Providence. But, with all the uplift that recollection gave her, she saw that it would still be a task to do this and a temptation to leave it undone, and her heart cried out, "O Lord, how long, how long?"

She had often spoken about her inner unrest and confusion to Noemi, and quietly Noemi had listened. But that night, when they both were sitting on the doorstep of Deborah's house before retiring, the mother at last opened up her mind. She began with seeming casualness, feeling her way.

"Another harvest is almost here, my daughter," she said. "Soon Rhea will be going into the fields. Will you be going with her?"

"Not into the fields of Boaz," answered Ruth regretfully. "There are other places where I can glean."

"There are no others where you should. Boaz has been providing for us."

"But I must not go, my mother. Don't you see —"

"I see more clearly than before. You want a life of oblation to the Lord, if the Lord wants it for you; and that is good. But is it his will that you deny yourself to his servant Boaz who has too long been alone? Could you not offer yourself to the one through the other? O Ruth, my good and gentle daughter, we love God but the more when we let ourselves find his image in the misery of man. Think you not that he shares the suffering of his creatures? To relieve that suffering, insofar as we can, is to lessen his."

Ruth twined her fingers over her knee and bowed her head, but made no reply. And Noemi went on. "In Orpha's house, that day when Elimelech died, that night when Chelion and Mahalon were slain, I had little feeling that the Lord was distant but rather an increasing certainty that he was very near, making every pang his own and somehow turning evil into good. Otherwise I could not have lived on."

Ruth took the thin hand. "I know," she said.

"And now, out of the misunderstanding that has made Boaz so miserable, will the Lord not bring a new and deeper understanding? Can we let ourselves be an obstacle instead of a help to it?"

"But I had thought that he was using our griefs to turn us the more to him —"

"That effect, my daughter, is in you, but not in Boaz. I, too, believed that his pain might be for his good, and that was why I kept silent. And now I speak only because, after much thinking, I see that the same trial that is good for one person is bad for another. Where you have found patience, Boaz is still finding only bitterness. He no longer visits the high place of worship. Life is worse for him than ever before, and I fear it will end in despair. He has been too long tried. You must help him."

"How, my mother?"

"I have learned and unlearned many lessons," said Noemi. "But this I now hold sure: Though we may harm others with too much help, we harm them even more without enough. The Lord would not have put so strong an urge in his children to assist one another, if he did not intend it to be used. He would not have us say, 'Lord, Lord,' and do little or nothing. He shares his energy and would work through us. It is only when we misuse or misapply that energy, intentionally or not, that we fail. You should go to Boaz —"

"I have gone, my mother."

A silence, emphasized by the faint sounds of the breeze in the night, fell between them. Noemi knew what Ruth was thinking and let her think on. But at last she spoke once more, eagerly repeating her question. "Will you glean with Rhea in his fields?"

Ruth pressed Noemi's hand.

The following evening, two men and a woman were standing and waiting for Ruth just outside the town gates. As she approached, the men retreated a little, but the woman — the same who had denounced her on the day when she returned to Bethlehem from Jerusalem — swung forward, hand on hip, and gave her a contemptuous stare. "I've seen you going regularly to the hills and coming back at sunset," she said. "Such mystery! Do you worship the false god of your wretched people in some black corner up there?"

"I worship no false god," replied Ruth.

The woman grunted. "You've done enough against Bethlehem, without still casting your spell on the hero who took our defense into his two hands. He is apart from us, because of you; and though he hates us for opposing you, we'll act. You must leave here and never show your face again."

"But I cannot leave — yet. My work is not finished."

"Your scheming is not finished." The woman came closer. "That's why you shall go."

One of the men interposed. "The Moabitess is overcome. We should give her some time, a fortnight or so, to think the matter over and see that we are right."

"I agree," said the other.

"No!" The woman's tone was harsh and grating. "More time, more trouble. She'll never let herself see anybody's way but her own."

Then the first man spoke again. "It would be far better if she went of her own accord. Boaz called us beasts when we raised our fists to her. He would never forgive us for forcing her; but he could neither say nor do anything if she should leave quietly and willingly."

"Moabitess, consider our position," said the other. "We

esteem Boaz beyond any man in Bethlehem and owe him more than we can ever repay. He has long been unhappy, and we cannot bear his increase of misery. Have you no heart, that you go on tormenting him by being here, after abusing his trust and consorting with our enemies? Those enemies were taken and sent back to Moab. You, who betrayed us, ought to be with them. Too long we've awaited your going. If there's any good at all in you, give Boaz a chance to forget you."

"She'll never do so, unless we make her," said the woman. "She even went alone to his house. Not until Boaz firmly shut the door in her face did she go away. Yes, and she went back again today — with the same result. His better judgment is against her being here. I know for a fact that he hasn't spoken a word to her or given her an opportunity to speak to him since she reappeared in Bethlehem. He'll eventually thank us for casting her out."

"The thanks could come too late. That same wrath of his that ended Banaias might be our own undoing. Personally, I am not fully resigned to running the risk, unless the Moabitess proves too obstinate. Now that we've warned her —"

The woman reflected. "I like not this delay," she said, "but it may be well." She snapped at Ruth, "Think, idolater!"

Then the trio let her pass through the gates.

She told Noemi nothing about the encounter, wishing to spare her the worry, but she thought of it almost constantly. She still lingered in the cave each day, hoping for the music that never came. Twice more she tried to speak with Boaz, but in vain. She thought of sending Rhea to him or of having Samuel communicate with him from Jerusalem, but decided in favor of more patience. And time passed on to the beginning of the harvest.

As of old, the wind from the western sea moved cool and invigorating through the land, and the sun came up from the depths of the Jordan Valley to gild the walls and the hills of Bethlehem. And, on the morning of the first day for reaping, Ruth left Deborah's house with Rhea.

The spaces just beyond the city gates were aflame with poppies which contributed to her pensiveness as she walked along. When she reached the fields of Boaz, all the workers who were already there turned from her, muttering their resentments; and darkest of all was the face of the woman who had warned her.

Rhea would have raised her voice in a defense, but Ruth restrained her and followed the harvesting at a distance.

Morning wore away to high noon, and Ruth's gleaning was only a few wisps of grain, for the sullen reapers had purposely left almost nothing behind. Rhea, looking, recalled the bushel of barley that Ruth had gathered in another harvest. "You are wasting your time here," she said tersely, in an effort to conceal her pity. "You might better be at home with Noemi. If Boaz were around, he'd command those wretches to treat you well. I wonder where he is."

Ruth did not reply.

"Since you won't have me speak for you, I cannot stay any longer. If I did, I'd let everything out in a blaze that would burn the ears off them. Are you coming with me?"

Ruth shook her head. "Don't go," she said. "Patience —"

"Patience! The time for that is over. I'll burst, I tell you, if I remain a minute longer. I'm going."

Ruth gazed after her wistfully. Then her eyes sought the harvesters resting under the trees. Some of their children caught her glance and smiled, but the parents glowered. When one very little boy started to toddle toward her with outspread arms, his mother drew him back and slapped him soundly on both cheeks. Sadly Ruth moved away.

She seated herself in a sunny spot surrounded with lilies, and waited for the work to begin again. Her eyes closed. Her head, heavy, drooped to her left shoulder. The warmth of the air and the soft buzz of insects lulled her senses, and soon she was lying on her right side in a doze.

It was then that Boaz, who had wandered from his house where, with no zest for the harvest, he had been languishing all morning, saw her. His impulse was to pass on, and he succumbed to it; but after a few paces, he looked over his shoulder. Turning fully, he came slowly to her, his eyes down. She seemed so helpless and forlorn, lying there with her veil blown foamlike by the breeze, her hair exposed, her cheek resting on her outflung arm, the arch of her throat unprotected. His countenance changed. Suddenly his eyes strained and he was kneeling beside her, seeing for the first time the injured hand, outstretched from the ruffled loopings of the sleeve. Under Noemi's care, it had healed completely; but the scars were still livid in contrast with the pale smoothness of the slender wrist. The last time he had seen that hand, there was only the mark of happy toil on it. But now. . . .

Thoughts, both sweet and stinging, buzzed in his mind. Could she have been seeking him that night of the enemy's approach and been taken captive — and tortured? True, she had turned from him when he found her in the Moabite camp, and smiled at the soldiers; but might that have been her attempt to divert their attention? This thought had occurred to him repeatedly before, only to be rejected by his memory of Hagar's comment that, for one taken against her will, Ruth looked "very much at home in that camp."

The scarred hand among the lilies seemed to be beckoning the thought back and pleading that he understand. Yet his conviction, so long fostered, could not be readily shed.

He regarded her for many moments with brimming eyes; then hurried off to the farther side of the field.

When Ruth awoke, she resumed her gleaning and was surprised to find that many ears of grain were being left behind for her. But there was no change in the hostility of the harvesters. From every side sharp looks were hurled at her. She felt rather than saw them; and she seemed to feel, too, a softer gaze coming from a distance. Once she glanced up from her work a little and thought she discerned Boaz beyond; but the sun was in her face and she could not be sure.

At sunset, she pressed her sheaf to her and began her return to Bethlehem, still solitary and shunned. The light had faded, but her spirit was far less depressed than during the earlier hours of the day.

At a bend in the homeward path, the same three figures that she had seen almost two weeks before emerged from the dusk with the stealth of wolves and confronted her.

"Our warning fell on deaf ears," said the woman surlily. "Not only did you defy us by coming into the fields this day, but you wove your spell tighter around him, throwing yourself wantonly among the flowers and pretending to be asleep after you saw him coming!" She turned to the men. "Are you convinced of the folly of giving her time? Had you listened to me, she'd be far away by now."

"She'll never see another dawn in Bethlehem," replied one of them. "It's well that her guile was not enough to get him to accompany her home tonight. He has gone his own way."

"And thinking of her! Tomorrow she'd be drawing him to her again with some new trick. But this hour belongs to us."

As Ruth listened, she had the same feeling of life closing in on her as when the gates of Bethlehem were locked and she was lost in darkness. She started to flee.

A blow struck the back of her head. A thick cloak was thrown over her head and shoulders, and she was bound with ropes like a sack of grain and carried a little distance. She felt herself being lifted into some kind of conveyance. She heard the lowing of oxen, the creaking of wheels, the breathing and muttering of her captors, a sigh on the night wind. Her senses blurred. She tried to cry out, but her voice was muffled in the folds of the cloak and a hand pressed her mouth through the cloth. Vaguely she caught the words of one of the men: "She'll suffocate, and that's not how we want it." Then all sensation ceased.

When she revived, a fresh breeze was sweeping over her. The mantle and the ropes had been removed, and she was lying on a bed of straw in a cart. She made an effort to sit up.

"Where are you taking me?" she asked the driver, hunched like an image of fate on a narrow seat above her.

He turned slightly, and she glimpsed his profile sharp against the light of the moon. "I am taking you where you can do no more harm," he said, and let his whip fall on the flanks of his plodding oxen.

"Who are you?"

"One who gives thanks for what he has been chosen to do. I am Rei, the son of him who was murdered in your pagan land. You knew Hagar, my mother, and you know me. I drove you from her grave where you dared to come to mock her spirit. She detested you."

Ruth sank back, smitten with the evidence that hate, after it leaves one victim, is still an arrow to lodge in another.

The driver now halted the animals and climbed down from his seat. "Get out!" he commanded.

She could not obey; so he reached into the cart and drew her roughly from it. Then putting her on her feet, he thrust her before him.

She gazed from a precipice out on a sea of blue space. The moon, a molten disk, seemed to be shining from under water. It cast a whitish sheen through the heavens and all the way toward a deep, dark valley. There was no line of horizon but only a far haze where sky and earth met and imperceptibly merged, and she felt that she was standing on the very edge of time, or that time itself stood suspended in air.

He came behind and pointed a finger down. "The Moabites would have slaughtered all of us," he said. "We were too foolish, too misdirected by Samuel, in merely sending them back where they'll scheme their schemes all over. We're not making the same mistake with you. I'm not going to kill you, though. You shall do that yourself."

Ruth turned and gazed on him. Though muscular, he appeared to be only in his teens. His face, now in the light rather than against it, might have been handsome but for the scowl which he wore like a mask. His lips were not cruel. And thinking of his mother, she yearned to help him by removing the mask and revealing him to himself; but to do that she would have to break the silence to which she had committed her suffering, and even now she hesitated. Her hand, out of the sleeve in which she habitually concealed it, was at her throat. It held the slender taut neck between thumb and fingers, and he stared curiously.

"Hagar beheld this hand," she said, making no appeal for sympathy but merely stating a fact, "when it had been almost burned to the bone."

"Who—?"

"Banaias, the leader of the Moabite invaders."

"But why? You are of Moab."

"I'd chosen Israel. I'd refused to speak to him the things of Bethlehem that he thought I knew."

"On the brink of death, you're lying to me! You'd never have protected Bethlehem. You hate it just as my mother hated you."

"Hagar had no hate toward the end. When she crept into the camp that last night of her life, she helped me to escape. I was near her when the arrow struck. She died in my arms."

He retreated a step or two, openmouthed, the mask slipping slowly. The moonlight showed him the sincerity of her face, and she could feel his heart going out to her. "But why," he demanded hoarsely, "did you keep silent so long, letting us think you were a traitor and tormenting Boaz, who is said to care for you?"

"I tried to leave all things to the Lord. And I speak now only because he must will that I listen to the voice of your mother from the grave. Her soul could not rest if you fell into crime."

He hung his head. Moments passed. "How can I go back to Bethlehem and tell the people? . . . I was to have goaded you to throw yourself from this cliff; and, if you refused, I was going to —"

"You can tell them I have gone. Just — gone. That's all they wanted, and they willed my ending only as a means to it. Their hate for me is love for Boaz. I thank them for that love and I share it. I'd have left before this, but I was hoping for music that never came."

His eyes turned awkwardly, shamefully, up at her. "What music?"

"The kind that, perhaps, is heard only within. But when there's too much fear, too little faith, it can't be heard at all. I can see now that the Lord wants me to go where I first found belief; back to my native land, such as it is. He has closed Israel to me. My sister Orpha, who remained in Moab, chose more humbly than I. Noemi, our mother, begged that I remain there, knowing me better than I knew myself. . . . Only a little life is left her. She no longer needs my arms, with the Lord's own around her. Say to her I'll always love her, and help Boaz to see that her few wants are supplied."

He plucked at his tunic. "I will. But Boaz — what of him?"

She could not reply.

"May I tell what you've told me?"

She turned her face to him, but the sudden eagerness in her eyes faded. She shook her head. Better that Boaz, from thinking her unfaithful, should come to regard her as dead. If the Lord willed the end of trial, would he not have healed all wounds by now and sent his music?

Drawn by her abjection, Rei knelt at her feet. "Can you forgive me?"

She laid a hand on his shoulder and held it there.

He pleaded for permission to take her as far as the shore, but again she shook her head, and bade him farewell. Then she found her way along a winding path to the valley; and the words that she had spoken to Noemi in what now seemed the long ago, came back to her tauntingly. *Whithersoever you go, I will go — where you stay, I will stay — where you die, I will die.*

And yet, as she walked on, she grew calm with a feeling that, in spirit, there neither was nor could ever be a parting. When those words had welled up out of her heart, she had been thinking in time: but now her thoughts were tending to eternity. Still, for all that, her heart would ache for the touch of Noemi's hand, the kind old eyes, the quiet words of wisdom. So many of her dreams, more human than she had realized, were scattered! She looked up. Through the sky, the pale stars also were scattered; but they were nevertheless unified in the fact of their being sparks of the great light of God, and not any was lost in the void. Was not every clean hope and thought below, however human, a sort of star? Could any be in vain? Asking her soul these things and groping through the shadows toward the Salt Sea, she thought of him who was to come and would surely gather together out of the darkness all the strange fragmentary gleams into a single, clear meaning: a meaning that would at last echo its healing melody through the vast lonely cave of life.

The sun rose and set, set and rose, and through days Ruth continued on the long road back. Strangers readily directed her. Here and there they shared a meal; and each night, as when she had journeyed with Noemi, she slept in the open. A mood of reconciliation was enfolding her; but beneath it a longing for Bethlehem steadily beat. She now faced frankly the extent of her love for Boaz. There was no longer any point in blinking it for, away from Bethlehem, there was no possibility of its preventing the life of abnegation to which God, in his own mysterious way, seemed more certainly leading her. She kept repeating to herself what Noemi had years ago said to her sons: "May his will, and his alone, be done." And her strength lay in her resolution to apply the merits of her future to Boaz, that his spirit might find light and rest.

When she finally reached the shore of the sea, a flat vessel of pitch and mud-calked bulrushes was waiting to cross; and a man, about to go aboard, noticed her standing and gazing from under her veil at it. He approached, looking keenly, and spoke to her. "Peace be to you," he said. "I am a Moabite and, at a summons from Samuel, the judge of Israel, have been visiting Jerusalem to make a report. Are you not Ruth, who, with Noemi, left Moab for Bethlehem?"

"I am," she said; and, lifting her veil, recognized the long, lean face with its thoughtful gray eyes and grizzled beard. Here was Hebel, Banaias' former steward and chief of the converts who used to gather at Orpha's house. She had not seen him since Mahalon and Chelion were slain, but remembered the rumor in Moab that he had been stripped of office and sent into exile. He was now regarding her hand from which a passing breeze had lifted the sleeve. She no longer thought to cover it up, being so far from Bethlehem. And she looked at his hand, tears coming to her eyes; for she saw that it was disfigured even worse than her own.

"We have both been victims of Banaias," he said. "He tried to make me sign away my faith in Yahweh; and when I refused, he forced this hand of mine into a brazier of live coals. What he did to me must have prompted what he did to you."

Her glance put a question. Had Samuel spoken to him?

"It was some of the soldiers, returned from the aborted siege, who told me," he explained. "By that time, I was again

active in Moab, since Samuel's good influence was prevailing
there and I had been recalled. O daughter of grace, wondrous
things have come to pass. Do you know that the gold that
Banaias hoarded in the temple of Chemosh was found by men
of Israel?"

"I have been told."

"But do you know, also, that it has already been distributed
to the people? Not an ounce of it was kept from them. And
Hotham, our king, who now employs me, seems a new person.
All the virtue in him that was buried under Banaias' influence,
has been uncovered now that the evil high priest is dead.
Justice and mercy at last. Great is the praise of Israel and
Yahweh among our countrymen."

Ruth's face reflected the radiance of his. But she was thinking rather of the words from the scroll called *Beresith*, which
Noemi had often quoted: *In the beginning, God created
heaven and earth. And the earth was void and empty, and
darkness was upon the face of the deep; and the spirit of
God moved over the waters. And God said: Let there be
light. And light was made.*

Hebel reverently gave her his arm and led her toward the
boat. "Orpha has been mothering the faith in Moab," he said,
"but the family of the faithful has so increased that we need
yet another. Are you returning to us for that mission?"

"If it be the Lord's will."

And during the crossing, he told her more about the blessings that Israel, through Samuel, had brought. "Chemosh is
still worshiped and will be worshiped for a long time yet,"
he said. "Deep-rooted beliefs cannot be destroyed in a day.
But Israelites walk our streets in peace and honor and are
building a tabernacle near the temple. They know that darkness can be overcome only with light; so they are content
to give a silent but vivid example of their faith and leave the
rest to time and the Lord. Already the worst of heathenism
is dying." He drew a parable from the treasure that had been

hidden in the temple. "There is good even in the false faith of Moab. The father of our people, from whom our country derives its name, was the son of Lot's eldest daughter; and some of the truth revealed by God to Adam passed on into our treasury of belief. But it was so buried in error that it became almost forgotten. Now it is being raised to public consciousness on a large scale, just as the hoarded gold has been exposed, and Moabites are coming to see that they have much in common with the faith of Israel. As this knowledge increases, so will the harmony between our races." He watched, for a few moments, the wake of the ship on the smooth water and then said, "If all men would only see the similarities that link them rather than the differences that divide them!"

She smiled, grateful not only for the substance of what he was saying, but because here was a wish that she had often heard Noemi falteringly express.

"May the Lord ever bless Samuel who thinks in terms not only of his own people but all mankind!" he exclaimed.

She replied, "Amen," and silently prayed, "May the Lord ever bless Noemi, who, coming to us, gave the blood of her husband and sons, far more precious to her than her own."

In the quiet of the early evening, Hebel accompanied her on the road to Orpha's home. And when they were in sight of it, he said, "Send word to me at Hotham's palace if ever you need any help." Then he left her, having decided that the scene of reunion should belong solely to the two women themselves.

As Ruth approached the great fig tree that grew near the familiar door, she heard voices and saw that Noemi's old garden, still blooming, was humanly enriched; that a sort of school was in session. Beneath the branches the teacher — Orpha herself — was sitting in a semicircle of olive-skinned children. The flickering leaves sent little shadows dancing on the small faces. A fragrance rose from the flowers and, high above, some blue herons were in flight from the far west, seeking a mild season among the marsh grasses of Moab.

Ruth stepped back in the mellow, golden light, so that she might ready herself by looking and listening, without being seen.

Orpha was telling about a certain book — *Creation* — which even a child could read. "God is written on every page of it, and it has pictures that speak."

"What do they say?" asked the smallest of the girls, her head on Orpha's lap, her dark hair falling over it, her bright unblinking eyes staring up at Orpha's face but seeming rather to be seeing a spirit.

"Flowers, souls, and stars proclaim his beauty, Esther," replied Orpha. "I call you Esther because that's the Hebrew word for star. Storms and the mighty sea tell of his power; the generous harvests prove his care; and the parents he's given — they show his love; he made everything good."

"He made you!" Esther exclaimed, as if making a discovery. She raised a hand to Orpha's veil. "He must have. You're good."

"But there are bad people, too," said a small, pinch-faced boy, a catch in his voice. "They laugh at me and push me out of the way, because I'm lame. They make me feel that I'm nobody. Did God make *them?*"

"They have let themselves become different from what he made them, Jeteth," said Orpha. "And that is sinful."

All wanted to know about sin. And she carefully explained it as a wandering away from the divine will, a turning of the back on light, a journey into darkness.

"Why does anyone want to go into the dark?" Jeteth frowned. "I'm afraid of the dark."

Esther smiled a strange little smile.

"People lose their way," said Orpha. "Then they do terrible things in their fear, as the darkness increases with the distance from God. But he does not abandon them; he always sends beams of light from himself to show them how to get back to him. There's the book I mentioned. It's full of beams! And, there's a letter which he wrote us through Moses; a long letter that tells about the beginning of things, and our first parents, and how he cares for his children in all their trials. I myself have, so far, only heard our Israelite friends quoting parts, but I hope to hear all of it some day. And he is such a generous God that, as if the book and the letter were not enough, he is going to send us in time his own personal Messenger who will make as clear as day everything we should know about him."

"What will the Messenger be like?"

Orpha gazed on Jeteth, the questioner; then down on Esther; then at the others. "He will come — I believe — in the form of a child," she replied.

Ruth drew in a long breath. She remembered what Noemi had once said to her in Bethlehem about the King being born of woman, and she tried to form in her mind a picture of that woman, as Noemi must have often tried to do. The effort made her think of everything beautiful she had ever known, and all the notes blended into a single impression: *Sinlessness.*

At that moment, Orpha caught sight of her and gave a joyous cry. Gently placing Esther aside, she got up and ran to meet her. They held each other close, then at arm's length, searching for whatever changes the period of separation might have effected. Ruth saw that pain had left Orpha's dark eyes and that peace lay in the depths of them; but Orpha discerned that the blue of Ruth's eyes had deepened almost to violet with an unmistakable sadness. Without a word, she led her to the children, feeling that, where she herself had found so much solace, her sister would find it too.

The children were on their feet, waiting; and when Orpha presented them, they clustered around. Ruth kissed each one.

Their touch sent a warmth through her, and her nature went out to them.

Their candid looks played all over her. Esther reached up and seized a finger. That served as a signal. The others similarly had to prove to themselves that this visitor was real, and immediately every fold of her skirt was in a tight tugging grasp. Orpha endeavored to free her.

"Where are you from?" Esther asked.

Ruth answered, smiling, "From a place called Bethlehem."

"Tell us about it," said Jeteth.

Somehow, with these fresh young faces before her, she forgot all suffering for the moment and said, "It is a town so sweet that I'd not be surprised if the Messenger, when he comes, chooses it for his very own."

The children wanted to hear more, but Orpha interposed. "It is almost time for your evening meal, children," she said, "and your parents will be worrying about you. Return tomorrow morning, and I'm sure Ruth will then find the chance to tell you everything you want to know. She's tired now and must rest."

Not before Ruth had embraced each one again did they start to go. They kept turning and waving. Jeteth and Esther were the most reluctant. Ruth placed Esther's hand in Jeteth's. "Guide her well," she said, "like a big brother." And he gave her a smile of adoration, for she had not even noticed that he was a cripple.

With their arms linked, Ruth and Orpha watched them leave. "Chelion and Mahalon caught the springs in the meadow and kept this soil producing when all the rest of the land was dry," said Orpha. "The Lord has had me draw these young lives from Chemosh before they could be lost. How much better this is than smashing an image! It's building up a faith. But you, my sister, can do it better than I. With you here, I already feel I should give my attention rather to the elder sisters and brothers and the parents. Sometimes

I think that grownups are the real children — so weakened in soul by their added years of living, more helpless in their bigger world than children in the smaller. The very young ones take to the truth as easily as they breathe, and they seem so wise in their little way."

"Couldn't we both care for them?" suggested Ruth.

But Orpha, still conscious of the veiled sadness in Ruth's eyes, and bent on dispelling it, answered, "One mother at a time is better. Two would confuse them." And she finished a little lamely but very sincerely, "You understand?"

"I understand, my sister," said Ruth, "what I have always known — your selflessness. Could my own equal it! I have been finding it very hard to give up all thought of a particular earthly happiness that could have been mine; but your strength shames my weakness."

Womanlike, Orpha wanted to probe. She had wondered much about Ruth and Noemi in relation to Boaz, the kinsman; whether he had been kind; whether he had done for them as a kinsman should; whether he had been captivated by Ruth. She was aware of the Jewish custom whereby the next of kin was granted the right to wed a widow and raise up children in living memory of the dead.

Ruth sat with her under the fig tree. It was very quiet there, now that the children had gone, but warm and inviting with an echoing memory. Quietly and fully Ruth answered Orpha's first question: about Noemi. Then, slowly, with only a slight quaver in her voice, she told briefly of the events since the morning of farewell. She ended by saying, "I had to leave. And here I am."

Orpha managed to cover her emotion by the simple resource of plucking a blade of grass and running it through her fingers. From under her lids, she watched Ruth's profile and noted the trembling of the lower lip, the tears in the eyes; and she asked very softly, "Are you sure you did right in coming here?"

"You told the children how to see the Lord's beauty and power and love in creation. I have seen his will in what has happened to me."

"What happened outside," said Orpha significantly. "But have you looked — sufficiently — within? Do you know yourself?"

Ruth's head lowered and she murmured, "There are two desires in me opposing each other."

"They might be molded into one."

"O my sister, my misfortune seems to have a voice of its own which directs me to a path of sacrifice like yours."

"My path has not had much sacrifice," said Orpha with a hollow little smile. "I've wanted no other since I lost Chelion; and I've found more relief than I ever thought possible. It is different with you."

"But I've chosen. Since I may not serve the Lord in Israel, I will serve him here."

"A perfect choice — a real pledge — would have subdued any yearning for something else, my sister. It would have brought peace. There is sorrow in you."

"If I have sorrow, it is less for myself than for Boaz and Noemi. But I've left them to the Lord. He cannot fail them."

Orpha reflected. "He uses us to comfort one another," she said. "Your presence here is comforting me. Does mine mean much to you?"

Ruth's answer was a firm handclasp.

"But what of Noemi and — Boaz?" asked Orpha.

"I think of them always. If the Lord wanted me in Bethlehem, I'd have died rather than leave. But he gave no sign. The cave remained so silent! And the silence seemed to say, 'All your efforts have brought no harmony.'"

"It takes more than one to make harmony." Another smile, faint but wise, slipped across Orpha's lips. "Sometimes two — just two — are enough."

Ruth seemed to ignore the implication. "You spoke to the

children of your belief that the Messias will come in the form of a child," she said, gazing off into the gathering night. "But the mother of such a child would have to be singularly worthy, would she not? Purer than purity itself."

Her face was now upturned, and the early starlight was on it. Orpha thought that she had never seen another countenance so chaste and fair. And, drawing Ruth to her, she said: "We shall pray and work together, and await here in Moab the sign that was not given you in Bethlehem."

Ruth readjusted herself to the life of Moab with at least an outward ease. Work in the fields and association with the children sped the days. And the childish voices seemed to bring her the music that she had sought to hear in the cave. Their affection mounted and sometimes she felt that it almost made up for what had been lost; but the feeling was transient, for her mind and heart were ever turning to Noemi and Boaz and the scenes she had left.

She described those scenes so often and minutely and with such a glow to Jeteth, Esther, and the others that they all came to know Bethlehem almost as well as their own surroundings. Whenever a dove flew out of the leaves of the fig tree, she would tell about the homes in Israel that sheltered nests in their walls, under stairs, or in clay pots on roofs. She would point out the partridge nests in the tufts of grass and tell of the mother birds in the fields of Bethlehem, that she had seen guarding the fledglings even of broods other than their own; and she would draw an object lesson that Israel's goodness was not limited to Israelites but shed itself far and wide like the rays of the sun. Often she led them to the graves of Elimelech, Chelion, and Mahalon and told them about the three. Over and over again she pointed out the same varieties of flowers growing here that grew also beyond the Salt Sea. And they found out her especial liking for the white bloom, the "star of Bethlehem," which opened its six-

pointed petals wide at noon; and they would happily pick
it for her, just as Mahalon in his childhood used to do for
Noemi, and as he had done for his bride on that spring wedding day.

News of the torture to which Banaias put her had spread
in Moab from the lips of the returned soldiers; and people
could not do enough to honor her for withstanding the high
priest. If the complete extent of her service had been known
to them, their esteem would have had no bounds. But she
had imposed silence on Hebel just as on Samuel, and she used
what homage she received only as a means of strengthening
the faith.

Orpha watched her influence growing: the attendance at
the little school of religion daily increased, the sick being
soothed, the poor being assisted, the love of Yahweh taking
on more and more life. She had deemed her as near to perfection as one could be, but now she saw that there were
numberless degrees and that Ruth, led by the Ideal of Ideals,
was ascending steadily. There had always been a difference
to Ruth, even from earliest days. Orpha could remember a
little ethereal girl holding a sea shell to her ear while other
children romped and played. She remembered a maiden who
never took part in the unbridled festivities of the town but
liked to wander in the open; one who seemed happiest with
the wind in her hair and nature twirling its fresh clean colors
around her. She recalled that in the beginning Ruth had not
been without the faults of an only child; but she had seen
her plucking them out every time they cropped forth, and she
suspected that it was in order to relieve her of any lingering
trace of them that the Lord had tried her in unusual ways.
Was he letting her be tempted with a love for Boaz, only
that, at length fully triumphing over it, she might be the
better fitted for his richer favor? Or had he implanted this
lesser love in her so that, living on, it might serve the greater?
Somehow Orpha could not bring herself to believe that the

lesser could be lost. Having longed so much for the fullness of Chelion's love, she realized the pangs of Boaz and hoped that Heaven would permit Ruth to heal them. As much as she wanted her to remain in Moab, she felt that this should not be. Ruth belonged to Bethlehem, and everything she said or did was an indication.

And early one morning, several months after Ruth's coming, when a breath of perfume from the garden that Noemi had started years ago was blowing through the open windows of the old house which had become one of the best known and most honored in Moab, a young man appeared at the door. He was weary and spent and his lips were pale, but a light burned in his eye. Ruth had gone into the fields, and there was only Orpha to receive him.

She waited for him to put into words the question with which his look was filled.

He fidgeted with the waistband of his tunic as she led him in and assisted him to a chair; and he scarcely noticed the bread and wine that she then set before him. She busied herself with a household task, letting him take his time. He watched her as she added to a bowl of fresh milk on the table a bit of leaven to make it ferment. In his boyhood, he perhaps had seen his mother doing that. The milk would turn to *ghaib,* which, when shaken well in a goatskin bag, would become *sheninah* or buttermilk. Then the *sheninah* would be put into small cloth sacks, and the water squeezed out, and the cheeselike substance rolled into little balls which could keep indefinitely.

Orpha glanced at his face. It was an attractive face, bronzed with the sun but not yet toughened from exposure. The brown-black eyes were round and large. The full lips glistened from a constant tipping of the tongue to them. That he was nervous and troubled she could plainly see; but she knew that his best relief would be in spontaneous expression, and still she waited.

"I am Rei," he at last told her. "Ruth knows me as Hagar's son, who tried to get her to kill herself."

"But she understood. She forgave you. Was it necessary to come from Bethlehem?"

"More than necessary! Even if she's forgiven me, I cannot forgive myself. She's held me to silence, and all in Bethlehem, except Noemi, think that, driven by me, she plunged to her death and that secret friends of hers found the body and buried it. I am a kind of hero back there. Me — a hero!"

Now that he had begun, his words came fast. And listening, Orpha detected something about him of which, apparently, he himself was not yet quite aware. She saw that, from living with the memory of Ruth, he had become devoted to her.

"Boaz is not worthy," he asserted, an evidence almost of hate invading his expression. And forgetting that he, too, had been guilty of misjudgment before his eyes were opened to the truth, he went on with a dark intensity to denounce what he considered a willful blindness. "Only an evil man could hold her faithless! She is as good as she is beautiful. And to think that I — we — in Bethlehem would have destroyed her so that he'd no longer be disturbed by her being there! I'm glad he's suffering. The worst is not enough. No matter what he did for us, he's no hero. He can't face the loss he brought on himself, and he's run off to Samuel in Jerusalem like a whimpering child. If she'll let me, I'll tell everyone how innocent she is; and they'll all welcome her back with open arms. That is why I'm here, to beg her to let me. She should be with Noemi whose life is empty without her. Each Bethlehemite needs to know the facts about her and help right the wrong that's been done." And he asked piteously, "Will she come with me?"

"That," said Orpha with a sigh, "is for her to say."

Then Ruth entered the room. Rei, hearing the faint step, swung around and, at the sight of her, fell on his knees, his hands extended. He bent until his forehead touched the floor.

She knelt beside him, as she would have knelt beside Boaz
in the cave, and drew him to her. "Why have you come?" she
asked gently.

"To bring you back." He seized her wrist and held on. "If
you won't let me, I myself cannot return." A tremor went
through him while she urged him up. On his feet again, he
became challenging. "I'll do to myself what I intended to
make you do that night! I won't go on, letting Bethlehem think
falsely of you. My mother came to me in the dark — she
pointed to her wounded breast and told me, 'It will never
be healed until . . .'" His voice broke.

Ruth got him reseated and quieted him as best she could.
Then she turned to Orpha. "Go to Hebel in the palace, my
sister," she said, "and he will come to me. With him and
Hagar's son, I'll leave for Bethlehem this day. This is the sign!"

Moving about for the last time in the room where Mahalon
and Chelion met death, and making her preparations for the
journey while awaiting Hebel, she thought back over her
stay in Moab. It had given her an opportunity to look on life
calmly and clearly. Here, while teaching the children, she
had learned important lessons herself. Their qualities had
made her feel that, to please the Lord, she must be much more
like those who were so fresh from his hands, so pliable in
their simplicity. She now realized that even goodness could
be exercised badly and that the right course, without wisdom,
could be rendered wrong. Had she been wise? Had not
a subtle pride, perhaps, entered into her? Examining herself ruthlessly, she suspected that, though she had left
Noemi and Boaz to the Lord, she might have presumed to
dream beyond his plan for her. Who was she, a former child
of Chemosh, to have aspired to live in a sanctuary in Jerusalem? Who was she, the least of the Lord's servants, to have
been superior to repute and to have imposed silence on
others? And so, with a new humility gained by her reflections,

she was at last able to arrive at a decision to permit Rei to say what he would about her in Bethlehem, and also, through Hebel, to release the prophet Samuel in the Holy City from withholding enlightenment from Boaz.

That afternoon, she stood at the threshold to bid Orpha good-by. "You have been more than sister to me, even as Noemi has been more than mother to us both," she said.

The children, unhappy, gathered near the door. She caressed them with her look. "I am going to the place I have so often told you about. Whenever you think of me, just close your eyes and you will see it."

Esther instantly closed her eyes tight, and her face was tense with earnestness. She counted off aloud on her fingers the things she saw: "The hills all around — the white walls and houses — the fields of barley and wheat — the sheep — the cave —" And a radiant smile covered her face. "There's a light in the cave! It's coming down through the top, and it's full of angels. Their mouths are open just like they were ready to sing. . . ."

Bending, Ruth took her into her arms. "Oh for the vision of a child!" she said, glancing at Orpha.

And Orpha thought: "How little Ruth credits herself with giving this child that vision, infinitely better than earthly sight!" For Esther had been blind from birth.

After embracing each of the children in turn, Ruth noticed that Jeteth was missing. She was about to ask for him, when she saw him approaching from the garden, a small dejected figure. He came straight to her and, hanging his head to conceal his feelings, he opened his small moist hand with an offering of the flower called "Star of Bethlehem."

Pressing the gift to her, she started with Rei and Hebel, down the road to the sea. Once, not far from the fig tree and the garden, she turned and looked back. Orpha was in the midst of the children. Again, the lame child, Jeteth, was holding the hand of the blind one, Esther.

Chapter Eight

THE SONG OF THE CAVE

THROUGHOUT the journey back, Ruth thought not only of Boaz and Noemi, but also of the tabernacle in Jerusalem; and regretted that a life of service there was not for her. She must choose the lowlier way. But, as she had found in Moab, there could be much light and warmth even in the lowlier way; and she reasoned: "Because of the lesser demands it makes, it can be the more perfectly followed." And, as she neared Bethlehem with Rei and Hebel, her spirit rose.

At the town gates, Hebel said good-by to her. "I shall go on to Jerusalem and deliver your message to Samuel," he said. "What joy he will give Boaz in telling him the truth about you! Certainly, before another dawn, Boaz will be back here."

She looked off toward the hills and said nothing; but Hebel noted the color that came to her cheeks, the eagerness that shone in that look. So did Rei.

The rheumy eyes of the same old gatekeeper almost sprang from between their sockets at the sight of Ruth. "The Moabitess — risen from Sheol!" he cried.

"Have a care, old man!" warned Rei, stepping up to him. And he thereupon relieved himself of such a vigorous verbal defense, together with such excessive praise, that Ruth was almost sorry for having freed him from silence.

The scene was repeated in the streets of the town several times before they reached Deborah's house; and a group of astonished people followed them right to the door. Rei stood on guard when Ruth entered; and he faced the Bethlehemites

180

once more, telling them in ringing tones that, because of their
treatment of her, they were not fit to draw breath.

Within the house, hearts beat fast. Noemi put her finger
tips to Ruth's face, her hair, her veil, her breast. "My eyes,
my daughter, have gone nearly blind with weeping," she
quavered. "But why should I have wept? This is better than
any of the Lord's previous blessings. And all the time you
were away, I had the consolation of being able to picture you
with our Orpha in Moab, helping her to spread the light. The
Lord did that for me, and I knew he would do more; he has!
. . . If only Boaz were here!"

In Jerusalem, late that night, Hebel, Samuel, and Boaz
came together; and the place of their meeting was the roof
of Samuel's house high above the sleeping city. A surround-
ing low wall of sun-baked brick cast a wide border of shade;
but the center of the enclosure was white with moonlight, and
there the prophet-judge sat with his guests.

"— she kept all these things within her," said Hebel,
"choosing to be despised rather than acclaimed."

Boaz struck his breast as Samuel turned to him.

"Henceforth you will esteem her more than ever before,"
said Samuel, who, availing himself of the permission that
Ruth had granted him through Hebel, had already told Boaz
the facts about her. All but one, which he was at last ready
to reveal. "I am taking it on myself to disregard her wishes
and mention her special yearning to serve the Lord in a life
apart from the world and hidden in the tabernacle."

The words were uttered softly, yet they fell like a funeral
knell on the ears of Boaz. He had already arranged to depart
before dawn for Bethlehem, there to ask for Ruth's forgiveness,
daring to presume on a complete reconciliation, and already
imagining her in his arms; and he had received Samuel's
story of her loyalty with a feeling of relief which seemed like
a rebirth. But now, in this new knowledge, all hope seemed to

leave him, for he drew from what Samuel said, the full significance of that margin of reserve which she had always maintained in their association during the joyful harvest that had merged into such a welter of gloom, and he recalled how she glanced away to the hills the night when he asked her if the Lord would have them go different ways. He recalled, too, the fear that then had come upon him at her silence. She had certainly inclined toward him, but something had held her back. And now at the thought, the very moonlight on the parapet seemed to him a mockery; the sparkling sky, smug and indifferent. How could a God be just who gave solace and hope only to taunt and stultify it?

To be sure, he would henceforth esteem her even the more, as Samuel had said, for her great worth. He could not blame her. She had served Bethlehem most nobly. But he blamed the Ideal for dazzling and alluring her; the Divine Robber who had stooped to strip him of his last chance of escape from the ever heavier weariness of existence. There was no way, as yet, for him to know the change that had come to Ruth, and he could think of her only as snatched from him forever.

His nails dug into his palms as a strange desire went clammily through him, an urge to fight back at the Ideal. To fight back with whatever weapon he could grasp. Having endured so much, he could be passive no more.

Suddenly he thought of a statue of Chemosh which Bethlehemites had brought him, the slayer of the god's high priest, for a trophy from Banaias' tent after they had raided, with Samuel's soldiers, the camp of the Moabite invaders. While Banaias' body was being consigned to a dishonorable grave by the town's folk, he had performed a rite all by himself: taking the idol to the cave where he had sheltered the harvesters on the night of Ruth's supposed betrayal, and burying it deep under the stones of the floor. For, then, Ruth's love had seemed as ephemeral as the music of the cave, as false as the god and the religion of the land from which she came; and his mood had caused him to feel a certain grim appropriateness in committing falsity to falsity.

What if, returning to Bethlehem, he should unearth the idol? . . .

Samuel watched the stillness settling on him like a thin coating of ice. "You are taking this too personally," he rebuked. "Your mind is dark."

"The Lord has left me only darkness," replied Boaz with cold wrath. "Moab's god could not have done worse. Perhaps I should not have dishonored him so much. He would have had reason to afflict me for killing his priest, but the Lord afflicts me without cause. Ruth might have really loved me —"

"Her love of God does not mean that she has none for you. What he takes he keeps in treasury for us."

Boaz raised his drawn face and stared at Samuel. "The gold in the dungeon of Moab did the people there no good until it was released and shared. So long as it was withheld from their needs, they knew wretchedness and despair. You've told me so. Your sympathy inspired you — a mere human being — to help them by releasing and distributing it. Is God less sympathetic to our hunger and need than man?"

"He made man."

"He has forgotten me! I'll go back to my fields in Bethlehem. I'll wrest the grain from the soil as before and think as I will." He rose, his voice harsh with the discords of his spirit. "The lies that are fed us! The famine that never ends!"

Samuel and Hebel, also on their feet, started to reason with him; but he silenced them with a gesture and, turning, moved along the shadows cast by the wall of the roof. For an instant, he stood outlined against the night sky. Flinging a tormented glance to the moon and stars, he hurriedly began to descend the steps that led to the courtyard below.

"You long misjudged Ruth — to your shame!" Samuel

called down at him, leaning over the parapet. "Would you misjudge the Lord?"

Boaz groaned, sinking from view.

Ruth visited the cave the morning after her return. She had set forth in high hope that Boaz would seek her there where he and Mahalon had so often come and she had once seen him weeping. She had felt that this would be the best place for the reunion, but now she was unsure. A chill, like bloodless fingers, touched her flesh. The light from above was a dull gray. Something evil and arrogant seemed to be stirring to life under the very stones, and several times she had a distinct sensation that, as she tried to pray, she was being derided. In a growing fear, she called on God and became more certain than ever before, while the weighted hours passed, that only in a life of exclusive relation to him could she ever be secure. Why was he apparently so far away from this spot where Boaz and Mahalon used to hear his music? The harp strings that she had fashioned months before were still in place, but the silence remained unbroken.

Near sunset, she left the cave.

At the door of Deborah's house, an excited Rhea greeted her. "Boaz is again in Bethlehem," she exclaimed. "I saw him on the street. . . . But he made me think of someone out of a tomb. Such a blank, cold look! He passed me by and didn't seem to hear when I called after him. He brushed everybody aside who came near; and all were so anxious to apologize to him for their attitude toward you, because Hagar's son has convinced them of their cruel folly. Noemi waited and waited. She would have sent him to you." She caught her breath. "But here I'm talking on, and maybe you've seen him yourself."

Shaking her head, Ruth entered the house.

Noemi was seated on the bench in the corner, her veil drawn over her face, her veined hands in her lap; and Ruth went to her and, kneeling, she let the old arms enfold her.

"I know, my daughter," said Noemi sadly. "You did not see him. . . . Your message must have reached Samuel. Our poor kinsman's immediate return to Bethlehem is proof enough."

"Why wasn't he with me, my mother?"

"Something is on his mind, deterring him."

"Maybe Samuel, not knowing all that has been going on within me, told him that —"

"Samuel is wise. No, it must be that Boaz is still sick in soul. When a trial passes, the effect remains, at least for a time. And, like all Bethlehem, he is perhaps so ashamed of himself that he cannot yet face you. Night and rest will help him."

In the following dawn, Ruth set forth again. The sun was touching the dark tree-clumped hills with scarlet, and the serrated summits appeared to her as a great twisting crown of thorns, so unlike the diadem that she had once fancied to be resting on the brow of Mount Moriah in Jerusalem. Notwithstanding Noemi's encouragement, she had a presentiment of further sorrow, and it increased when, beyond the town gates, a young man stepped into her path. He was Rei. His lips were white and the hand he held out to her was shaking.

"Don't go up there," he begged, his eyes giving even more warning than his words. "I'd been uneasy about you since his return and couldn't sleep this night. I followed him."

"Whom?"

"Boaz. Hours ago in the dark he went up alone. He entered a cave."

Ruth was all eagerness and alertness.

"Oh, I beseech you: if that's your direction, take another. The Lord and my mother's spirit must have wanted me to head you off. Boaz is evil."

"Evil? That cannot be!" Her eyes flamed with the first

anger Rei had ever seen in them; and instantly, gathering
the folds of her tunic, she began to run, her veil flying behind.

He overtook and tried to restrain her. She shook him off.

At the cave's entrance, she paused, and with an effort
forced herself to look inside. Then the color left her face and
her heart stood still.

Beside a hole in the center of the floor, from which rocks
had been removed, Boaz, with his back turned, was kneeling
and holding up, in the weary manner of one who has kept
in the same position too long, and whose nature has been
forced too strenuously to a deed, a replica of the red-
stone image that used to occupy one of the small arched niches
of the main room of Orpha's house in Moab. In the oblique
rays of the sun from the open space above, the glass eyes in
the calf-shaped head seemed alive.

The sight evoked all the horror Ruth had ever known and
locked her throat against any outcry. Bahila's insane crime on
Elimelech, Jared's brutality, Mahalon's forced dealing with the
slave Manred, the violent ending of two brothers, the high
priest Banaias' inhumanity, a hand held in burning embers, the
arrow piercing Hagar's breast — all, the design of Chemosh!
And now Boaz, who had destroyed the god's chief minister,
was incredibly raising the god himself. . . .

The whole scene became a ghostly blur to her, with only
the eyes of the idol, wickedly triumphant, coming through.
Turning, she stumbled and would have fallen, but that the
arm of Rei, who had followed her, was waiting and ready.

He helped her down the hill. Not a word was spoken until
they were standing in the meadow below.

"I wanted to spare you," he said.

"I needed to know." Then she murmured to herself, "It ex-
plains the awful persistent silence there. No harp has ever
played for Chemosh. — And the image must have been lying
under my very knees while . . ."

The drained look of her frightened Rei. "I must get you

back to Noemi," he said hurriedly. "Later, when you're stronger, we can come back to the cave together and try to undo what's done."

She let him take her hand and lead her on toward the gates of Bethlehem.

All that morning and afternoon she sat with Noemi. She could not tell her what she had seen. She hardly believed she had seen it. Was it still night and was she caught in the meshes of an uncouth dream? Noemi, Rhea, and Deborah, because of her mood, did not ask any questions but waited for the thawing that, they prayed, would come.

Toward the close of the day, Rei reappeared. It was Rhea who admitted him. His eyes met hers. Her plain face, lit with sympathy for Ruth, appealed to him; and she blushed at his momentary gaze. Then he looked at Ruth. "Now is the time," he said to her. "Boaz is drunk. Back in his house he sleeps like a swine."

"I would have you speak differently of him!" she rebuked almost passionately, rising. "You know him not!"

Noemi tried the more to deduce what had happened, but Rhea and Deborah were too puzzled to try. Together the three watched Ruth and Rei leave the room.

Rhea went to the door. She wanted to think only of Ruth, but her eyes were rather on Rei, for he had glanced again at her in passing and no other young man had ever so much as noticed her before.

When Ruth and Rei reached the cave, dusk was massed deep in it, but a little light from above revealed the image on a heap of the stones that had been taken from the flooring and built into a kind of altar.

Ruth shrank back, but Rei, gritting his teeth, went forward. With one hand, he grabbed the object and, with the other, a stone. Using the altar for a table, he brought the stone down again and again. The air shook with what might have been a demoniac, dying wail. A breeze swept through the entrance and from the open roof, bearing a fresh scent of woodland and driving out the odors of must and decay which Ruth, with all her previous ablutions, had not been able quite to destroy. The image readily fell apart and was reduced to small fragments. But Rei pounded on, grinding the pieces to powder, until he and Ruth, suddenly aware of a heavenly sound, looked up.

The strings of the aeolian harp were stirring under the seeming touch of invisible fingers, and a singing was rising from them; soft-swelling, exultant, harmonious with a star trembling out of the evening sky and sending down its beams in a rain of silver through the cleft in the rocks.

With Rei, Ruth stood still until the wind and the music ceased.

"I have never heard anything so beautiful," whispered Rei in amazement. "What can it mean?"

She did not reply. Her gaze was on the lyre, her veiled head tilted back, her face transfigured.

When they left at last, they heard leaves rustling and stepped beyond the entrance to the cave, so as not to be seen. They saw Boaz groping through bushes and branches. "Should we not stop him?" whispered Rei.

"No," she breathed. "His conscience is drawing him this time. He would do what you have done."

And a moment after Boaz had gone into the cave, they heard his sobs.

"He must be grieving for the loss of his false god," said Rei.

"Not so. He has come back penitent." Her hand was at her ear. "He is being pardoned."

In apparent proof of the pardon, once more the wind had risen, and the notes of the harp again were on the air.

Both listened and then Ruth said, "We must leave. This hour is just for Boaz."

And silently they descended the hill.

The next morning, Noemi called Ruth to her and said, "My daughter, shall I not seek a place of rest for you, that it may be well for you? Your faithfulness should at length receive its reward. Today is the start of another harvest." She inhaled the breath of the fields coming through the open door and window. "Now, therefore, is not Boaz, with whose maidservants you once were, our kinsman? And can a kinsman be forgotten? If he comes not to you, it is for you to go to him. He will be out there this day, hard at work. When a man is troubled, he must lose himself in toil."

"He is no longer so troubled, my mother," said Ruth confidently, taking Noemi's hand and bringing it to her lips. "Last night I wanted to tell you something, but I was too filled to speak."

"I sensed it, my daughter, when you came and leaned over me, thinking me asleep."

"Music has returned to the cave!"

Noemi waited a moment in awe. "Did the music turn your mind to Mahalon, Boaz, or solely to the Lord?" she asked.

Ruth smiled. "To the three, my mother. And to you, Elimelech, Chelion, Orpha, and all those I've ever loved. It blended them in a beauty that left no trace of sadness." She sighed. "And one note sounded above the rest."

"What was it?"

"Strangely, the softest and sweetest of all. It seemed to be the voice of a child . . . my own child. . . ."

Noemi's finger tips moved over the smooth contour of Ruth's face and her old eyes were as if a long-sought light had come to them.

Wrapped in thought, she spoke no more through the morning and the afternoon. But toward evening, she again called Ruth to her and said, "Lave and anoint yourself, my daughter, and go down near the threshing floor and wait in the gathering night. The first harvest feast will take place. Do not make your presence known to Boaz until after he has finished eating and drinking. It is when the body is sated that the soul is loneliest. Watch where he lays himself down to sleep; then go and uncover his feet. You have a right to be near him. As our kinsman, he is bound to you by the custom of our people; besides, a time of implicit betrothal has passed and the contract is written in our hearts. The cool night air will slowly awaken him and he will take you for his bride."

Ruth answered, "All that my mother says, I will do."

Rhea, overhearing and instantly eager to assist, had an inspiration. There was one really good garment in the house; a *khurkah* or full, long dress, made years ago by Noemi herself and given to Deborah to be kept until the time when the little daughter would be grown up and ready for marriage. From a plain wooden chest, the girl now drew it forth. She fingered it fondly. "I'll never be a bride," she said to Ruth, shrugging her shoulders, trying to look resigned, "and this has been going to waste. Now it can be used."

"It may have a further use, too," said Ruth gratefully. "I think I surprised something in Rei's look when you and he met at the door last evening. You are so good and true, my Rhea. Were Hagar alive, she could not select a better wife for her son. He, too, is full worthy. May you know for your own the joy that is beginning to creep around me!"

Rhea's cheeks were roses as, holding the garment with one hand, she smoothed the folds of it with the other. It was made of crash and tinted as blue as the sky; and there were little stripes to it, scarlet as the lilies of the field and yellow as the salvia which might have furnished the design for the seven-branched candlestick of sacred ritual. Gores of green were sewn into each side. "Boaz will more than admire you in it," she said. "It was woven with a love for Bethlehem and it has the very colors."

Finally arrayed and ready, and with a parting blessing from Noemi, Ruth stepped from the house. A breeze played on the veil that covered her hair and shoulders, and the last light of day touched the whiteness of it.

Rei was standing beneath the branches of the tree near the doorway, where Boaz had stood the morning after his first sight of her. Wistfully he watched her going down the street toward the town gates. She needed him no longer, and the ending of his championship left him lonely. But he must not let it end quite yet. Noticing Rhea watching too, he slipped out of the shadows and joined her. He had to speak to one who would understand. Their hands and eyes met.

No longer the Moabitess but Noemi's daughter and Bethlehem's friend, Ruth was reverenced by the town's folk who happened to see her as she passed by. If any of them wondered at her attire, no sign of criticism was given. Children ran to her and she received them warmly. The gate-keeper bent a knee at her approach and waited. As she paused to greet him, he took the hem of her veil in both hands and kissed it. The air was bland and the moon was rising to light the way. And so, with a prayer on her lips, Ruth passed on to the fields of Boaz.

She drew her veil across her mouth and chin and held it in place so that now she might not be recognized by anybody. The flowing length of it covered much of her wedding garment. And because Noemi had told her that, in this proverbial season of good feeling, even some uninvited guests would be there in their best attire to share in the feasting, she was fairly sure that she would be given no special attention. But even so, she kept to the shadows.

A great fire had been kindled. The leaping flames sent their glow over the eager faces of a circle of reclining, singing harvesters, and the song carried its theme of fertility and abundance like an offering to the risen moon.

The barren reign of winter, broken, yields to the mothersway
    of spring.
Waters whisper and earth's dark womb, unlocked,
Pours forth its richest treasures to mankind.
Now do the hands of nature drip with gold;
Now do the heavens shed serenest light;
Now, like a newborn babe,
Joy holds the heart as King.

Ruth saw only Boaz. He presided over the circle, yet seemed remote from it. His face kept turning to the west, and his eyes were seeking the hills. Was he hearing in memory, as she was hearing, the melody there beyond the songs of men?

Many more songs were sung while the feasting proceeded; but she noticed that Boaz did not join in and that he ate and drank little. And after a while, his head drooped a trifle, as if the fatigue of a long day's work and a heavy burden of thought were too much for him. At length he rose, signaling the harvesters to continue if they would, and going to lie down at the edge of a grain heap beyond the reach of sparks.

Without him, the others felt their celebration should cease. After collecting wineskins and fragments of food, and strewing the dying flames with wet leaves, they drifted off, some to places of repose in the fields, others to their homes in the town. And the night was still.

Ruth sat beneath a tree, waiting. Her gaze remained on Boaz beside the pile of grain. She could see the restless movement of his limbs and knew that mind was still awake in the body that craved sleep. Soon she beheld him again rising; and this time he walked toward a low hill above the fields, where the booth in which he had night-watched the harvest in the time of her first meeting him, framed itself against the sky. There, under the little roof of boughs upheld by four slender poles, he sank to the ground once more and drew his camel's hair cloak for a blanket around him. How well she remembered that cloak from having washed it in the brook and mended it seasons ago! It was of a texture so fine and light, though warm and serviceable, that the whole could be gathered up in two hands.

After a while, she went as noiseless as the breeze itself to him, uncovered his feet, and humbly lay down at them. Raising herself with her elbow, she gazed at his face in the moonlight filtering through the laced boughs of the shelter. Drained of emotion and with the features relaxed, it had something of a childlike quality. A maternal sentiment moved her, and she had a strange thought which brought the vaguest of smiles to her lips: that a woman's first child is the man she weds. Petulant, hurt, bewildered, impulsive, Boaz had been; but, in sleep, he seemed reborn; and she wanted to shield him as she would have shielded a child from all the hurts of existence. Her love for him did not lessen her love of the Lord. She now knew at last that love destroys nothing. Loving the Lord the more, she could not love his servant the less; and the love of the servant, like a stream flowing into a river, was tributary to her love of the Lord.

At midnight, Boaz awoke, sat up, and rubbed his eyes as he sensed the veiled figure at his feet.

"Who are you?" he breathed, now kneeling.

The answer came like an echo of the music he had heard in the cave, "I am Ruth, your handmaid." She lifted her veil.

He leaned back on his palms, his lids wide apart. Then he bent forward, longing to believe but unable. Surely this apparition was born only of his yearning and the moonlight. . . .

"My lord is a kinsman." She spoke low, half rising and leaning toward him. "As night spreads above us, so may my lord's mantle spread over his handmaid."

Moments passed, and they held within themselves the endings of all the winters and the beginnings of all the springtides he had ever known. His arms would have held her; but then he drew a little away, remembering what Samuel had told him about her desire to give herself to the Lord, wondering if she might not be here only out of generosity and pity.

"May Yahweh bless you, my daughter," he said, lingering on the last word. "But years divide us. . . ."

She extended her hand.

He took the hand in both of his. "You have made this last kind deed of yours better than the first," he said hoarsely. "You twice left your homeland, that you might be with Noemi, and tonight you come to me. . . ." The very earth beneath him seemed changed — soft, diffused. His tongue had no art for what he wanted to say. This perfect woman offering herself, whom he wanted beyond all else, ought to have a spouse worthy of her, if it should really be that the Lord at length willed that she wed. "You are desirable to every young man, poor or rich, in Bethlehem."

"None other would your handmaid have."

"Not my handmaid, but the Lord's."

"The Lord would have me serve my lord."

"My daughter —"

"Not 'daughter.' God grant that I may give you sons."

Bending, he pressed his lips to her fingers. She was trembling. "Fear not," he told her. "Virtue has spoken in you. All my people at the town gate now know your merit, and shame for our mistakes will ever haunt us. How can I make amends, except by forgetting my wretched self and remembering only what is best for you? No man deserves you, least of all myself."

"Through Noemi, Heaven directed me here."

"Could it have been Heaven?" He lowered his head. "Hardly knowing what I did, I offended the Lord by uplifting an idol. I feel he has forgiven me, else why would he send me such a gift; and what have I ever done with my life that I should be so rewarded?"

"You have endured it," she said.

A light passed over his set face. "Yahweh indeed reigns! He did bring me through to this proof of himself and his mercy. That you are with me is beyond all my deserving; but that he should grant me also the grace of having you for my wife is. . . ." Again he edged away and this time his lips worked strangely. For many moments, he was silent, his brow furrowing as if warding off a memory. Then he said slowly, almost inaudibly, "An obstacle, which I did not even consider when I first met you, for I believed it to have been removed, lies between us." He hesitated, and then forced himself on. "You call me kinsman, and I am that. Yet there is a nearer than I."

She started. A nearer? Suddenly she recalled Noemi's occasional mentioning of a certain Hobab, younger brother to Elimelech. But this person had long been out of touch with the family and become merely a name even before the news reached Noemi of his being stabbed fatally during a street brawl in Jerusalem. Once Mahalon, reminiscing, had mentioned to Ruth a dispute between Elimelech and Hobab; a matter of a legacy, which was never settled. "I think I know the 'obstacle,'" she now said to Boaz. "But it has passed. Hobab is gone."

"No. The report of his death was false. He fled north during the famine; then wandered from town to town, seeking better opportunities but squandering his means, always getting into trouble. Recently he returned to Bethlehem and learned about Elimelech and his sons. Only yesterday he came to me, aroused me from sleep, and urged his old claim to Elimelech's land. I told him I was holding and cultivating it for Noemi. He mocked me and spoke with contempt of her. In anger, I forgot his years and struck him. Maybe I'd have done worse, but one of my men came between us. Full of disgust for him and myself, wanting to be done with evil because it seemed to me that I'd seen something of Chemosh in Hobab's

eyes, mocking me as Hobab himself had mocked, I hurried
to the cave to atone my sacrilege there. . . . Heaven must have
sent me. I found the idol already destroyed — by what hand
I know not — and heard again the music that I used to hear
in the days of Mahalon. But now —"

"That music should cast out every fear," said Ruth eagerly.

"I do not fear Hobab himself, though I confess that the
feeling of the malice in him has lasted since he left." He
threw a quick glance around. "Even here his eyes seem to
be on me. And, with your coming to me, I fear what he
may do. As next of kin to Mahalon, he would have a right to
you, if he should somehow convince the elders at the gate
that, Elimelech and his sons dead, his title to the land is good.
Though he could relinquish such a right before the judges,
I know he will not, once he realizes how much I want
you. He has none of the virtues of Elimelech. He's what I
myself, from looking down, seeing only the soil, have been.
O Ruth, what darkness I was in until I met you. . . ."

"And by misreading the Lord's will, I increased that
darkness."

"Do not blame yourself," he begged. "That would be
unfair to the very goodness you sought in all things."

Again silence encompassed them, and the night wind was
the only sound.

"If I may not be your wife," said Ruth at length, "I will
refuse to be another's. We could have the kind of union — not
of body but soul — that I had with Mahalon. Perhaps that is
what the Lord intended all along, and he was preparing
us. . . ."

He gazed fixedly at her, and in a moment his old resentment at life surged back. Why should he, who had not spared
Banaias, the enemy of his country, give in to Hobab, the
enemy of his happiness? Why had Ruth been sent to him, if
she was not to be all his? Might he not take her in defiance of
the law? His prestige in Bethlehem would guarantee him the

privilege of doing whatever he pleased. Not even Samuel in Jerusalem could successfully oppose.

But Ruth's hand on his arm calmed him, and soon he was able to think more reasonably. He had forgotten the Lord and the law long enough with his brooding and rancor; and now that the divine pardon and her presence had been granted him, why could he not be fully grateful? This question, however, seemed only to make way for still others. If Hobab should want Ruth, how might she refuse? Though her heart rejected, her hand would have to accept. Hobab, if sustained by the judges, could compel her. And if she and Hobab should wed, how could she have even a spiritual union with another? She would belong entirely to him, since the law granted the husband a power so great that the wife might not enter independently into any engagement, even before God.

"Rest this night," he said, taking his mantle. He covered her with it as, obediently, she lay back exhausted with emotion. "Morning may bring its own answers."

His hand still holding a part of the mantle so close to her throat that a warmth from her wreathed around his fingers, he looked down on her saddened face, her closing eyes. The moonlight added to the pallor of her features and the pathos of her wedding finery.

Ruth's sleep was disturbed by dreams. Toward morning she awoke.

Boaz was sitting by. Evidently he had kept vigil through the night. His eyes had a glaze to them and the shadows beneath were like bruises. She wondered what thoughts had held him in the hours of watching, and she feared even more than she wondered. But a kindness combined itself with his unhappiness and somewhat reassured her, as he helped her to her feet.

"It must not be known that you came to me," he said, glancing toward the first streaks of dawn in the east. "The harvesters are still sleeping and none will see you, if you return to Noemi without delay." He stooped and gathered up some measures of barley which, during the night, he had brought from the threshing floor. "Take this, so that you may not go empty-handed."

Thanking him with a look, she made an apron of the front of her outer skirt. As he poured the grain into it, she again noticed the circles under his eyes. "Has my lord had any rest?" she asked.

"There can be no rest for me until —" He checked himself, swallowing hard, his lips pressed tight.

"The Lord has brought you through much, as you yourself have said," she reminded him. "He will continue to be with you, if your own hands do not thrust him away."

"He gave me these hands. What can I do but use them, when those of another would seize what is mine?"

Some of the grain spilled from her dress. "Violence would make matters worse," she warned, her tone a pleading, for he seemed to be listening only to the tumult within him.

"Sometimes, it is the only way," he replied. "When Samson, the judge and hero of our nation, could not have his mate, he cried out, 'From this day I shall be faultless in what I do, and I will do evils!' And he set fire to vineyards and olive yards and made a great slaughter of the Philistines. Shall I do nothing against one who would stand between me and you?"

"There is no certainty that Hobab will stand between us. Go to him, my lord, peaceably and with reasoning."

He stepped back. "Reasoning — peace — with him who insulted Noemi and rejoices that Elimelech and his sons are dead? His eyes are small and hard. His hand is greedy."

"As a son of Israel, he cannot have quite escaped the influence of the faith. There must be some good in him. As a tiller of the soil, you have brought barley and wheat up out of its stubbornness —"

"Not when the seed fell on stony ground."

"Even in the crevices of a stone, a seed my sprout and grow. Mahalon often pointed out to me in Moab a tree whose roots had worked down into a mass of rock and were splitting it. He used this as an example of how the faith of Israel could overcome the worst resistance. And he lived to see the victory more than start. I myself know its progress." Her earnestness increased. "There may be more strength in meekness than in force."

He tried to smile sardonically. The soft approach of a good woman — a weak thinker — to hard facts! But her hand, in the rays of the rising sun, was permanently marked with the proof of what she had endured for Israel; and, seeing it, he was ashamed.

"The dawn increases," he said. "Hasten to Noemi and leave me to do what I must."

His shoulder slanting, he strode away.

Noemi, sitting in her accustomed place, stirred as Ruth entered Deborah's house. Her eyes were opaque in the parchmentlike face. She reached out. "Is it you, my daughter?" she said. Surprise at the early return and chagrin at the failure that it seemed to imply were in the question.

Ruth went to her, after hastily transferring the burden of grain to Rhea and giving Deborah a wan greeting. Kneeling, she placed her folded hands in the awaiting lap and bowed her head.

Noemi put her palms on the bent shoulders.

"He did not receive you?"

"He treated me with all kindness, my mother. He covered me with his mantle and watched over me while I slept. He gave me six measures of barley so that I might not return empty-handed to you."

Noemi slid her fingers along Ruth's cheeks and raised the chin, bringing her own close. "But did he take you to wife?"

"He could not, my mother. He told me with sorrow that Hobab, who still lives, stands between."

It took Noemi a while to gather enough breath for words. "The dead living — the past throwing its shadow on us —"

"Hobab is now in Bethlehem and has talked with him."

"Strange, then, that he did not come to me too. But — perhaps not too strange. He must still be resenting me as the one who, nearest to Elimelech, could have had the most effect. If he only knew how much we wanted to understand and satisfy him! Elimelech did try and try. For the sake of peace, he would have given him everything he wanted, only that he could not bring himself to deprive Chelion and Mahalon of their future inheritance. It was a case of having to choose between a brother and two sons. Oh, that he had seen how brief, in any case, is man's hold on anything earthly!"

She shut her eyes and rocked a little, her mind ranging the long series of conflicts of brother with brother, kin with kin, that had marred the history of a people from Cain and Abel down to the present. And she puzzled that this should have been so. United in worship and endowed with a vision of eternity, why should they have been divided by the things of time? And she longed, as she had longed so often before, for the coming of him who would teach men how to live their short hour on earth in harmony.

She felt Ruth trembling. "What is it, my daughter?" she asked quickly. "Is there something worse?"

"Yes, my mother. Fear! Boaz has quarreled with Hobab. He is holding Elimelech's acres for you, but Hobab wants them for himself. Boaz thinks he can save me and the land by doing away with him."

Noemi took a fold of her robe and pulled at it with her bony fingers until the texture almost parted. Her old eyes narrowed. "This must not be!" she cried. "The morning is young. Do you think he has gone to Hobab yet?"

"I doubt that he yet knows where Hobab is dwelling in

Bethlehem. To find him, he would likely have to seek him where all disputes are heard and settled; and there at the gates in the presence of others, he could hardly do violence. No, I think he will merely make inquiries this day; but when night falls. . . ."

Noemi rose unsteadily. Ruth, rising too, watched the blinking of the old eyes and a twitching in the cheek.

"We ourselves will find Hobab," said Noemi. "I have something to say to him. May Yahweh grant that this time my attempt to — manage — will bring no regrets!"

Rhea, standing by, offered to accompany them. But Noemi, set on being mistress of herself and the situation, refused. "Deborah needs you here, good Rhea, and I can handle myself well enough," she said, tossing her head. "I am able. It's only waiting, doing nothing, that's made me seem helpless."

As Ruth led her from the house, she had to walk slowly, knowing that, for all the burst of would-be energy, Noemi was physically weak indeed.

People greeted them along the way and paused to watch. "Bethlehem will always be Bethlehem, so long as the old receive such loving care," whispered a woman to a neighbor.

And Ruth walked with Noemi through streets lined with adobe houses to which clusters of honeysuckle and roses clung. The scent of the flowers mingled with that of bread fresh from ovens and cooling on window sills. Women were sitting on the steps, and children were playing. Seeing the simple, domestic life of the town, Ruth yearningly pictured herself as part of it; and Noemi, instinctively understanding, declared, "I cannot fail you, my daughter. This day your place in Bethlehem must be fixed once and for all!"

When they were nearing the gates, she spoke further: "You will be my sight. Hobab, as I remember him, had medium height; russet, curly hair; small, black eyes, one with a cast in it; a slight twist to the nose; a crooked mouth. Time has no doubt changed his appearance in some respects, but

I'd well know him if I got near. Be alert for him, my daughter."

At this hour, the elders and several spectators were gathered together at the gates for the administration of justice. The process was simplicity itself: there being no set officials to dispense it, no police to defend it, no formal court to enthrone it. It rested merely on right as written in the law, on truth as evident in the very nature of things, and on the regard that brother should have for brother. Ruth, standing with Noemi a little aside from a group of litigants, listened to a case that was being tried, and she marveled at the swift and easy settling of it in a degree of calm which contrasted with the emotionalism of similar scenes that she had occasionally witnessed in Moab. And she espied a man in the crowd who seemed to answer Noemi's description. He had plainly been awaiting his turn to air his grievance, and now it was come. As he faced the elders, all striking looking in their long, white trousers and sky-blue jackets with full sleeves, he appeared not ungainly himself. An evident purposiveness added to his stature, and he showed no fear.

Ruth did not have to tell Noemi that this might be Hobab. He no sooner raised his voice than the old head nodded, the dim eye lighted. "Lead me nearer," she requested sharply.

Hobab had fastened his gaze on the chief of the elders — tall, with deep-set eyes; dignified, with a bronzed beard shot through with gray — and was addressing him. "I am the wronged half brother of one who, in the time of famine, left his fields to rot."

"There was not much else to do in those days," returned the chief dryly. "All our land already lay waste."

"But, abandoning Bethlehem with his wife and sons, this man sought the fleshpots of Moab!"

"He sought that his family might survive. I know you, Hobab; and I knew Elimelech. A God-fearing man, respected by everybody, himself a servant of justice at these very gates; how could he have wronged you?"

"Our father had two wives, and I was the son of her whom he less favored," explained Hobab briskly. "It is written in the law that such a son, lacking his father's love, shall be compensated by a double portion of inheritance."

"But this is so only when the unhappy son is the first born. You came some years after Elimelech."

"Nevertheless, I insist that I was cheated. There is a spirit as well as a letter to the law; and according to the spirit, I should have been dealt with."

The elder stroked his beard and his cool eyes narrowed unpleasantly. "There was a spirit to you, too, Hobab, and it might hardly have been called good. I recall how you treated your father, and how given to squander and revel you were."

"I was beside myself. He cared not for me."

"He cared much and did all he could to reclaim you. It is written that if a man have a stubborn and unruly son who will not hear his commandments, and being corrected slights obedience, such a son shall be taken and brought to judgment."

Hobab ran a finger across his sweaty throat, but he did not lose his defiance. "My father never had to go to that extreme," he said with a sneer.

"Your father was patient."

"You have no real proof that I was not a dutiful son."

"I have a perfect memory — the best of proofs." The elder's voice had become deep and stern. "Know you not that, according to the law, the penalty for a disobedient, rebellious son is death? It is written that the people of the city shall stone him, that they might take away the evil out of the midst of them, and all Israel hearing it might be afraid. Your father, who left you no legacy, granted you your life by forbearance. Have you no gratitude for that?"

Hobab was silent.

"Go in what peace you can," said the elder. "Forget your claim."

But Hobab, pulling himself together, took another stand.

"Now that Elimelech and his sons, as everyone knows, are no more, why should I not receive at last what was denied me?" he cried. "I've discovered that Boaz, a mere cousin, availed himself of the time of famine to get hold of the property; and when I went to him to demand what ought to be mine, he fell on me with blows and I was driven thence."

"Boaz stands high in the esteem of Bethlehem. What he did must have been provoked less by your demand than your attitude. He is a just man."

A wry smile crossed Hobab's lips. "Just?" he echoed, scratching an ear. "How deceived you are! I set watch on him, that I might have further proof of the sort of man he really is. Last night, my mantle covering my head, I mixed with strangers at his harvest feast; and when the celebrating was over, I remained behind after the others had fallen asleep or departed. Hidden from view, I saw with my own eyes your — just one. As God is my judge, there in a booth above the field of harvest he secretly received the woman who came out of the land of Moab with Elimelech's widow!"

Ruth pressed close to Noemi who, in a gesture of agitation, tried to smooth down her veil on her head with both hands.

The elder's countenance was very grave, and his eyes were piercing. "The woman from Moab, as you call her, is honored in Bethlehem because of her sacrifice and service to us during the threat of siege. Her virtue is unquestionable." He looked to his fellow elders and the people for confirmation. In the act, he noticed Ruth herself with Noemi and pointed. "Behold, there she stands, hearing your vile accusation."

All eyes were now on Ruth, and Hobab's stare was the keenest. Fair as she had appeared to him in the moonlight, she seemed even fairer in the light of day; and, with the inner relenting that any man is apt to feel at the sight of feminine appeal, he almost wished that he could spare her. But he held to his offensive. "What I say is truth. They remained together until dawn."

Then Noemi, throwing an arm around Ruth and drawing her through the little space that the spectators opened up, confronted Hobab and the judges. Her shoulders and chin had squared. The bygone stateliness had returned. "It was I who sent her to Boaz, having heard and believed that Hobab was no more," she declared in a clear, strong tone. "Boaz has wanted her in wedlock for many long months, and knew that I — her foster mother — approved. So the condition of a period of espousal was fulfilled. It seemed to remain only that the marriage be completed by her being received."

Hobab thrust himself forward. "Marriage between an Israelite and a non-Israelite is forbidden," he protested loudly. "It is written that the Ammonite and the Moabite are an abomination to the church of the Lord."

Some of the elders muttered agreement. But the chief asserted, "It is unseemly that you, Hobab, who have lived so lawless, should persist in telling us so glibly what is written. The laws that regulate our lives are reasonable and may admit of reasonable exception. Know you that Ruth has forsworn Moab and adopted the faith of Israel, and therefore is she one of us."

Silent for a second, Hobab scowled. "Then I, not Boaz, being next of kin to her husband Mahalon who died without issue in Moab, have the right to wed her, if so I will," he said.

"And do you so will?"

Hobab rubbed his hands. "The point is that, last night, this Boaz took her in violation of my right."

"Did Boaz really — take — you, my daughter?" the elder asked Ruth.

"He treated me with all respect," she replied in a low voice, "and spoke of this other's possible right."

The elder cast a glance of triumph at Hobab. "As I have told you, Boaz is a just man."

"But you are a credulous one," continued Hobab boldly, his eyes red with anger. "Her answer is but a screen, and shame is on her cheek. Once more, whether you like it or not, I'll quote the law. It is written: 'If a man takes another man's wife, they both shall die.' This woman, along with the land, should be considered mine. Boaz took her and she let herself be taken."

"One witness shall not rise up against any man," said the elder, bringing his finger close to Hobab's nose. "But in the mouth of two or three witnesses every word shall stand."

"I am witness and so is she herself. There you have your two! Ask her again, this time not softly but with stern command; and she cannot deny that she remained with Boaz the night."

"Did you, my daughter?"

Ruth bowed her head.

"She admits it!" cried Hobab. "He spread his mantle over her —"

"But chastely," broke in a voice. The speaker was Rei, who, having gone to Deborah's house to talk with Rhea, had been bidden by the anxious girl to follow Ruth and Noemi to the gates. "I was in the fields of Boaz last night and saw both him and Ruth. The attitude of brother for sister, or of father for daughter, was what I found. I've been watching over Ruth since her return to Bethlehem, because I cherish her as my mother's friend and because of the great good, now open to all of us, that she rendered Bethlehem. If Boaz had dared to lay an unclean hand on her, I'd have tried to kill him. But there was no need whatsoever for any fear. After conversing with her, he had her take rest, the hour being late; and he covered her with his cloak against the chill of the night, and then sat apart, guarding her as any of us would guard a sleeping child. I remained unseen until dawn, when she awoke and took her leave."

A hush had fallen on the group.

"This young man's testimony, combined with Ruth's, shows

your own false, Hobab," said the elder severely. "It appears that, having hate for Boaz, you would defame him. Where a man has told a lie against his brother, the law decrees that it be rendered to him as he meant to do his brother; and, further, that there be no pity, but an eye for an eye, a tooth for a tooth, a hand for a hand, a foot for a foot. What say you?"

Hobab, seeing the frank, honest face of Rei and the effect on all the elders and the people, knew that any attempt at a refutation would be futile. Choked with confusion, he yet managed to reply, "Believe what you will. My word means nothing here." He spat. "I would withdraw."

"Withdraw?" said the chief witheringly. "Hear you this. Inasmuch as you have sought to slander two of our most honorable Bethlehemites, you are odious to all Bethlehem. If Boaz should proceed against you for this, expect no protection from us."

Then Noemi raised her voice again. "I demand that a guard be given Hobab this day," she said, holding Ruth's hand, "so that Boaz may have no stain on his account. Legal or not, violence is violence, and it only causes more passion in which nothing can ever be truly solved or healed. If this belief of mine seems to you men of Israel to be just an old woman's fancy, let me tell you that it has been forged for me in grief. Ruth and I have seen so much outrage — things too terrible to tell! — that we crave the end. It is our due and the due of our dead." Her voice broke. "Oh, I know, too well I know, the law of Moses is hard; but that's because the hearts of men are harder still. The Lord would rule us only with love, if we but let him." She turned to Hobab. "You want land. Having it, would you hold your peace and help the poor as Boaz has been doing?"

"I would."

"Hear then. Boaz is not keeping Elimelech's property for

himself but for me. If I can, I will pervail on him, through Ruth, to let you have it — on condition that you meet him here tomorrow morning and make friends."

"But Boaz hates me."

"Hate — hate." A weary scorn was in her tone. "Bethlehem should know only the love of God and the God of love. Hate would have burned itself out long ago, if it weren't kept fed with folly. Stop feeding it!"

"But Boaz — will *he* stop?"

Noemi glanced off toward the hills which her faint vision could no longer reach. Ruth knew that she was thinking of the singing cave, and she was stirred by her reply. "Hearing the Lord, how can he continue to hate?"

"Elimelech's widow utters wisdom," said the chief of the elders to the others. "You, Hobab, shall be guarded. And tomorrow, again gathered here, we will see that a quiet course is not beset."

Later that morning, after taking Noemi back to Deborah's house, Ruth went alone to the cave. Her heart grew lighter on the way, her steps quickened, and a smile was on her lips; for the sun was shining, and something inside kept saying, "He will be there."

She found Boaz standing in the light from above. "I knew you would come," he said, taking her hands. "As I listened" — he looked upward — "I felt that you were already here."

She lost no time in telling him, "Noemi and I have seen Hobab."

He stiffened. "I came here to banish him a while from my thoughts. Why speak his name?"

"It touches our lives."

He was silent.

"Hobab wants only land," she said. "Noemi would have you give him Elimelech's."

"And deprive her?"

"She wants it not. She would have you, tomorrow at the gates, seal the transfer."

"And then?"

"Then," said Ruth simply, "shall I not be yours?"

He put his arms around her. She put her palms to his chest and started to withdraw, but stopped before she was free. She saw the hunger of the years and the ache of it in his eyes, and let him hold her close. With the rising of the spring-scented breeze, the harp began to sing.

After a few moments, she spoke. "Too long has the tilling of the soil claimed my lord. Having Noemi, a few sheep, and this hilltop home with its music, would we not be free to offer ourselves to him who brought me out of the land of Moab to you and Bethlehem?" Her voice seemed to blend with the melody from overhead. "Samuel called this cave a tabernacle of nature and said that its worth would remain hidden in Israel until the fullness of time. . . . Do you not feel that, someday, something full of meaning for mankind will happen here?"

"I know that here I feel peace drawing nearer."

"Peace — the shadow of him who is to come." She looked up, her eyes reflecting the clean blueness of the sky. "He will be born of woman. I've often wondered where, and have had the strangest thought that. . . ."

They shared their minds and hearts in silence, exalted by their theme and the strains of music. And at last, as they started to leave, she said: "Be not content, my lord, with letting Hobab have Elimelech's land. Why not find full release from the soil by matching Noemi's goodness and giving your own fields to Rhea and Rei? They have been so loyal! How pleased they would be to live with Deborah in your old home while Hobab occupies Noemi's! Mindful of the virtues of Elimelech and his sons, as he dwells where they used to dwell, and tilling the earth that once nourished their bodies, Hobab might well acquire those virtues; and Rhea and Rei would take away sadness from the house where you had only loneliness." As if fearing that she seemed too solemn, she added with a happy little smile, "That bridal chamber on the roof of it would at last have its use."

"But then," he said, "what could I offer my wife?"

For answer she looked up toward the source of the music.

Early the next morning, Boaz went to the place of judgment. He was holding a flowered twig from the white almond tree. And though he was almost unconscious of it in his hand, its significance lay like spring in his heart. And while he waited, Ruth seemed to be close to him.

The elders and several others assembled. Greetings were interchanged. Then Hobab, accompanied by his guard, appeared; his look chastened, his shoulders drooping.

"Come here beside me," said Boaz to him.

Without a word, Hobab complied.

Boaz looked respectfully at the elders and especially their chief. Then he said to Hobab, "Noemi, who has returned from the fields of Moab, and has been living here for many months, is willing to dispose of the fields that belonged to Elimelech. You and I have had our differences, but now we can strike an agreement. You may redeem the property with a pledge that you practice the virtues of those who once held it. If so you will, give sign; for there is none near to Noemi but you, and I after you."

Hobab, with bent head, answered, "I redeem."

"On the day you acquire the land from the hand of Noemi," continued Boaz, "you will also have acquired with it Ruth, the widow of Mahalon, to raise up the name of the deceased upon his inheritance. His elder brother Chelion, also gone, left a wife in Moab; but that wife, unlike Ruth, holds to her birthplace and therefore seeks no part of the estate. Would you claim Ruth?"

"Why do you ask me that?" said Hobab, lifting his bloodshot eyes. "You love her. Only love would have shown the decency and restraint which, here in public, I confess and attest I saw you exercise when you were with her the night before last." Bending down and lifting a foot, he loosed and drew off a sandal, handing it to Boaz in token of surrender. "I've no right at all to the land. If Noemi lets me have possession, it is out of the goodness of her heart, and I will never forget her, but try to make myself worthy. As for Ruth, she is yours and you know it, and in the presence of these judges I waive my claim."

Then Boaz turned to the elders and the people and said, "You are witnesses today that I acquire Ruth for my wife, to raise up the name of Mahalon upon his inheritance, that it may not be cut off from his brethren and these gates. I repeat: You are witnesses this day."

"Witnesses!" cried the chief of the elders. "May the Lord make the wife, who is to come to you, like Rachel and Lia who reared the house of Israel!" He glanced at the blossoms in the hand of Boaz and smiled. "May her goodness ever fill your life!"

And a joyous shout rose from the people.

A year passed. The month of Marsheshvan had brought warm breezes from the great western sea and had strewn the meadows with lilies; and now the last fall planting was in the soil, and winds blew cold on the hills of Bethlehem. But warmth filled the cave where Boaz, Ruth, and Noemi had made their home, for the sun shed its rays so abundantly through the opening in the roof by day that the effect remained even when the shadows fell. And one night, when the skies were brightest, and a great fragrance exhaled from the evergreens near the door, and the strings of the lyre were stroked by the air to sounds even sweeter than before, Ruth brought forth a son.

The following morning, women came from the town and the valley to see the child, and found him cradled in Noemi's arms. Her eyes were as bright as in the days of her own motherhood. And the women said to her: "Blessed be Yahweh, who has not let Elimelech's name be forgotten in Israel. This babe shall be new life to you and sustain your age, for she who loves you and is better than seven sons has given birth to him."

And Noemi, holding the infant close, as Mahalon used to hold his harp, declared in the eloquent voice of a prophetess, "This is a gift of the Lord, belonging to Moab and Bethlehem, linking a foreign country with our land of faith; for the world is one, as God is one, and souls everywhere under the sun are dear to him. Just as this child brings two bloods together, so shall the Messias bring all people into a larger Israel — into a single fold; and fear will die, love will take its place." Her gaze turned to Ruth lying on a bed of straw while Boaz knelt beside her with the devotion of a pilgrim at a shrine. "Behold my daughter. Is she not — must she not be — as the mother that the Lord will choose for him who is to come?"

And the harp strings above gave out a seeming affirmation.

EPILOGUE

At Noemi's suggestion, the child of Ruth and Boaz was called Obed, which means "servant," because he served to bring to Bethlehem at least the beginning of a consciousness of Israel's mission to the world.

When he grew up and had a son of his own, this offspring in turn was named Jesse, which signifies "wealthy," because, rich in spiritual heritage, Obed desired him always to be impressed that, having the love of God, no man may be reckoned poor.

And Jesse begot David, which means "well-beloved," for the love of Ruth and Boaz in the Lord had flowed down through the years like a stream of living waters, gathering strength from each generation and mirroring the heavens in its course.

As time passed, the cave in the hills became almost forgotten, for the strings of the lyre had frayed away and Ruth and Noemi and Boaz were no more. But music lived on in the soul of young David and, shepherd that he was, like Mahalon before him, he would watch his flock and hear voices in the very silences around him. And, fashioning a harp which eventually filled all Israel with song, he bequeathed his gift to his son Solomon, who composed a canticle of canticles such as Boaz had longed to be able to pour forth to Ruth, and he built on Mount Moriah the temple of Ruth's dreams.

At length, in the fullness of time, the skies were pierced with a great star, and the cave of life itself opened flush on the light, and yet another Child was born of the fruitful line of Ruth and Boaz. At the midnight hour of his birth, when the world was sleeping and nature was wrapped in a timeless hush, the heavenly singers, whose notes had long been a prelude in hearts that loved, came into view. And they sang to simple men in the hills of Bethlehem the certain dawn of that which, since the beginning of sin and sorrow, had ever been the most prayerful hope of the race.

When, directed by them, the shepherds reached and entered the place of the Nativity, the last of their fear left them. They were at home: having been prepared for the sight that greeted them by the story of Ruth, which, that holy night, they had been recounting and reliving under the star.

And in Mary's beauty, they saw a Moabite maiden; in Joseph's devotion, another Boaz; and in the Child, the new life, ending all woe, that once lay in old Noemi's arms.